# Fake Fiancée for the Grumpy Billionaire

## An Off-limits Enemies to Lovers Second Chance Romance

### Lily Cross

# Contents

# Chapter 1 – Jay

"Sounds like the young lady doesn't want to buy what you're selling, buddy." And with those words, I pull the stranger off the struggling dark-haired girl he's trying to keep lying down on the bed.

It's a fairly easy thing to do. The fitness level I obtained while on tour with my marine unit overseas has been rigidly maintained.

Yes. I'm that guy. The one you don't want to mess with. The one who makes it his business to win at all costs and then makes you live to regret taking me on.

The man begins to swear at me when he hears my voice and feels my hand tighten around the back of his neck. But, he simmers down when he finally manages to stand up and sees who he's dealing with.

"Jay? What the fuc—? Who the hell invited you here?"

I ignore him. My focus is on the young girl sitting on the edge of the bed as she wipes all traces of tears off her face.

"I could have handled that bumbling fool my-self," she mutters, staring at the man behind me with daggers in her eyes. "You're lucky I didn't give you a good kicking in the family jewels, mister!"

I like her immediately. "Are you okay?"

She's not hysterical or outraged. The young girl sits straight, running her slim fingers through the long strands of pitch-black hair, shooting a glare of hatred at the man who had been on top of her.

"I knew there was something hinky about this yacht and this man just confirmed it!"

She's wearing one of those bikinis made out of four triangles of material—two for the top part and two for the lower part—it's skimpy in a really eye-catching way. The color—red—suits her suntanned skin tone.

Her body is sensational, curved, and toned in all the right places. But no man has the right to take what he likes without getting a solid "yes" first.

Trying to act as dignified as she can, the girl adjusts the bikini triangles to cover the exposed parts of her body. I can't help it, I turn around to give Brent Morecambe a piece of my mind. Maybe I should rough him up a bit so that he can see what it feels like, but Brent has sneaked out already.

I can't hold it against him. This young woman could melt wax off a candle with the scorn smoldering on her face.

The girl looks at me, shooting me a hesitant glare with those deep brown eyes of hers. It's as if she needs to make sure that I'm not like the other men—the ones who don't take no for an answer.

Instinctively, I reach out my hand towards her. I want to give her a hug to comfort her, but she's as skittish as a whipped foal and shifts away quickly.

"Please tell me you're okay, miss."

"I am, thank you. This whole day has been one huge mistake." She sighs as if the weight of the world lies on her pretty shoulders.

Somehow, I feel myself reacting to the sound of her voice. She has a husky, sweet little voice and there's a musical inflection to every word she says.

"I'm sorry to hear that. Don't have a yacht of my own, but if I did I wouldn't host these kinds of parties on it, that's for sure."

"Do you mind?" She starts to edge past me, pointing to the bathroom en suite. "I want to wash."

I am used to getting this kind of reaction from women sometimes. I'm a big guy, six-four in socks with shoulders so broad I have to go through narrow doors sideways.

A body built for combat as my old drill sergeant used to say, and a mind designed for military strategy.

You can bet I use my mental and physical advantages at every chance I get. And I pick my battles carefully.

"Sure, go ahead, Miss...?"

Before closing the door, she manages to muster up a small smile. "Forrest. Just Forrest."

For some crazy reason, I stand staring at the bathroom door for a moment or two after she shuts it. Damn! If she catches me doing that when she comes out, she's going to think I'm a tom cat too.

Get a grip. There is no way she would be in the mood for a cozy chat with you just after being groped by Brent Morecambe.

I should leave and go back on deck. There's a contract to be signed. Things to do. People to see.

Then why am I still staring at the bathroom en suite door like one of those mesmerized acts at the circus?

I counted about a round dozen cute girls on this yacht when I landed my helicopter, and all of them were wearing bikinis too. But for some inexplicable reason, I've fixated on this one young woman.

The blame lies squarely on me. I've been working too hard and neglecting those parts of my body that come naturally to a man in his prime.

Miss Red Bikini wakes the hunter in me and I'm enjoying the sensation of how it arouses my body. I've never been rejected by a woman since high school. This hunt won't take long.

I'm ready to pounce when she comes out of the bathroom. Her skin glistens with water from the shower, slick pearly droplets dripping down towards her breasts.

Damn! I must make sure not to screw this up! I've never approached a woman after she's been treated badly by another man before.

That only happens in the movies. When a man rescues the heroine and then she falls into his arms with gratitude.

"Want to join me for a drink on the deck?" One of my patented charming smiles should seal the deal.

The young woman looks me up and down and then lifts one eyebrow.

"Seriously? Do you think I want anything to do with any man after what I just went through?"

She gives a little grrr sound and shakes her head. "I just want to get off this stupid boat."

My stomach flips as my cocky attitude adjusts to her rejection of my proposal.

"After what you've just been through, I thought a drink would be exactly what you needed."

She scoffs and smirks, looking me up and down again after folding her arms. All her body language is negative. "I said I was thankful. And this is not a fair conversation anyway."

For some strange reason, I'm getting mad and defensive.

"How is this not a fair conversation, Forrest? I think I treated you fairly. And if you are delusional enough to think that you could have 'handled that bumbling fool' yourself," I say, putting on a mocking high-pitched voice to mimic her, "you are a million percent wrong!"

That smirk is back. "Ugh! Are you trying to cash in your chips with me for being the dude who came to my rescue? That's so lame."

This woman is very exasperating! "No, I am not so crass. And I am still waiting for you to tell me how this is not a fair conversation. I don't like that, you know."

"You don't like what?" Now she's curious. Her arms are folded in a protective, hugging gesture around herself.

"When people make a glib statement without anything to back it up."

"Ha!" Throwing back her head, she laughs out loud, fully as mocking as I was towards her. "This—" She taps the middle of my chest with a sharp poke. "—is not a fair conversation, Jay, because I'm wearing a bikini and you're wearing some kind of combat fatigues."

She moves to the door, shooting me a cheeky look over her shoulder. "Like I said, G.I. Joe, I am grateful for your intervention, but there is no way I want to have a drink with any of the fake-ass Romeos on this pleasure cruise!"

I'm dumbstruck, my gaze fixed on her smooth back, tiny waist, and round ass jiggling under that red triangle of her bikini. I have to give myself a shake to snap out of it.

"I flew here by helicopter!" I shout after her retreating figure. "These aren't combat fatigues. They're overalls!"

But all she does is give a little wave with her hand and disappear down one of the spiral staircases leading to one of the lower decks.

Reluctantly, I leave the cabin and climb back on deck. Part of me wants to shrug off what just happened, but the young woman's attitude haunts me.

My host comes to greet me with a glass of champagne in his hand. I shake my head. "No, thanks, Kevin. I'm piloting myself out of here just as soon as I get the papers signed."

This is Kevin's yacht. He bought it for himself after earning his tenth billion dollars. Like Kevin, the yacht is expensive and a little bit flashy.

It has two helipads—one belonging to the yacht and a second one for a guest. That's more helicopters on this sailing vessel than they have at the White House. How crazy is that?

I read somewhere in the promotional literature that gets sent to my email that there's a parking spot for a couple of sports cars in the hull as well.

"Stay the night," Kev suggests, jerking his head behind him in the direction of the Jacuzzi. "Better take your pick of the girls soon. I ordered them personally—tried to cater to all tastes."

The young women in the Jacuzzi seem to be having a good time. Screaming with fake laughter as two men hop into the tub with them and begin to splash water at one another.

When he sees the look of distaste on my face, Kev gets defensive.

"They aren't escorts, Jay! I'm not the Wolf of bloody Wall Street! These girls are models and influencers. Some are even actors with solid acting credentials. They have jobs, just like us."

Yes, Kev. You keep telling yourself that. Yacht girls are notorious for attending crazy sex parties in exchange for money and self-promotion.

"All you need is for one of those girls to be underage and you'll get into some serious trouble once you re-enter US waters, Kev," I remind him. "And anyway, I have no interest in shooting fish in a barrel."

"I'm not stupid, Jay," Kevin says, "I trust the service who gets me the girls. My yacht trips have never been this much fun before. They aren't fish—these girls are all primo kitty-cats."

"Thanks, but I think I'll stick to my helicopter." Shaking my head when one of the waiters comes forward with a tray of champagne flutes, I stare out at the blue sky and gentle lapping waves.

Dammit! I can't get Forrest out of my mind. I have never been this tempted in my life.

She's like a delicious sweet treat I want to hunt down and eat.

"Did they all sign up for sex?" I can't help myself from asking and then hating myself the minute the question comes out of my mouth.

Kev shakes his head. "No way! That's the beauty of using this service. The girls don't have to do anything they don't want. They come on board in pairs, so they have a nice buddy system going."

I guess Forrest's buddy must have let her down, allowing her to get trapped below deck with Brent Morecambe.

"Is that what you believe in your heart, Kev," I say, smirking and narrowing my eyes, "or is that what you tell guests like me—the ones with a moral compass?"

Kev hangs his head just a little bit. "Okay. Jeez. Don't be such a pain in the ass. The girls have to give a little something if they want to get paid before they leave. Satisfied?"

No, I'm not satisfied. "Where's Amir?" I have to keep my head in the game. I came here for business and business is what I will do.

Raising his glass in a mock toast, Kev moves towards the Jacuzzi. "I'll tell him to meet you in the conference room, shall I?"

"No, I'll be in the media room. I need to catch up on the news cycle." I never use my phone for information when I can help it. Looking down at a tiny screen for entertainment is not my favorite thing to do.

I'm a big man and I like to spread myself out while I wait.

Kev has one more parting shot before he goes back to his party. "There are colored rubber bands in every cabin side table. If you get with a girl, give it to her so I can keep tabs on how... friendly they are. If you change your mind."

Giving a careless wave, I'm already heading below deck.

Like the rest of the yacht, the media room is splendid. I'm not that interested in decoration or furniture—I pay people to do those kinds of things for me—but the highly polished veneer on the massive mahogany table in front of the television screen almost blinds me.

Finding the nearest black leather recliner chair, I sit back and wait for Amir. We're merging two of our companies. Amir wants to break into the Western markets and I will be expanding into the Middle East.

The luxury resort hotels will be called First Ensign. And the budget option will be called First Pennant.

Instead of following the newsfeed on the screen, I find my mind drifting back to the girl in the red bikini. Physically, I am tempted, but that sassy attitude of hers needs some schooling.

I really want to be the man to put a smile back on her face. But is she too much of a challenge for me to take on at this busy time in my billionaire life?

# Chapter 2 – Forrest

I know that guy saved me from the most unpleasant experience of my life, but damn! He's so cocky!

No, he's definitely not like one of those smug bastards splish-splashing around on the upper deck. What's the best way to describe him? Bossy?

One of the timid crew members darts off to the side. I stop them.

"This floating palace is like a maze! How do I get away from the bedroom area?"

"You mean the cabins?"

I try not to notice the way the sailor's eyes struggle not to look down at my breasts. This red bikini is an excuse for clothing!

"Yes, whatever. The cabins with beds in them. I have to get away from them."

I'm trying hard not to let him see how upset I am, but I can't stop the waves of humiliation washing over me.

"At the end of every corridor is a spiral staircase. You can go up or down."

His eyes sweep up and down my body too. I don't hold it against him. I'm sure he knows I was ordered to wear this stupid bikini.

"Hey, thanks," I shout over my shoulder as I run for the spiral stairs.

Immediately, my mind flips back to thinking about the tall man in overalls who helped me—Jay. Did he save me? Ugh! Makes me feel so weak.

He expected me to fall over him like a damsel in distress, sobbing on his chest and wailing for help. Doesn't he understand how embarrassing it is for me to be here at all?

I can feel my teeth grinding as I remember the idiotic agreement I made with my best friend, Mary-Kay. But now that I'm here, I may as well bite the bullet and suck it up.

Mmm, so yummy....

For a fleeting moment, I imagine what it might be like licking and sucking that fabulous man who saved me from Brent Morecambe. Jay might be the last word when it comes to giving off serious master and servant vibes, but he is gorgeous.

Giving myself a sharp shake, I tell myself to get my head back in the game. All I have to do is get through this weekend and then I will be set financially for my first year at university.

Instead of going to the upper deck, I remember why I was below deck in the first place.

I was on the phone, listening to my bestie, Mary-Kay, with complete disbelief.

"I can't make it, girl. You're going to have to go on without me if you want all that lovely cash!" Mary-Kay gave me the news calmly.

This is not what I wanted to be hearing from my BFF. Not when I was already on the darn yacht! "But Mary-Kay, you promised me you would meet me on board. Now what am I going to do?"

"Haul ass off the bloody boat if you're too chicken to go through with it, you idiot." Mary-Kay has never been known for her subtlety. "Maybe being a yacht girl is not something you want to do on your own!"

This careless attitude is typical of my erratic, flaky best friend, Mary-Kay Banner.

"We've been besties since I got my scholarship to study at that fancy school in New York City," I say, fuming mad. "I would have thought you had my back! You couldn't have chosen a worse time to let me down."

Mary-Kay is not put off. She knows I will forgive her. "The 'sexy temptress Forrest - yacht girl.' You know, it has a nice ring to it!"

I can't help wincing when she says the words out loud. Yacht girl. Depending on who you listen to, hopping on a superyacht full of rich men and pretty models could be a dream or a nightmare.

As open-minded as I like to think I am, I can't help being a little bit suspicious about a group of men who are willing to pay thousands for the pleasure of my company.

"I don't think I can leave now," I hissed into my phone.

I was standing in one of the dozens of guest bathrooms, in front of a cabinet full of La Prairie skincare, gemstone-encrusted Guerlain cosmetics, and Chanel perfumes.

"The bloody yacht had to anchor outside the marina because the slips weren't big enough to handle its length! Me and ten other girls were brought here from the pier on a speedboat."

"Ooh, Ivy. You're sounding like a yacht girl already, talking about slips and length. That's all they want you know, the men. Some flirting and dirty talk. Someone to laugh at their jokes. But whatever you do, do not go near the railings. I've heard of some girls getting drunk and falling overboard."

"No, that is not the only thing they want!" I hiss, struggling to rein in my temper. "The host made it clear to us that we must put out if we want to be paid. You should have seen his face when he tried to watch us change into our bikinis. Randy old sausage. Yuk!"

"Have a martini and simmer down," Mary-Kay tried to soothe me. "If a man can afford a yacht, he can't be all bad."

"I am not about to get shitfaced without a friend by my side, MK! How could you do this to me? You promised!"

I was ready to explode with anger! Mary-Kay is not so nearly as badly strapped for cash as I am. She will always have a roof over her head when we start college. My parents live in Maine and exist on a strict budget!

"MK! You knew I needed to earn money for my accommodation next year. And this was your idea in the first place."

My friend was acting so chill about the horrid surprise she was springing on me.

"I'm sorry. I just heard my brother's in town, and I can't risk being away for the weekend without him asking fifty questions about where I went.

He's an ogre. And he has this uncanny ability for finding out the truth. I daren't come with you!"

Mary-Kay hates her brother, Fletcher, so much, she even refuses to have photographs of him in the accommodation we share. To an eighteen-year-old girl just out of senior high, he sounded like a really scary individual, controlling and manipulative.

"Screw your horrid brother!" I huffed before disconnecting the call. I couldn't help being upset. I was torn between the money and the risk of staying on the yacht on my own for the weekend.

Looking at myself in the reflection of the giant pane of glass leading to one of the lavishly decorated cabins, I came to a decision.

Maybe wearing last season's clothes is a hell of a lot better than entering international waters with a bunch of strangers, Ivy. You were clueless to accept this gig without knowing more about things!

I heard a helicopter landing above my head, probably here to offload more wealthy passengers.

My mind is made up. Looking with disgust at the tiny Brazilian-style bikini I'm wearing, I head for the deck. Time for me to hop aboard that speedboat and get the hell out of here.

My feet lurched underneath me as the yacht engine purrs to life. And when I looked out of the nearest porthole, I saw the Manhattan sky-line slowly getting smaller behind us.

The captain seemed to have made my decision for me. Running outside, I bumped into a pretty girl wearing a similar micro-bikini to my own.

"Tell them to stop!" I grabbed her arms, my eyes wide with desperation. "I don't want to do this!"

The girl scoffed. "Lie back and enjoy it, newbie. Whether you like it or not, you're a yacht girl now."

Five minutes later, I was nabbed in the corridor and hustled into one of the cabins by an ea-ger-looking man with busy hands.

"You're new, aren't you?" He licked his lips while looking at me. "Lovely."

He's talking about me as if I'm a work of art that he wants to buy.

I am so not in the mood for this—and this cabin is starting to make me feel claustrophobic.

"Well, I don't know about you, mister, but I'm going back to the top deck." I made a move for the door, but he blocked the way, pushing me back towards the bed.

"Come on, you little tease. There's no need for you to leave yet. At least give me a quick blowjob."

I gasped, not out of shock, but disgust. "That's not in my job description, mister!"

But when I tried to leave again by walking around him, he gave me a hard shove down on the bed.

Hot tears of frustration leaked out from under my eyelids. How dare he! How dare this man think he can feel me up!

And then the weight of his body was lifted off me.

The man called Jay entered my life with a bang. Or was it a whimper? That brute who was trying to kiss me was certainly whimpering as he checked with his fingers to see if his neck was all right after Jay squeezed it so hard.

The man looked at Jay with his body in a sub-missive posture.

Half-scared, half-resentful. All respect.

And then the tall man in combat casuals looked at me with pity in his riveting blue eyes. That made me spitting mad!

Does he have any idea how embarrassed I am? I can't wait to get out of here and hide my blush-ing cheeks.

And now here I am, running for the hills, look-ing for a way out, just because I was too em-barrassed to accept the tall, dark-haired man's help. Remembering what the sailor told me, I start climbing back up to the top deck using the spiral stairs.

Hang on a minute. Maybe I was too hasty to bite the hand that saved me.

I catch a glimpse of that recognizable cropped hair and broad shoulders as I walk past one of the lower rooms.

The man called Jay is slumped down in an easy chair, staring blankly at the screen, papers piled up on the massive table in front of him.

It would be cool to hang around here and kill some time until the people upstairs have paired off. The view from the railings is beautiful, and I know the other men won't bother me if I'm in close proximity to a man as intimidating as Jay.

I'm totally out of my depth, but I don't have a problem with the other girls.

They are friendly and professional. And they don't look like they need money for college res fees, that's for sure!

I simply cannot resist smiling as I go past. When I get off this yacht, I think I will remember Jay fondly.

I am going to have to hide and wait it out somewhere, so it might as well be here. The staff I spoke to when I came on board confirmed that I won't get paid if I don't sleep with someone.

This is the first and last time I ever agree to do something without having all the facts!

I was told that what I do on the yacht was voluntary. If I stay hidden, I can avoid observation and then lie that I was with someone.

"Hey! Forrest!" Spinning around, I see Jay leaning halfway out the door. "Do you still want to leave?"

He must have seen me breezing past. I guess he was encouraged by the small smile I had on my face.

Edging a bit closer to him, I try to look like I know what I'm doing. "Go on. I'm listening."

His megawatt grin really bowls me over. He jerks his thumb, indicating the cabin with the screen. "The documents are signed. I have nothing more to live for. Come have an iced tea while my program finishes?"

It's a question, not an order. It seems we're off to a good start.

Charming as hell, as well as being super good-looking. This man certainly knows how to bury the hatchet.

"Will you take me home afterward?" I am slightly hesitant. He is too good to be true. I'm waiting for this particular prowling leopard to show me his spots.

I can't help noticing that he has removed the khaki green overalls he was wearing. His outfit of jeans and a white Henley shirt suits him so well. His work boots look like they might be handmade.

But that all fades away when I gaze into those stellar blue eyes of his.

Yes, he's an arrogant SOB, but he's a gentleman underneath it all. I can tell.

"If that's what you want, Forrest. I will take you home."

It's way too tempting for me to refuse. I try not to get too suspicious when I go into the room and the first thing he does is lower the blinds!

"Hey!" I am regretting this already. "I didn't come in here for some hanky-panky!"

He grins. "Yep. I don't know about you, but I don't want old Brent walking past and being able to see you."

Falling into the recliner next to the one he was sitting in, I huff. "You and me both! What are you watching?"

The enormous screen shows lots of charts and statistics while a man's voice drones about market shares and predictions.

"Never mind." Slumping down in my chair, I pretend to fall asleep. "I'll just leave you to enjoy it in peace."

"You don't follow the stock market?" He goes to the fridge and gets two bottles, but I can see that his face is lit up after my little comedy routine.

"Why should I?" My smirk seems to challenge him to change my mind. "When there are so many other more interesting things to follow."

"Like what?" Standing in front of me, he presses the side of his cold bottle to his face. He is definitely too hot to handle. I can see the outline of his abs stuck against the thin material of his shirt.

"The fresh foods market?" I make the suggestion and then flutter my eyelashes like a ding-bat.

Passing me my bottle of iced tea, Jay sits beside me, chuckling. "You have great comedic timing. So, tell me, Forrest. Where's home?"

I have to think fast. "Manhattan. Where else? I'm a city slicker through and through."

He frowns, his laser focus trying to pick apart my casually sophisticated statement for clues.

"I find you fascinating," he finally admits. "Why did you agree to come on board and then back out? Have you run into some financial difficulties?"

Ooh, mister, wouldn't you just love to know! But there's no way I'm going to tell you my sad "fish out of water" sob story.

"You know, I heard about it on the grapevine and thought it sounded fun. Worth doing for the chunk of change and the chance of making some great business connections."

The way he is concentrating on me is making me nervous! It's like he can see right through me and knows I'm putting on a brave front.

"But the reality never lives up to the hype, does it?" He touches my hand. It's not a kind gesture—it's dominant, almost predatory.

I was not expecting how my body would react to his touch. That light brush of his hand against my finger is enough to make me melt.

Instantly, I am sexually excited. Like a frightened rabbit, I give a small jump in my seat and laugh nervously. "Mm? I-I guess I'm still a bit skittish after Brent."

He does not take his eyes off me. "I'm not Brent, Forrest. Tell me, do you still want me to take you home?"

Stammering, I try to stick to my original decision. "Yes... yes!"

He smirks. "I would love to hear you saying that while you were naked—and I was on top of you."

Oh, yes, Jay. I would love that too.

Why am I even bothering to pretend? I want this man and it's clear that he wants me too.

"Well?" He cocks one eyebrow as he waits for me to reply. "Should we stay or should we go?"

# Chapter 3 – Forrest

We should stay. That's what I want to say. The melting feeling between my thighs increases as he runs one finger over my wrist.

Just one touch, and I am acting like a rabbit in front of the headlights. Frozen in place, watching and waiting for what comes next.

I wish I had the experience to turn him on the same way he is doing to me, but I don't. Every part of my body is insisting I stay put, but I have no way of showing it.

"Why me?" I manage to get the words out.

The confident smile is gone from his face as he allows the physical attraction he is feeling to show through. It thrills me to see how badly he wants this.

"Why you?" His voice is gruff as if he is reluctant to expose his desire. "Rather, I should be asking you why you aren't giving me the bum's rush, just like you gave old Brent."

Slowly, his fingers move up my arm, teasing and tantalizing me to want more. I close my eyes so I can concentrate on his touch. A moan escapes my lips.

"Mmm, because..., it feels like this was meant to be."

"My thoughts exactly," he murmurs, "but if you want, we can wait until we get back to New York. Tell me what borough you live in and I'll find a helipad close by there."

No, no, no! There is no way I want to take this man back to the untidy student accommodation I share with my best friend!

My eyes fly open. "It's now or never, Jay."

Oh my God. He looks absolutely delicious as he leans back in his recliner and pats his lap for me to join him. Scrambling up from my chair, I straddle him with no hesitation or preamble.

The thin covering of my bikini bottom is all that separates me from his crotch. I can feel his cock is rigid underneath my mound. Suddenly, I'm happy I got that bikini wax last week.

I'm as soft and sensitive as a baby kitten down there.

His hands grip my waist. "You comfortable?" I can't stop myself from grinding up and down on the hard outline of his erection.

"Yes." Dammit, I wish I knew more sexy things to say. I want to tell him to "fuck me hard right now, you gorgeous stud!" But I don't have the nerve.

Jay knows how badly I want this, though. Using his thumb, he brushes it over the front of my bikini bottoms. "Ahh," I gasp as my clit reacts and floods with excitement. "That feels so good."

"It's going to feel even better if you give me a kiss."

It turns me on the way he tells me what to do. Bending my head, I dare to kiss his firm mouth. It feels so different compared to the two boys I got with during senior high.

The bristles of his scruff prickle in a very stimulating way. Oh boy, my pussy almost melts when his tongue licks my upper lip and then my lower one.

"I'm so turned on," I confess, "just to let you know that this might not last as long as you want it to."

"Is that so?" He is so dominant in the way he brushes his fingers over my bikini in all the right spots. "If you want, we can try to fix it."

"I kind of like the sound of that." I giggle a little bit at the thought of him fixing me good.

"You will," Jay promises me, his kisses getting a bit deeper and the stiffness under his jeans zipper jumps as I rub myself over it. "Because I am going to make you come right now. Then you will be able to relax and enjoy what follows after."

"Lock the door." Whatever this man wants to do to me, I don't want interruptions.

As if I weigh nothing, Jay picks me up as he stands, and places me on the edge of the big wooden table. "Don't move. This won't take more than a second."

He goes to the door and slides the bolt, locking us in together. My heart skips a beat. I really, really want this, but I can't believe I'm being so blatant!

As he prowls back to where I am perched on the edge of the table, he says, "Do I need to use a condom, Forrest?"

I shake my head. "I'm on the pill. But I don't mind if you use one." I'm kind of glad that we are having this conversation. I can add "takes responsibility" to this man's list of highly desirable traits.

But his most desirable "trait" is still zipped up inside his jeans. I'm panting with eagerness to see and touch his cock. I want to stroke it and taste it.

The excitement inside my belly does a little flip when I think of him unzipping.

And then he pushes me back onto the table and starts to eat me out. The way he pushes the crotch of my bikini to one side and lowers his mouth down there is one of the most beautiful things I've ever seen—or felt!

He unties the bows on either side of my bikini bottoms and the triangles fall away, exposing my slit for his expert attention.

Bending my knees, I rest my feet on the edge of the dark mahogany table. The highly polished surface feels smooth and cool under my skin.

"Oh, Jay... this has never happened before. I never knew oral felt so good."

The tip of his tongue flicks delicately over the hood of my clit. I just about go through the roof with ecstasy. Then his mouth lowers over my pussy and he sucks and licks me as if I am the most yummy thing he has ever tasted.

The passion mounts quickly inside me as the blood rushes to my clit, adding to that pounding urgency pulsing inside me.

And then he somehow manages to make it even better. With his mouth and tongue busy with my clit, he slowly inserts his finger into the tight wetness of my pussy.

It's a tantalizing feeling. That little bit of friction moving in and out as my plump, hairless labia gets all soaking, glistening wet.

I think about how rampant he must be inside those jeans of his and my desperation to see his cock tips me over the edge.

"I'm coming, Jay. Don't stop."

I grab for his hair. My need to hold on to something tight is so strong. My thighs grip his head as he gives me the business with his mouth.

Leaving my clit to come in amazing waves of orgasm, the warmth of his mouth covers my aching mound.

The feeling is perfect—not too sensitive and not too light. Just the pressure of his mouth over the front of my slit.

"I-I need you to say something." I am panting, flailing on the table, desperate for him to stick around long enough for me to repay the favor as my crashing orgasm fades away.

"My turn." He's no longer satisfied to be the source of my pleasure as he reminds me what he is here for. "Is that what you want me to say?"

Cocky bastard! But he is also a bit of a mind reader too!

"Fair is fair," I smirk, licking my lips as he unzips and hauls a gorgeous girthy cock out of his jeans. "Is that what you want me to suck?"

"It's a good place to start, Forrest." He grins, but then gets serious again as I slide over the table towards him. "Is that your pussy juice lubing up the table like that?"

I check the shining trail I have left on the expensive polished surface. "Wow, yes. I must have come in buckets."

"That," Jay says, unbuckling and unbuttoning too, "is the sexiest fucking thing I have ever seen in my life."

It pleases me to know that. Lying on my belly, I beckon him to come closer. Giving blowjobs is something I definitely know how to do. But I want this one to be unforgettable.

I have to open my mouth all the way to fit him inside. And that's just the head of his cock.

"I wanted this to happen from the first time I saw you," Jay growls as I begin to suck and lick the stiff member, cupping his balls as he lowers his jeans.

Just as I suspected, he tastes and smells as good as he looks, like sandalwood and fresh-washed cotton.

"Mmm," I moan, wanting him to know how badly this is turning me on. He's more than a mouthful, thick, veiny, and lengthy as a porn star. This man could drive a woman wild with just a dick pic!

Holding his shaft, I pump the cock, keeping the tumescent head in my warm, wet mouth and running my tongue around the rim. I can feel he's not going to last long. I'm amazed he has even lasted this long after eating me out so nicely.

He leans forward, rubbing his large hands on my back and then massaging my ass. "Ready?" he lets me know this is happening right now. He stiffens and seems to get even bigger before I feel the warm jet pulsing into my mouth.

His fingers grip the round curve of my ass as he lets the orgasm flow over him.

Just like the rest of him, he is yummy. And after spending this short time seeing how delicious his cock is, I am ready for him to slide inside me.

"I'm ready for more if that's what you mean." Our sexual communication is flawless. It is as if we were always meant to be together.

Stepping back, he pulls the Henley shirt over his head and throws it onto the recliner. His cock is still rock hard in all the right places, only losing some degree of acuteness after coming in my mouth.

I can't take my eyes off him as he kicks off his boots and socks. Next, the jeans come off. And then his tight briefs are tossed aside.

The only thing I have on is the bikini top, but the triangle covers have been pushed to the side, displaying my pert breasts and dark brown nipples.

He crawls onto the conference table like a ravenous tiger, crouched to spring into action.

"Play with yourself," he demands because he can tell that I am all too eager to obey. "Don't touch your clit—that's mine—but you can slide your fingers into that tight slit of yours."

Holding my breath, I wait as he moves towards me. I have come to learn with great happiness that with Jay there will never be a slamming penetration. He has way too much finesse for that.

Sliding his hands along the inside of my thighs, it feels like he's appreciating a beautiful work of art as he stares at me.

"You're sensational, you know that?" Lightly, his fingers caress my hairless mound, causing me to shiver with excitement. "I've never wanted any woman as much as I want you."

The intense way he says this takes the words out of my mouth. "I-I love your body," I manage to say with a nervous giggle. "You look like an athlete."

This is the truth. His muscles rippled when he removed his shirt, and there was not an extra inch to pinch anywhere on his taut body.

"I have stamina, Forrest," he smirks, "but you are difficult to resist, so this is going to be a long ride."

"You're right about the long part anyways," I whisper under my breath, but he hears me and smiles.

"I'm a big man." I love it when he runs his hands through my hair. "Are you sure you can handle me?"

I'm sure of one thing, Jay. I think I will burst if you don't get busy fucking me right now!

But all I say out loud is "I'll let you know if I'm in discomfort, Jay, but please don't confuse sex moans with pain, especially if I don't want you to stop!"

"Pleasure and pain during sex is such a turn-on," he growls, and I gasp when I feel him entering me. His girth is incredible, but he takes it slow as I brace myself for his thrust.

And just like that, my body readies itself for another climax. That lovely melting feeling pours over me, concentrating on my clit and my tight slit.

"God, girl, but it feels so good inside you," Jay grunts as he feeds every inch of himself into me. "You're all warm and wet."

"I'm dripping," I share, "because I'm so turned on right now."

I don't have to touch my clit. I don't need to. The friction of his cock sliding in and out of my pussy is vibrating my clit in the most sensational way.

My eyes widen as he pushes deep into me, but I adore the feeling of receiving as much of this man inside me as I possibly can. His technique is superb, masterful. I forgive him for being such a cocky bastard because he certainly knows how to use that amazing equipment he keeps hidden in his jeans.

His strokes get faster, and his urgency is obvi-ous. "That sweet snatch of yours has really got me going," he growls. "Can I come inside you?"

I would love to watch him spurting as he pumps his cock, but I don't mind him coming inside me either. "Yes." He can tell from the way I shut my eyes and hold my breath that I am also close. "Do it."

I swear I can feel it when his orgasm shoots deep in me. It must hit my G-spot or something because my climax rolls over me like a tidal wave.

We are joined together, desperate for this to continue, but crazy excited that it's happening at all.

He rolls off me and we lie next to one another as our breathing returns to normal.

"So, Forrest. Tell me everything about yourself." He helps me get down from the table and we laugh a little bit at the steam on the polished wood. "We've got all night."

# Chapter 4 – Forrest

After dressing, we go looking for a cabin together. Here I am, a fully-fledged member of the yacht girls club—and I'm loving it.

After the great sex we just had, I think I would follow Jay anywhere.

Finding an empty suite, Jay asks if it's okay he slides the lock on the door.

"Yes," I say. "I trust you—to show me an amazing time in bed at least!"

He chuckles. "I love the way you can still joke after what happened to you with Brent."

I head for the shower. "Men like him are a joke, that's how!"

After pulling the drapes shut, he turns on the lamp on his side of the bed as I slide under the crisp linen sheets, my bikini discarded on the floor. My body is still damp from the shower, but the cabin temperature is set to perfect ambience.

Turning onto my side, I look on as Jay strips naked. This is a floor show I will never get tired of watching!

"Well?" he gets into bed with me, a simple action that somehow has the ability to make me insanely happy.

"Well, what?" I can't wait for him to initiate more sex. "Should I put the bikini back on?"

Jay lifts up one arm and waits for me to snuggle into its crook, nestling my head on his shoulder with one hand on his chest.

Yes, folks. This is me, Forrest the yacht girl, officially in paradise.

"No, you look great, with or without a bikini. But I want you to tell me everything about yourself, remember?"

"You first." I'm trying to delay the inevitable. I really like this man, but there is no way I am going to tell him the truth about myself.

Settling down more comfortably on his pillows, Jay frowns as if he finds himself boring. "Ex-Marine. Set up a nice little business before training started. It flourished while I did two tours overseas."

"Two tours?" I am impressed. "Isn't that scary?"

Chuckling, he hugs me a bit closer. "No, Forrest. That's what the training is for."

"I don't like the thought of having a target on my back." I give a little shudder, pulling the cover up.

"You're cute, I hope you know that. I mustered out for family reasons. Expanded on the business I left behind. And here I am."

Stroking his flawlessly perfect chest, I smile. "Here you are. In bed with me."

He kisses the top of my head. "On a superyacht with my first yacht girl. Something I never dreamed I would ever do."

That makes me huff and pout. "I'm not a professional yacht girl, Jay."

"Then do you mind explaining how you came to be here?"

\*\*\*

Ten days before

I had my doubts about being a yacht girl from the time Julian Stratford suggested it to Mary-Kay and me.

Last week, we took our headshots to the Strat modeling agency just off Fifth Avenue. After Elite and Wilhelmina, the Strat is considered to be one of New York's best beauty talent representatives.

The receptionist took one look at Mary-Kay and me and immediately got on the phone. "Mr. Stratford? Can I send two young ladies through? A dark, long-haired brunette, about five eight, golden suntanned, perfect skin. And a shoulder-length wavy blonde, looks to be five six, pale skin with some freckling."

His answer must have been yes, because the receptionist got out of her seat and walked us down the plush carpeted corridor to the wide double doors at the end. After knocking, she opened the door and stepped back.

I can't believe Mary-Kay and me might be chosen to be models! I wonder how soon I will be paid? I am so broke; I really need some cash stat!

Julian Stratford was sitting behind his enormous desk. He would have been good-looking in my books if he hadn't come across as so fake. His veneers were slightly too white.

His outfit was clearly meant to scream Versace. And his fake orange-brown tan was hideous, only making his Botox more obvious.

For a successful New York businessman, he looked more like a used car salesman. Or a newscaster. Someone who liked to call the shots if you gave them the chance.

"Welcome to the Strat, ladies." Julian's eyes lit up like Christmas lights when he said the words.

"Hello, Mr. Stratford."

"Thank you for seeing us, Mr. Stratford." It must have been clear to him that Mary-Kay and I were fresh off the block.

We passed our headshots to him and politely waited for him to ask us to sit down. He looked us up and down as we stood awkwardly in front of him.

"I'm not going to lie." Julian got straight to the point without bothering to offer us chairs. "You're both too short and curvy, but you've got it here." Using his two thumbs and forefingers, he made a square shape around his face.

I am so not having that! I decided to make a stand.

"With all due respect, Mr. Stratford, I think the industry parameters have expanded over the last ten years. The only area height is a requirement is the catwalk. Everywhere else, the models can be photoshopped taller or slimmer."

"Yes!" Mary-Kay backed me up. "You can photoshop someone's dimensions, but you can't fake pretty."

A wide grin spreads over Julian's face. "You're right—and I like your moxie." Flicking over our headshots, he checked our ages. "Eighteen. You're a bit old, so let's get you started quickly before you age out. Um...."

He shuffled the papers on his desk and stopped looking us in the eye. "With the ongoing addiction crisis, I can't risk adding two girls to my books if they have health issues. Throwing good money down the drain to promote you if it turns out you're hooked on something. I'm going to need you to have blood tests."

Darting looks at each other, Mary-Kay and I figured that makes sense. "Sure," I said, "Whatever makes you happy, Mr. Stratford." I had nothing to worry about on that front.

After a couple of disastrous hookups in high school, I never went near young men again. Boys are too eager and desperate with zero experience.

There is something about bad sex that can make a girl lose interest fast. I was holding out for a man with all the right moves. I wanted a guaranteed orgasm the next time I had sex!

Julian clapped his hands after hearing us agree. "Excellent! I'll pay for the tests, of course." He handed us two forms over the table. "Just get your sweet asses down to this clinic. They'll let me know if you're clean. Then we can talk."

I should have walked out then and not looked back, but Mary-Kay and I desperately needed money, MK, because her brother was a tyrant when it comes to giving her a livable allowance, and me, because my folks were typical middle-income salary slaves.

Whenever I have needed anything, my parents told me to earn it myself. Like I said, middle class much?

All my exceptional schooling had been funded by scholarships. I was going to be the next Margaret Atwood, which was why I did my senior years in New York.

MK had always called her brother Scrooge Mac-Duck because he didn't let her have a credit card.

There are models needed for everything now—adverts, music videos, and expos. Whatever was needed, we would do it.

After the Strat agency, we were headed for a casting agency to try and get work as movie extras. I'm all about the hustle when it comes to crazy money-making schemes!

"The last thing I want is for our first day at college to be a bust because of the shoddy way we are forced to present ourselves," Mary-Kay reminded me. "I'm prepared to have dozens of injections if it means I get to buy some designer brands!"

Several days later, Mary-Kay and I were lazing around our student accommodation wondering if we had enough money to rent something to watch on our streaming service when my phone rang.

"Hello? It's Julian Stratford. Just calling to let you know your tests came back clean."

"No surprises there." I was so hoping for a modeling job, and all this man can focus on is that I don't carry some weird disease.

"You girls live together, don't you? It says here your addresses are the same."

"Yeah. Roommates. We're here during the summer vacation, because we're still looking for a budget-friendly college dorm—at least, I am."

The new semester was starting in a couple of months. I needed money if I was going to be able to afford res on the college campus.

"Cool, cool." The way he said it, I can tell that Julian Stratford doesn't give a shit about my housing crisis.

"We're always available, Mr. Stratford." I tried hard not to sound too begging.

"I might have something for you girls this weekend if you're interested."

Beckoning Mary-Kay to come closer, I put the phone on speaker. "We're listening, Mr. Stratford," Mary-Kay said, giving me the thumbs-up.

"Have you heard of yacht girls?"

Mary-Kay and I looked at one another and shrugged. "No, sir. We have not."

"Let me explain." Julian's voice adjusted to being all coaxing and nice. "Billionaire businessmen take their yachts into international waters, and you get to party with them. Does that sound like something you would be interested in doing?"

"Define 'partying.'" Mary-Kay looked dubious.

"Yes, please do. We're not into drugs or wild bedroom antics, Mr. Stratford," I said, just so we were clear.

He chuckled. "You wear a bikini and chat to wealthy billionaires. Be friendly, cute, just your average weekend night out. And it pays fifty thousand dollars per."

We nearly fell off the couch in shock. "F-fifty thousand dollars each?! And there's no sex involved?"

"Not unless you want it," Julian said, his voice teasing. "I know dozens of yacht girls who met her Prince Charming during one of these gigs. Imagine being married to a billionaire, girls. How exciting your lives would be."

Mary-Kay shoots that image down. "I dunno. My brother's really wealthy. I can't imagine some poor woman being married to him. It would be a complete nightmare."

I snort with laughter, and the two of us giggle at Mary-Kay throwing shade at her bully of a brother.

Mary-Kay continues. "He's a tightwad—holds on to a penny so tight you could turn it into copper wire."

Julian chuckles. "Yes, Mary-Kay! It's jokes like that the men on these yachts want to hear."

He has no idea that my friend is being serious. "So, can I tell the captain to expect you at the marina? You'll have to share a cabin, but I have the feeling you might not spend too much time in your bunk beds. Ha-ha."

I wasn't a fan of his suggestive comments, but fifty thousand dollars was a life-changing amount of money for me.

Mary-Kay looked at me and we gave the thumbs-up. "Sure, Mr. Stratford. Count us in."

It seemed like it could be a walk in the park—me and my best friend, flirting with a group of middle-aged businessmen on a yacht in the middle of the ocean—how wrong could I have been?!

\*\*\*

That is so not the story I am prepared to tell Jay. "I'm with the Strat Modelling Agency. They asked me if I wanted to earn a lot of cash doing this. What girl is going to turn that much money down?"

Jay whistles. I love the way his hand strokes my arm in a soothing, repetitive motion. "I thought you must be a model. You're so... beautiful, but in a unique way."

I'm loving this. "How so?"

He obliges me, continuing his compliment. "Well, first of all, you're no walk in the park. And I love a challenge. The cherry on top is your lovely, long suntanned legs, bodacious body, and that hair! It's like black velvet."

I think I'm falling in love with you, Jay!

"Will I have seen you in anything? Ads, print, media?"

Let me get that idea right out of his mind! "No. I'm fairly new to the modeling game. I joined the

Strat with my friend, but she couldn't come with me this weekend, so I came alone."

"How many times have you been on a yacht?"

The way Jay asks the question, I can't quite work out if he means if I have done this before—had sex with a man for money—or if I have been on a yacht in general.

"My parents are middle class, if that's what you want to know!" I answer, a bit snippy. "Even though I live in Maine, we can't even afford to have a rowboat!"

"Are my questions rude? I'm sorry. I just want to know more about you."

Pulling me close and turning me onto my belly to lie on his chest, he waits for me to settle. Tucking my hands under my chin to make myself comfortable in this new position, I stare at his face to my heart's content.

"I don't like questions when they get too personal."

Jay stares right back. "Is sex too personal? Because I would love to fuck you again. As soon as possible, in fact."

I feel him thickening and stiffening between my legs. My body responds with a writhing, sensual feeling.

"Now you're talking," I whisper seductively.

# Chapter 5 – Jay

Only the supreme discipline I learned in the Marines enables me to leave Forrest the next morning.

My body has that well-used feeling of lots of sex and very little sleep. I haven't felt this exhausted but happy for a long time.

"One more for the road—or the skies?" Forrest asks, her husky voice teasing and tempting as she pats the side of the bed next to her.

I have a towel wrapped around my midriff and another around my shoulders to dry my short light brown hair. "I have to go, sweetheart," I don't look at her when I say this because she has the ability to change my mind. So, I keep staring at my reflection in the mirror.

In the reflection, I watch her perfect lips start to pout. "It's still early, Jay. You told me you use VFR on the helicopter and the sun is barely over the horizon."

Crossing her arms, she sulks, fuming with anger that we can't sail away and keep fucking forever.

I sit on the edge of the bed and I caress one of her long shapely legs. "Did I bore the pants off you last night talking about Visual Flight Rules? You must hate me for that."

Bursting out into sincere laughter, she's suddenly all smiles without a hint of frown. "You don't have to bore me to get my pants off, Jay! Besides, it was interesting."

I am satisfied. But I still have to go. My business is not allowed to make a single decision without my go-ahead.

Leaning over, I kiss her forehead. "Are you coming? I only need to get this one meeting out of the way and hand the contract off to my legal team—and check the Nippon markets—but after that, I'm all yours. My offer to drop you off at the helipad closest to your apartment still stands."

Shaking her head, she looks down at her hands and begins to play with her fingernails.

"Er... that's okay. I think I can handle myself here for the remaining few hours and return to the marina with the rest of the girls. It's Sunday, Jay. Can't you stay?"

She is so adorable. I kiss the end of her nose. Any more than that and I definitely won't make it back to the city today.

"Can I have your number, Forrest? Can I call you later in the week?"

And what are your plans for the remainder of the summer? The Christmas holidays? The rest of your life?

Damn! I have got it bad.

"I don't know if we're allowed to hand over our phone numbers, Jay. Mr. Stratford seems kind of strict about how the yacht girls are allowed to interact with guests. He said too many girls contact married men without permission and that can get them into trouble with their wives! But I would love to see you again."

"How about if I call your agency and ask them? I can pass a message on to you that way."

"That might be the best way." She bites the end of her thumb when saying this like she's nervous or something.

"Julian fucking Stratford better pass my message on to you, Forrest, if he wants his agency to continue functioning as normal!" My stomach tightens at the thought that maybe she is giving me the brush off. "Let me know if you don't want to see me again! I can take it."

She chuckles. "No, you can't! I bet you have never been turned down by a woman before in your entire life!"

We laugh, and I want to hug her again. "I have, I promise. Before I joined the Marines, I was a skinny boy. Lanky and skinny. They called me 'Spider' in senior high. Not even when I blasted out the rest of the competition on the basketball court did they change their minds!"

Her chocolate-brown eyes sparkle. "I had you down as a footballer."

"Yep, that too. Thank God I liked sports because the fitness level demanded by the Corps is off the charts."

Forrest pushes down the sheet and straddles me, sitting on my lap again, pressing her forehead against mine. "That's an excellent descriptor for you, Jay. Fit."

She runs her hands down my arms, and I can tell that she is taking great pleasure out of feeling my muscles. Her breath starts to come in short gasps. I know she's thinking about all the crazy sex we had last night.

This pretty lady certainly knows how to make me feel like a million bucks—in bed and out of it. Then she gives a wicked little smile.

"No, wait. Did I say 'fit'? Because I meant to say 'spider'!"

We laugh and fall back onto the bed, kissing and romping. I haven't felt this young and lighthearted since my folks died. I needed this.

I need this young woman in my life. And when I see something I want, I take it.

That sobers me up fast.

We're lying on the bed, our legs intertwined, our arms in a tight embrace. It's special.

"Promise you don't mind if I contact the agency for your number, Forrest?"

A lovely lilting smile curves her lips. "Promise you will contact the agency and send me a message, Jay?"

We kiss one another gently, sealing our promise to each other. I don't want to tell her the real reason why I am leaving so early.

I don't want the other men to see me creeping out of a yacht girl's cabin! Not that I hold myself above them for doing it themselves, but I never thought someone like Forrest would happen to me.

Pulling away, I head for the door. "Don't forget to lock it after I leave in case any of the other men are still in the mood."

Her eyes are sad, but accepting. "Sure, Jay. Thank you for a wonderful time."

My beautiful brown-eyed girl. We will have so much catching up to do the next time we meet.

"Oh, I forgot!" Smacking my palm against my forehead, I say "duh" like I'm stupid. "Kevin says every girl has to show a colored rubber band before they disembark. I think they're in the side table drawer—help yourself."

Lifting my hand in a half wave, half salute, I leave.

***

I am a patient man when it comes to business.

Sometimes I'm a bulldozer, rolling over the competition. Sometimes I'm a pair of tweezers, picking a deal apart for all the information. But I am always patient.

So then why am I standing in the Stratford Modeling Agency lobby at ten the next morning? The moment the stuck-up receptionist unlocks the doors, I'm blasting through them like a hurri-cane.

"Julian Stratford. I want to see him."

The receptionist looks me up and down. I'm wearing a business suit today. Nothing unusual in New York.

It's summer, so the linen-wool mix is a light, breathable texture—dark blue with a plaid tie and white shirt. I keep casual wear for the weekends.

"Mr. Stratford hasn't come in yet, Mister…?"

This is not good enough for me. "Give me his cell number."

The receptionist shakes her head firmly. "I'm afraid I can't give out Mr. Stratford's private number to strangers, sir."

Growling in a low voice, I let her know that I am the last person she should be messing with when I am on a mission!

"Call him on his private number and tell him that Jay is here to see him."

"Jay who?" The receptionist is really feeling me now. I notice the dawning realization that I am the last person she would want to be denying appearing on her face.

This is the part I enjoy. "Tell him Jesse James is here to see him. Jay to my friends. He'll know who that is."

Turning away from me so that I can't see the number she presses; the receptionist waits for the call to connect.

"What the fuck?" She doesn't realize that Julian Stratford has a few things to learn about volume control on his voice. "You know not to bother me, Janet!"

"I-I'm sorry, Mr. Stratford, but there is a man here to see you. He... he says his name is Jesse James—Jay."

A loud yodel comes from the other end of the line. "Woo-hoo! I can't believe it. That's the man they call the Cowboy of the Conference Room, Janet. His advertising revenue is the same as a small country's! Tell him I'll be there in ten minutes. Get him anything he wants."

I step back from the reception desk before she disconnects the call. Janet is looking at me like the prize bull at a State Fair.

"Please take a seat, sir. Mr. Stratford won't be long. Can I get you anything? Tea, coffee, bottled water?"

I'm lucky. I'm one of those people who can stare at the wall for hours if I have something good to look forward to at the end of it all.

Blame it on doing sentry duty in the Corps. Twelve hours straight of standing at attention. And I hate playing on my phone.

"No, I'm fine."

Julian Stratford bustles through the glass doors fifteen minutes later. He's all toothy grin as he tries to shake one of my hands with two of his.

"Welcome! Welcome. Please come inside my office. Can I call you 'Jay'?"

When I am settled in the chair in front of his desk, I get straight to the point while Julian reaches for a pencil to make notes on the yellow legal pad in front of him.

"I visited Kevin's yacht over the weekend. I want Forrest's phone number. She wouldn't give her contact details to me—said you didn't allow that. So, now I'm here. You can allow it."

The pencil drops out of Julian's hand. A smarmy smile spreads over his face.

"I'm afraid I can't just do that, Jay."

I'm out of my chair in a heartbeat. "If you doubt my story, call her! Do you think that I would waste my morning coming here to connect with someone if she didn't want the same thing?"

Julian looks a little less smug after getting a taste of the famous Jesse James temper.

"Please sit down. I don't mean to upset you, Jay, but that is not how this works!"

Sitting back down, I let my anger simmer. "Fine. Tell me how it works and I'll go along with that."

"Miss Forrest is a valuable asset. I have her booked to go yachting with an Arab prince next weekend. Are you following me?"

"You mean she's not a free agent in her private life? That's ridiculous. You can't control that."

Julian shakes his head, pretending to be sad. "Miss Forrest actually pays me a lot of money to control that side of things for her, Jay. She doesn't want a relationship. She wants money—in her private life and her professional one."

I can't comprehend what this slimy motherfucker is trying to say to me. The way he says professional like that.

Julian continues.

"It's her job to make you think she's having a good time. And you had a good time with her, didn't you, Jay? But how would Forrest and I make our money if she were to go off on a date with a man for free?"

My blood was running hot, but now it's running cold.

"What are you trying to say?" I don't really want an answer to my question, but I have to ask it anyway.

Julian makes a temple of his hands in front of his mouth and leans his elbows on the desk.

"Hmm, I'm not sure what Miss Forrest wants to get out of this, but why don't we start with a booking fee of ten million dollars? I can book her out for a week with you for that."

"Are you telling me that Forrest is a prostitute?"

Julian acts shocked. "Absolutely not! She's a yacht girl. My yacht girl. And I wouldn't be able to say that, Jay, if she didn't want to be paid as much as I do."

I make a low growling sound, so Julian backpedals a bit.

"If you don't like the sound of that, why don't we book her to be in one of your brochures or online promos? Then you can pretend the money was for that. I'm a reasonable man. I want your advertising revenue as much as you want to see Miss Forrest again."

I feel dirty and disgusted. But worst of all, I feel stupid. I try one last time.

"Look, give me Forrest's phone number. I want to hear this coming from her own mouth." I just can't believe she wants me to pay to see her again.

I'm more than halfway in love with the girl. I can't believe she would do this to me.

Julian Stratford shakes his head. "Give me twenty million dollars, Jay, and I'll think about it. If not, there's always the Arab prince."

Lunging over the desk, I grab the sleazeball by the tie, pulling him halfway across the desk so I can snarl into his face.

"You better hope I never see you again, Stratford." Julian is wheezing, trying to call for his receptionist, but he can't breathe. I let him go and he falls back into his chair, gasping.

I'm out of here. I can't take this shit anymore.

"And you can pass on a message to Forrest as well. When I next see her again, I will call her an escort to her face!"

# Chapter 6 – Ten Years Later

"Is there any chance you can get a sitter for Daniel for this weekend, Mary-Kay?" I'm on the phone with my friend, trying to find a date for the weekend. "It's kind of an emergency."

I can tell Mary-Kay has her phone on speaker because there are definite sounds of my eight-year-old godson playing in the background. He's making superhero noises.

Mary-Kay's little boy is the light of her life—and mine. I never thought I was the maternal type until Daniel came into our lives. Thanks to her brother, MK was able to drop out of college and set up in a nice house in the suburbs with the trust fund money he gave her.

It was a struggle to finish my education without my friend by my side, but I've always been driven. And that drive pushed me into culinary and hospitality journalism the moment that my college diploma was placed in my hands.

"Pfft. Come on. You know that you're the only sitter I can truly rely on. Blame it on all those horrible podcasts. I listened to one the other day when the mother lets the neighbor's teenage—"

Once Mary-Kay gets started on listing all the reasons why she doesn't trust anyone but me or her to look after Daniel, we could be here all day. I cut her off.

"Yeah, I heard that one too. But none of this helps me find a partner for the weekend."

My friend loves hearing about my exciting life. "Ooh, where are you going this time? Bermuda? Hawaii?"

Her enthusiasm makes me chuckle. "It's not a junket. It's a restaurant review. The new five-star hotel opening in Vegas claims to be the next molecular gastronomy marvel. Rupert wants me to check it out."

Rupert is my agent. He syndicates my restaurant reviews around the world, edits my website, and books my TV appearances. He is London-based because I write about hotels and restaurants all over the world.

England, Italy, France, all of Europe, and a surprising number of places in South America too. I have written about all the top destinations to eat. Travel and good food excite me—kind of like a substitute boyfriend—which is maybe why I don't have a date for this weekend.

Mary-Kay sighs with longing. "What I wouldn't do to be able to hop on a plane and fly to Vegas for the weekend."

"You can! That's what I'm offering, you doolally! Just find a sitter for Daniel. Or bring him with and we can get one of those fancy Vegas English nannies to look after him at my hotel. You know the nannies I'm talking about. Chances are they'll teach Danny algebra or French while we go eat."

Mary-Kay goes off on another one of her horror story rants about sitters. I'm desperate to find someone to come with me.

I am what folks call "in-between boyfriends" at the moment. I have a fairly substantial list of exes whom I have managed to stay friends with, but I had to learn the hard way that suggesting a weekend away with a single ex is not a good idea.

It gets their hopes up for a reconciliation, but when I'm done with someone, I'm done. Also, a worryingly large number of my ex-boyfriends are now engaged or married. One by one, my pool of exes who are friends is dwindling.

This is because I'm not that girl. You know the one that insists on staying "friends" with an ex when he's dating someone else and she's not. I wouldn't put up with that happening to me, so I'm damn sure not going to inflict that on another woman.

But I can't let the fact that I'm struggling to find a date for my restaurant review a little bit worrying.

It's like the universe is trying to tell me something...

Mary-Kay stops mid-rant when she hears me huff. "Sorry, friend, but my son is my pride and joy. I can't risk leaving him with a stranger."

"What about Daniel's Uncle Flet?" I know I'm clutching at straws, but Daniel's uncle is my last hope. Mary-Kay hates it when Daniel chatters about his precious "Unca Flet," because it makes her realize how her son adores the strong male role model in his life.

She would never mention her brother when we were in high school together. If Mary-Kay ever had to reference him, she would call him "The Wretch."

"Seeing as he's doing so well in the business world, why can't 'Unca Flet' take some time off work and sit his nephew for us? He can bring his girlfriend and watch TV in the sitting room like a normal person."

Although Mary-Kay and her brother are friendly towards each other now, she still doesn't like to be reminded about what a success he is compared to her. Apparently, he's some bigwig businessman. He hardly ever comes to visit, and Mary-Kay says that's fine by her.

"Just so long as the old poop continues putting that money in my account every month, we have a cordial relationship" are her final words on the matter whenever I bring her brother up in our conversations.

I'm pleased brother and sister are getting along a bit better now compared to how much they seemed to hate one another when MK was in high school. Mr. and Mrs. Banner died in a car crash when MK was still a tween. It must have been rough on both of the siblings.

When we first met in junior high, Mary-Kay confided in me that her brother used to say he never wanted to have her as his responsibility. I'm guessing he changed his mind about hating responsibilities after Daniel was born because he suddenly became the perfect uncle.

"I think he's between girlfriends at the moment," Mary-Kay tells me. "The last one didn't stick. I can't say I blame her—not that I ever got to meet her. The Wretch likes to keep his cards close to the chest and I guess she got tired of playing a losing game."

"Gambling analogies! That's a sign that you must come with me to Vegas."

That makes Mary-Kay chuckle. "You're breaking my heart, friend. I really wish I could go, but I'm too paranoid to leave Daniel with anyone else. I know how long the meals last at those fancy schmancy restaurants you have to review. How long did that last one take?"

I have to laugh. "Are you talking about the 'dining experience' on the island in the middle of the lake? It took eight hours. If the food hadn't been so good, I would have been scared they had left me stranded there."

"Dining experience? Oh my God, is that what they're calling restaurants now? When is it going to end?"

"Hopefully never. It's my bread and butter, don't forget. Since my dad injured himself, I have two extra mouths to feed—that's one more than you."

Mary-Kay makes a rude noise with her tongue. "You keep your parents in luxury, Ivy. I think you forget how mean they were when you were struggling to make it in New York."

I don't like to talk about those days. That's where I got my appreciation for fine dining. There are only so many instant noodles someone can eat before they realize they want better things in life.

"I'm too old to bear a grudge now." As much as I love to chat with my best friend, I am reminded that she can do it all day from the comfort of her home while I have deadlines to worry about. "You're friends with The Wretch now. You should understand. I remember when the only name you would ever call him by was 'old grump.'"

That gets us laughing hysterically. I hear Daniel come closer as he wants to know what Mommy and Ivy are laughing about.

"We're laughing about the rude names I used to call your uncle when I was young, Danny," Mary-Kay explains.

Danny gasps. "I'm gonna tell on you to Unca Flet!"

My friend makes soothing noises. "Gotta go soon. It's his bedtime.

I appeal to her one last time. "MK, do you know any other single moms who might be interested in a free, all-expenses-paid jaunt to Vegas? Think, I'm begging you. Maybe someone whose child has sleepovers with Daniel, and then you can sit for them? I can't dine in the restaurant alone."

Mary-Kay hears the desperation in my voice. "Try one of those blow-up male dolls they sell online. I bet the servers won't even notice. Chances are it'll be more fun than most men. When my brother came here for Christmas, he hardly said a word. Talk about a poker face! Or maybe he had a poker rammed up somewhere else!"

I give a short laugh, but I'm really worried. Restaurant critics can't sit alone at a restaurant. It tips the staff off when a customer makes notes after eating every dish. My famous catch-phrase: "You never get a second chance to make a good first impression" would be meaningless if an establishment knew to make a good first impression in advance.

And that's what restaurants do. When they see a solo booking, they make a special effort in case it's a critic.

Sensing my lack of appreciation for her joke, Mary-Kay suggests something truly last ditch.

"Listen, maybe it's time you met the old grump. My brother might be close to Vegas. He's living in Los Angeles at the moment, I think. I don't think he would mind sitting opposite you while you ate."

I don't want to sound ungrateful, but I have been avoiding meeting her brother since forever. Mary-Kay made him sound loathsome when we were teens together, and I can't shake the feeling that he still is.

Yes, he looks after Daniel's every need and keeps tabs on their day-to-day necessities, but my dislike for him is hard to shake.

"I'm desperate, friend, but not that desperate. The Wretch is hella scary. I have to at least know a little bit about the person I'm sitting next to so that we have something to talk about. Does he even know who I am?"

"Full disclosure," Mary-Kay says, sounding contrite, "I used to blame a lot of the naughty things I did as a teenager on you whenever he caught me out."

I am utterly astonished! "What? That's not fair, MK. He must have a very low opinion of me. And I wasn't even the worst of your friends. You used to get up to some incredible nonsense with a couple of other girls too—why didn't you blame them?"

"It was so long ago. Relax. No one can bear a grudge for that long."

That is no comfort to me because I have the suspicion that MK's brother is the kind of person who can hold on to a grudge the same way he holds on to his money—with a steel-tight fist!

"No wonder he never came to Daniel's christening." I know I'm stressing, but I can't help it. "He probably couldn't stand to see me made an official godparent."

Mary-Kay tries explaining. "He didn't come to the christening because he's an old grump with his nose stuck in the money trough. Listen, I'm sorry for blaming you, but you would have lied too if you were me. You have no idea how intimidating my brother can be. Frankly, I ran out of friends to blame and you were the easiest to lay it on. I knew he wasn't going to bother scolding you."

That's where Mary-Kay is wrong. I have a very good idea of how terrifying The Wretch could be. When MK and I were teens, he hired a private detective to follow a bunch of us girls around once after he found out his sister was dating some older guy from the Bronx. So, I guess that makes him a snob too.

I snap back, "And this is the man you want me to take to a fine dining restaurant? Nice." I can't help being sarcastic, but I have run out of options.

"I'm going to send you his number," Mary-Kay says. "You better call him soon. What is it today…? Wednesday. Yes. Call him soon so that he can book a couple of hours out of his precious schedule to travel to Vegas."

"Nuh-uh. Nope. Nada. No way. The Wretch would make a wretched dinner date! And that was even before I found out that you blamed me for all those sticky situations you got yourself into as a teenager, Mary-Kay. If he doesn't hate me for that, he will hate me for not telling him how naughty you were."

Mary-Kay doesn't take no for an answer. "Too bad. What's the restaurant's name again?"

"Sabine at the Banderole. The booking is for eight-thirty. Peak dining time in Vegas, because it leaves time to go clubbing afterward."

"My clubbing days are over, friend." I'm impressed that Mary-Kay doesn't sound sad about it. I guess that is what happens when a woman embraces motherhood as completely as she has done. "I'm sorting this out for you the moment I get off this call. If Fletcher can't make it, I'll tell him to send one of his hot assistants to take his place."

I'm hopeful, but still vaguely disturbed. "Fingers crossed that it's one of the assistants. Thank you, dearest. I suppose that's the only thing I can do."

# Chapter 7 – Fletcher

One glance at my phone tells me it's my sister. I slide to accept the call.

"What?"

"A 'good to hear from you, Sis, and how are you' would be nice, Fletcher."

The noise I hear in the background tells me my nephew is still awake. "Why isn't Daniel in bed?"

Mary-Kay sighs. "He's allowed to have a delayed bedtime occasionally. I was on a call with his godmother and he likes to say 'hi' to her."

I have zero interest in another of Mary-Kay's troublemaker buddies from my sister's high school days. She managed to hook up with the worst airheads in seventh grade. Whenever Mary-Kay opened her mouth in high school it was to tell me she needed to do something ridiculous because "her friends did it."

"Tell her not to call so late."

Mary-Kay puffs into the phone to show me how put out she is by my abrupt dismissal of her goofy pal. "How do you even know how late it is here on the East Coast, anyway?"

Sometimes my sister can be a real dunce. "Because my Rolex tells me so." I like teasing her because Mary-Kay is so gullible.

"You bought me a Rolex for Christmas, Fletcher, and it doesn't tell the time in two cities." Mary-Kay suddenly realizes that she needs a favor from me because her tone changes. "Not that it's not a beautiful watch. I love it."

"I was teasing you." I glance at the watch in question to check how long this conversation is likely to last, already bored. "I know how many hours ahead you are because it doesn't take a genius to make that deduction. Spit it out. What do you want?"

She ums and ahs a bit before getting to the point. "I need a favor. Not me exactly... my friend."

Oh boy. Here it comes. One of her old pals has gone and fallen off the deep end and needs my help to get her out of a sticky situation. I knew this day would come around.

Ever since they were teens, Mary-Kay was continuously dragged into trouble by that bunch of unprincipled minxes.

Sneaking off to clubs together with fake IDs. Check. Hanging around shifty bars instead of being asleep in their residence dorm room. Check. Running up ridiculous amounts on my stolen store card. Double check.

The incidents were never-ending. It was hard for me to handle my sister at the best of times, but her out-of-control friends always managed to make it worse.

"Listen, Fletcher," Mary-Kay says, encouraged by my silence and taking it for granted that I'm ready and willing to help out her pest of a friend. "She desperately needs a date in Vegas for tomorrow night. You hang out in Vegas, right? And if you can't go, you can get someone from your office."

My sister has never shown the slightest interest in my work until it's time for me to pay for something. Then she pretends to be fascinated when I tell her about what I do, but it goes in one ear and out the other. It seems like the Vegas part of my business expansion must have stuck in her memory.

"You're right, Mary-Kay. I do hang out in Vegas. But I do not want to have dinner with one of your fiendish friends. If she can't get a date for a Vegas weekend, she must be a complete bore."

My sister goes silent and then begins confessing. "If you still hold all the trouble I got into against my friends, Flet, you shouldn't. I might have blamed them for a few things that were straight-up my fault."

I am unmoved. "Then I blame them for encouraging you to do it instead of stopping you. Those girls have never been true good friends to you, Mary-Kay. I can't believe you made one of them Daniel's godmother."

"I'm going to pretend you didn't say that, and I forgive you because you don't know her like I do. It's time you two met. Bury the hatchet. She's grown up now. She's got a career and everything. And she needs a date for this week-end."

The phone gets muffled as Mary-Kay flicks through her notepad. "It's at the Sabine this Saturday. Eight-thirty. Please, can you hook her up with someone?"

Sabine. That's interesting enough for me to play nice.

"Fine." I accept the fact that Mary-Kay is reaching out to me for this one favor that isn't money-related. "Let me talk to Daniel now."

She puts my nephew on the phone. "How's things going, Daniel? How's school?"

Sounding wide awake even though it's nearly an hour past his bedtime, Danial shouts. "Unca Flet! Mommy's friend called you an old grump!"

***

As it happens, I am in Las Vegas this weekend. My new hotel launch is happening right now. The official opening, not the soft opening. And I am curious to know how one of my sister's old school friends managed to get a table at my hotel restaurant on what will definitely be its busiest night.

I asked Mary-Kay to send me a photo of her friend so that I can recognize her when we meet at the bar. Typical of my sister, she sends me an image of ten teenage schoolgirls sitting on the bleachers throwing up gang signs and pulling faces. She added text: "Middle row in the middle," like I'm supposed to be able to work out who that is.

I took care in dressing this evening, not because I want to make a good impression with one of my sister's ditzy friends, but because I will be watching service at the restaurant this evening. I already know the food is exceptional, but it will be my pleasure this evening to know that the service is too.

"Mr. Banner?" One of the lobby staff is standing at my elbow. "A lady is asking for you. May I bring her to the table?"

I'm seated at one of the booths in the wine bar. Everything smells like leather and beeswax polish with a faint scent of cigar smoke. I have my head bent over my notepad as I check things off.

Sure, the notepad is actually a journal, a genuine Anya Hindmarch—the leading tannery artisan in France—and the pen is a Montblanc. I enjoy the finer things in life when they are worth it.

"Yes. And tell Evan to open a bottle of Krug. She's bound to like that."

"The vintage?"

"Make it a seventy-nine."

The man nods his head and leaves. That is the type of service I want to be on offer at the Banderole. Discreet and subtle.

The carpets are so thick I don't hear her approaching. She clears her throat. I don't know why she would think she was at the wrong fucking table. The server would have made sure to indicate my table properly.

I look up. And then everything except time goes into freefall. My mind seems stuck in slow motion as I see her black stilettos with red soles, smooth tanned legs, form-fitting black pencil skirt, and white silk blouse unbuttoned just enough to catch the eye of any red-blooded male within a twenty-yard perimeter. And finally, her face.

"Forrest."

I don't mean to say her name out loud, but I can't help myself. And I think I said it quite loudly as well because she blushes.

She opens her mouth to say something and begins to move away, but a server is blocking her escape with a bottle of Cristal in a huge silver bucket of ice.

"Mr. Banner?" Another server is standing by the table, two champagne flutes in his hand.

They are waiting for Forrest to sit down. I want to stand up. It's like a comedy sketch where everyone is frozen in place.

I stand up. Hell, this is my hotel. I can say someone's name as loud as I fucking well want to.

"Pleased to meet you." It's quite reassuring that my manners are still intact even though my composure is in pieces. "Would you care to sit down?"

This is her chance to step away and tell me that something has just come up and she has to leave. I am wishing with all my heart that she accepts my invitation.

"You're Unca Flet?" She is checking she's got the right table, the right man.

"Yes." I am acutely aware of the three servers standing around like a very interested audience listening to us. It's almost like they want to mock me. Well, you wanted discreet and subtle service, and now you've got it.

"Not Jay?"

"I mean...." Am I getting flustered? "I mean, that's my name too, but it's a joke. Because my business associates call me Jesse James—"

"Jesse James—Jay. The Cowboy of the Conference Room. I've heard about you in the hospitality merger business reports." Her voice is barely above a whisper, and yet I think everyone in the bar can hear her. I have to applaud her discipline. Girl would have made an excellent Marine—she knows how to stay cool under fire.

"Yep. That's me. But please call me Fletcher—Fletcher Banner."

Amazingly, she sits down. The poor guy carrying the heavy bucket sets it down on the small table another server places next to our table. Forrest and I stare at each other as the staff opens the bottle, offers me a taste, and then pours two glasses.

Forrest doesn't offer up a toast, but she does take a small sip.

"I love the seventy-nine," she says to me in a steady tone. "The lovely golden color, shimmering and clear. Sweet and fruity on the nose, but stunningly complex. This vintage Krug is healthy and mature, with notes of apricot, honey, orange blossom... and sugar cookie."

I notice she has the record function activated on her phone. Is she trying to shame me? It's she who should be ashamed.

"Switch that off." I point to the phone. "And might I remind you that secret phone recordings aren't admissible in court."

"I'm describing the champagne so that I can remember how it tastes for later," she tells me in an innocent voice. "It's my way of handling this. I'm not trying to entrap you, Banner."

"Too late, darling," I growl, "because you already did."

"Oh yes." She rolls her eyes to the ceiling. "I forgot. The creepy guy on the boat, the one who promised to call me but never did, thinks I'm the one trying to ensnare him. That's rich coming from the man who fucked me stupid and then disappeared out of my life forever."

I am stunned. "Me? I'm the one who was left looking like a damn fool. I went to Julian fucking Stratford and begged him to give me your number. Only he wouldn't, because that's not something pimps ever like to do."

Her hands bunch into tight fists and then stretch out into bent claws. She's feeling my insults like a raging tigress. I'm not usually rude to ladies, but as far as I am concerned, Forrest has never been one.

"You are so lucky we're in a public space right now, Banner, because if we were not I would teach you a lesson."

My bitterness makes me sarcastic. "What are you going to do? I was a Marine for Christ's sake. I could see one of your punches coming from a mile off."

That's about as far as my sarcasm goes. I have to suppress a yelp of pain as the toe of her pointed black stiletto catches me on the shin under the table. The pain is intense enough to make my eyes water.

# Chapter 8 - Ivy

There is no way that I can review Sabine restaurant now. I am way too upset. How dare this man speak to me like this after the way he let me down!

"Ugh, you know what? You might have it all going on up here," I say, motioning around his face with the palm of my outstretched hand and I am quite pleased when he flinches back, "and down there—" I gesture towards his muscular body and groin area. "But I can see why you're still single—because you have the nastiest personality ever!"

We keep our voices low, but we are in no doubt about how much pent-up emotion lies under our conversation.

"At least I never lie to my partners when I don't want to see them again," he claps back, quickly recovering from the pain in his leg. "Unlike you—sending me to that sorry excuse for a man, Julian Stratford. I always thought it was suspicious when you didn't just give me your number like any normal person would."

It bursts out of me like a dam breaking, made all the more painful by the fact that I have to keep my voice low.

"I couldn't give you my number because I was poor! I didn't have a fancy phone or an apartment with a fucking helipad. Why do you think I was on that blasted yacht in the first place?"

He grabs his glass, and for one moment I think that he is going to throw the champagne in my face. But he doesn't. He downs the expensive drink and motions with his hand for one of the servers. The man comes pronto.

"We're going to Sabine. Carry the rest of the bottle there and make sure to keep it on ice."

I shake my head, saying to the server, "Actually, no. Don't move the rest of the champagne over to the restaurant! I'm sure the Sabine sommelier would like to select their own aperitif drinks to go with the restaurant's set menu."

Recovering from my disappointment and anger, my professional attitude comes back into focus. My readers look forward to my reviews. Even if they can't visit the restaurant for themselves, they enjoy reading about the food and buying the cookbooks.

I guess I'm going to have to start calling him Fletcher Banner now. There is no way I am going to refer to the biggest disappointment in my life by the same name his business cronies call him!

Saying goodbye to my heartache and Jay from the yacht forever, I prepare to act like the successful culinary and accommodation journalist that I am.

"Mr. Banner, are you coming?"

He looks surprised when I speak to him so formally. "You still want me to sit opposite you at the table? It would be very difficult for you to kick me at Sabine you know—the lighting is quite good and the tablecloths don't go all the way down to the floor."

I roll my eyes. "Oh, ha-ha, Mr. Comedian. You deserved that kick. And you'll get another one if you dare talk to me again with anything other than respect."

Fletcher gives a sarcastic salute. All he does is bring the tips of his fingers to his forehead with a quick flick and a smirk, but it's all he needs to do to make my hackles rise. I can see this evening is going to be... challenging.

Picking up the beautiful leather-bound journal in one hand, he holds out his other hand towards me. "Respect, sure. But just remember that it swings both ways. Come on. Take my hand. I won't bite you."

Fletcher seems ready to put the past behind us as well. He's abrupt, dictatorial, and to the point as usual. He tells the server to take the bottle of Krug up to his suite later.

The man is acting as though this is any other blind date and I am the perfect dining companion. He's still that same cocky bastard who rocked my world ten years ago.

Why won't my brain stop reminding me about how it felt when he lay on top of me, staring into my eyes as he slowly inserted his—

Damn it, Ivy! Pull yourself together. It's time to file that mind-lowing sex in the past—where it belongs.

I wish it was that easy.

Is it my imagination or is he limping slightly as we walk to the entrance doors? I must have gotten a real good kick under the table, and I don't feel any sympathy for him considering the hundreds of sleepless nights I lay crying for this man when I never heard from him again.

I truly believed that Jesse "Jay" James was my exception to the rule. My knight in shining armor. The lightning that never needed to strike twice.

If I had been brave enough, I would have told him how broke I was and given him my real name, but considering the circumstances under which we met, I couldn't.

I blame it on my stupid pride. When I was eighteen, it seemed very important to me that Jay believed we could be equals. I never wanted him to see my shitty digs and my old phone with the smashed screen.

I didn't want his pity—only his love.

How stupid and fucking naive you were, Ivy! Now, pull yourself together for the sake of your readers. They want this Sabine review more than you want to rehash the past.

At Sabine, the staff part in front of us, smiling and acknowledging Mr. Banner and his dining companion. We are led to a sitting room and served champagne after a pleasant consultation with the sommelier.

One of the waitstaff brings us a plate of amuse-bouche. These delectable morsels are translated into English as "tease the mouth." But all I can think about is how Jay went down on me in the yacht cabin and the delicious way he ate out my pussy and the pulsing waves as I came over and over again....

I have to get my head in the game! Time for me to push "erase" on those tantalizing memories.

Looking at me with a frowning fixed stare, Fletcher wants to know what I am smiling about.

"Oh, nothing. I was thinking to myself how ideal this is for me. I'm in the shadows while you take all the spotlight. The famous Cowboy of the Conference Room."

His frown deepens. "So, why do you need to point that out?" I can tell from the way he is acting that he's still sore about that kick I gave him. Fletcher continues. "Every single member of staff in every hotel I own knows who I am."

"So, no appearances on 'Undercover Boss' for you, then." My tone is lighthearted, even cheeky. Lifting my glass in a mock toast, I take a dainty sip of the champagne with pursed lips. Adding air to the sparkling wine brings out the flavors.

Taking a small USB-compatible recorder out of my evening purse, I whisper a few words about my impression of the welcome we got, the interior of Sabine, and the quality of the champagne.

"What are you doing?" Fletcher looks at my recording device with scorn.

"Making a few notes. Do you mind? I have a blog—"

Fletcher makes a loud scoffing sound. "What is it with you guests? You all seem to think you can become an 'influencer' every time you use the camera on your phone."

Smiling politely, I nod. "Yes. I agree. People should live in the moment and experience the delight that one fleeting moment gives them. You never get a second chance to make a good first impression. It's the same with food."

"And sex." He growls the words in a low voice, but suddenly it seems as if the whole restaurant might be listening.

I blush. "That's not what I meant, and you know it. Ugh. I am so not going to discuss my sex life with you."

He sighs, leans back against the elegant cushion on his chair, and then clears his throat. "Please don't. That's the last thing I need you to be throwing in my face."

Doesn't he like the thought of me with another man? How weird. He doesn't seem like the jealous type, especially not after ten years of separation!

I push the pause button on the recorder. "Me too. But it would be silly of us not to acknowledge that too much water has flowed under the bridge for us to still be angry at each other. I mean, I was only eighteen, so mistakes would have been made no matter what."

"Christ!" Fletcher shakes his head. "What the hell were you doing on that yacht at eighteen—?" He stops short of what he wants to say before continuing in a steadier voice. "You're right. What happened that night was a giant mistake. Let's move on."

Somehow, when he says that, a hot wave of sorrow washes over me.

He thinks I was a mistake. A blip on his radar. He has no idea how head over heels I fell for him after our blissful, wonderful one-night stand.

Managing to smile, I agree. "Yes. Let's move on. That's for the best. I can't believe Mary-Kay never told me that her brother was connected to a Vegas hotel."

"My sister only likes to talk about herself—and she knows nothing about my business."

The server brings three tiny appetizers to the table for us to enjoy with the champagne. I jot down a few notes and take some photos. Fletcher seems interested in what I am doing.

He grins and leans forward with his hand held out. "Maybe I should introduce myself properly this time. Fletcher Banner, CEO of Insignia Consolidated Investments."

Insignia Consolidated Investments. One of the largest hotel chains in the Continental US. Who am I kidding? One of the biggest resorts and accommodation chains in the world.

Finally, the penny drops. "Banner. Insignia. Oh, I get it. They are all words for flags and emblems."

Fletcher grins and begins to relax. "Yep. This is the Banderole. That is a long flag with two points at the end. And then I have the Pennant budget hotels and Ensign luxury resorts.

They operate under different names according to which country."

I can't believe I am sitting opposite the legendary CEO of Insignia. "Why didn't Mary-Kay ever tell me this?"

He shrugs. "Damned if I know. She's always held a grudge against me."

"Why?" I've always been fascinated by family dynamics.

Fletcher finishes his champagne before replying. "Because I left her alone after our parents died. She was a kid, almost a teenager, and she irritated the shit out of me whenever I was out on furlough. So, instead of pretending to be her guardian, I stuck her in a boarding school."

I try to imagine how it must have felt from both sides. A young Marine, I'm guessing around twenty-three or twenty-four years old, left to care for his tween-age sister. Mary-Kay, on the cusp of puberty, was stuck in a boarding hostel while her elder brother toured with his Corps.

Ouch. I would not like to be their analyst!

Fletcher gives my question a bit more thought. "And I turned our parents' ranch into a hotel so it could earn an income while I was enlisted. Mary-Kay said she would never forgive me for bulldozing the family home. But she's mellowed since Danny came along—she sees how comfortable the profits have made her life."

I can't help looking around the beautiful restaurant and marveling at the decor. "You certainly managed to parlay the profits into something quite spectacular."

The maître d' interrupts us discreetly. "Mr. Banner. Ms. Woods. Your table is ready. Please follow me."

When we are settled at the table, I feel the excitement start to mount inside me. This is when the magic is about to happen. I press the button and start to record again.

"Do you mind?" I point at it. "If you like, I can give you a waiver and sign it if you are worried about privacy issues?"

To Fletcher's credit, he seems cool about being recorded now. "I want to know your real name. Mary-Kay calls you Ivy. What's up with that?"

"I publish under the name 'Holly Forrest.' It's a play on words."

The first course arrives and we eat in silence. I make a few notes and record my first impressions.

"Nori and salted caramel type sable biscuit covered in bitter chocolate, so perfectly tempered that it snaps easily. It's a new take on chocolate-covered pretzels with an Asian-influenced twist. A touch of sesame oil too."

Fletcher listens to my recording intently.

"Are you Holly Forrest, the food critic?"

# Chapter 9 – Fletcher

She gives me another one of her mischievous smiles. Her dark eyes sparkle. "Yes, Mr. Banner, I am. Yet another reason why I was so shocked to see you sitting at the booth. I've never had to sit opposite the hotel owner while critiquing one of their restaurants before!"

Another course is set in front of us as the server explains what it is. I'm only half listening. I am not liking the fact that this woman has the power to make or break my flagship Vegas hotel restaurant at all! For the first time in a long time, I am forced to face the consequences of my actions.

Looking at Forrest sitting opposite me, I kinda get the feeling that she is enjoying flipping the script on me. The server and sommelier have given up on me entirely and are busy putting all their focus on my gorgeous dining companion. All three of them are chatting and laughing together, discussing the best wine pairings.

This is one time when I don't have all the power. And I am not liking this feeling one bit. As before, there is something about this woman that makes me want to save her and then dominate her.

As if she was made to be mine.

When the waitstaff has gone, I get to work strategizing. "You've been busy since I last saw you. And I'm finding it difficult to see how a penniless eighteen-year-old girl who's prepared to go on a pleasure cruise with a bunch of strange men manages to become one of the most respected names in restaurant reviews.

Leaning back in her chair, Forrest observes me with that sexy, lilting smile curving the bow of her lips.

"Same as you, Mr. Banner. I worked hard."

There is something about the way she stresses the word hard that makes me think she's got other things on her mind.

"I like to think I'm gifted and hard-working." I leave the statement hanging just to see what she makes of it.

"I don't know about the conference room, but you are definitely gifted and hard-working in bed."

Damn! I was right. But is she flirting with me or teasing me? The young woman I met ten years ago has flown the coop, leaving this sophisticated siren in her place.

My urge to dominate her gets even stronger.

Typical of my nature, I don't acknowledge what she said. My ignoring her doesn't seem to unsettle Forrest at all.

Most women would be driven mad by a man not responding to a saucy statement. With supreme indifference to my silence, she continues eating.

I like the sound of her husky voice as she makes notes while speaking into the recorder. It's a throaty purr that I can't help wishing was being whispered in my ear—and in bed.

"I'm usually a bit more discreet when I do this," she says as if she's sharing a special secret with me. "But seeing as you already know why I'm here, I can do it in the open. That's why I needed a dinner companion, you know. It's easier to camouflage my true reason for being at a restaurant."

"Who do you usually take with you as 'camouflage'?"

I hate myself for asking, but the question comes out like an accidental gunshot.

She twists up one side of her mouth in a cute grimace. "Friends, dates, other food bloggers. You know—the usual."

Is Forrest deliberately trying to be opaque? It's driving me nuts the way she is giving me the runaround.

The sweet dessert wines are served. One of the waitstaff brings out a plate of exquisite petit fours placed on a silver cake stand wreathed with flowers. Forrest takes a small nibble out of each one and continues writing as if I'm not even there.

Reading her notes upside down, I can tell she has an impressive palate. She is listing some of the more obscure ingredients the chef has used.

Looking up and seeing that I am not eating, she smiles and holds a candy out towards me. "Want one?"

I don't take it with my fingers. I bite it straight out of her hand. For that one moment, our eyes connect like electricity.

I decide it's time to show my hand.

"What do I have to do to get a five-star review for the restaurant out of you?"

She freezes as her pearly white teeth bite into a chocolate. Swallowing and then licking her lips in a way that makes me wish we were in bed together, Forrest leans closer.

I feel her foot slide up the inside of my leg and begin to caress my thigh. "Are you suggesting what I think you're suggesting, Mr. Banner?"

Oh God. She's started massaging the crotch of my pants with the ball of her foot. It feels so good... but I have to keep my focus.

I manage to get the words out. "How much?"

If I wasn't so well trained, I would have groaned as her foot pressed down hard into my crotch.

"How much?" She is not talking in a husky, whisper anymore. She's seriously pissed, so it comes out like a hiss. "Are you offering to buy me?"

"No, Forrest. I'm not talking about how much for the night. I want to buy a five-star review from you for Sabine. How much for that?"

Before the pressure of her foot can get more intense, I push my chair away from the table so she can't reach me with her foot anymore.

"Don't act like what I just said is an insult. You sold yourself once before. Why not do it again? And this time, you don't need to put out—just make the damn rating five stars."

She doesn't stick around to give me an answer. Picking up her notepad and recorder, Forrest slips them back into her purse and walks out, flicking her long black hair behind her shoulder without a backward glance.

*** 

Ivy

I need to get away from that man before I explode with rage.

How dare he think that how we met ten years ago still defines me. What happened on that yacht still haunts my dreams. The nightmare circumstances and the dreamy outcome. And now Fletcher Banner thinks he can buy my good opinion too?

Screw him!

"Forrest! Wait!" That only makes me walk faster. If I didn't have my Louboutins on, I would be sprinting.

He catches up with me outside the hotel. I'm looking around for a cab, unsure where I can go to escape him. Fletcher spins me around to face him. "Can you stop running away for one moment? Stop acting like a child."

His uncompromising attitude riles me up. Lifting my hand, I smack him across the face.

"Let me go!"

A few passersby clock us as we struggle on the sidewalk, but they can see it's not escalating into more violence, so continue walking. I am so embarrassed. Never in my life have I been the kind of person to cause a public incident.

If a cop car had been cruising by, they might have arrested me for assault—and this horrible man could have pressed charges!

"It was a mistake to think you could forgive and forget, Banner! And it's clear that you don't respect my professional integrity."

His cheek is scarlet from where I let him have it.

Oh God. A kicked shin and now a slapped face. This man has turned me into a mad woman.

"What I said was out of order. And I'm sorry." After he says that, he drops my wrist from his forceful grip. "I... I'm impressed with what you've made of your life, Forrest. But I can't let you go before I tell you how much I love your reviews."

A bubble of hysterical laughter bubbles up inside me. I can't help it. This is so absurd.

"Please call me Ivy, Fletcher. And I'm sorry too."

Reaching up, I caress his cheek. In that moment, time seems to stand still as we connect without anger standing between us.

And then he kisses me. I fight against the hunger that rises inside me. It's almost a physical ache, it is so intense.

His large hands run around my waist and over my hips, reaching for my ass and then pulling me closer.

I yield to his touch, ready, willing, and very able to return his embrace kiss for kiss.

Running my fingers through his thick dark hair makes those old memories rise to the surface. It comes back to me so clearly.

We're lying in the cabin bed together, the gentle rocking of the yacht in the water reflected in our bodies. Side by side, we kissed and explored every exquisitely tender part of each other.

The old fire flares up in me again and my pussy reacts to his scent, his touch, and his rock-hard body.

Fletcher's voice is hoarse when he speaks. "Do you want to come up to my suite?"

Without removing my lips from his mouth, I whisper my eager reply. "Yes."

Stumbling back into the hotel with eyes only for each other, we return to Sabine. "Tear up the bill for table five," he tells the host waiting to greet guests at the entrance. He runs his arm around my waist, giving me a little hug. "This little lady is with me."

I can't help it. I have to giggle. He's still the same bossy man who wanted things his own way on the yacht. After all this time, he has not changed...

And I am loving it!

Impatient because we have to walk to the VIP elevator doors, I hardly notice the speed at which it zooms up to the top floor. We can't keep our hands off each other. All I know is the elevator seems to reach his floor way too fast. I don't want this to stop.

I hate Fletcher Banner so much—his arrogance, his bossy attitude, and his air of entitlement—but I think I still have feelings for Jay. Especially sexual ones.

We stumble out of the doors, our bodies intertwined. We're starting to unbutton our clothes already, desperate to see the other person naked.

"Let's go through to one of the bedrooms?" he asks me, half begging, half the same old bossy Jay.

Unbuttoning the buttons of my blouse, I am almost panting with excitement. "No, let's do it right here in the hall. I don't think my legs are strong enough to walk any farther."

I get a glimpse of the man I fell head over heels for when Jay grins and says, "Better not. I told them to bring the rest of the Krug champagne here. And what I have planned for us...? Well, I don't want to be disturbed by anyone."

# Chapter 10 – Ivy

I run into his arms and kiss him. I feel young and lighthearted again as if the tears and misery never happened.

"You promise you went to Stratford's and asked for my number?" I have to double-check to make sure. The pain of my broken teenage heart haunts me.

Leading me to the master bedroom, he jokes, "I nearly strangled him when he wouldn't give it to me! He told me you were booked to sleep with an Arab prince the next weekend."

Gurgling with laughter, I shake my head. "Ha! I never went back there, Jay. And besides, it was orientation at my college the weekend after we met."

He kicks off his shoes and hooks off his socks. Even though he is wearing a formal suit, he still has that debonair, slightly raunchy way he carries himself. Throwing himself onto the bed, he lies with his hands behind his head resting against the pillows.

"Now that we have a bit of privacy, you can continue taking off that blouse—" He stops. "What's your real name? I want to call you that. But I also want to know so you can never run away and hide from me again."

I have the grace to blush. "I promise it's Ivy Woods. Like I said, Holly Forrest is just a play on words. Please call me Ivy." I was just about to tell him that Mary-Kay and I chose the name "Forrest" as my model name when we agreed to become yacht girls together.

Then I remember just in time that Fletcher is actually her brother. He would go ballistic if he knew the yacht was Mary-Kay's idea!

He growls in appreciation as I slowly unbutton my silk blouse and shrug out of it. "You could have saved me a hell of a lot of wasted time if you had just told me that in the beginning."

"Patience is a virtue," I tease him, turning around so he can watch me unzip out of my pencil skirt.

"Get that sweet ass over here."

"Ooh, so demanding." I am loving this, being with him as an adult. Now, we can play our games as equals, no holds barred.

Keeping my stilettos on, I strut around in front of him in my lacy white lingerie. His erection thickens and gets big under the front of his pants. I remember how amazing that gorgeous part of him made me feel and a surge of arousal courses through my body.

It's been a very long time since I was so aroused just from looking at a man. Dare I admit to myself that it has been ten years? But I don't want to acknowledge that Fletcher is the only man for me.

After strutting around in my underwear and seeing how his cock is straining under his pants, I begin to dance seductively. Running my hands over my pert breasts and gently pinching my nipples into hard peaks.

"Do you like this?" I want him to be so desperate for me when I finally join him on that bed. I'm a big girl now and I want to play games with this hot stud. And maybe I want to punish him just a little bit for insulting me in the restaurant too.

One bra strap drops off my shoulder—and then the other one. Fletcher can't keep his eyes off me. He starts to unzip so he can haul out his cock and play with himself while he watches me, but I won't let that happen.

"Nuh-uh, naughty. Hands where I can see them."

Groaning with sexual frustration, he glowers at me. "This is driving me wild."

I give a little smile of triumph. "Cry me a river."

Turning my back to him, I jiggle my buttocks with my fingers, making them bounce enticingly. "What about this? Do you like this too?"

"Get over here and I'll show you how much I like it," Fletcher says, but I can tell that he's loving this.

With my back to him, I bend over and slide my panties down. I want him to get an eyeful of my shaved pussy and sweet ass. I've been working on my bikini tan too. A tiny pale triangle of skin sits neatly over my butt like a banner all of its own.

"Eek!" I give a little shriek of surprise as he jumps off the bed and grabs me from behind.

"Ha!" Fletcher is triumphant. "You want to play games? Then expect consequences!"

Crushing his mouth down on my lips with the perfect amount of pressure, he murmurs in his deep voice, "Sexy, tantalizing consequences, Ivy Woods... just like this."

I am already at the peak of desire, but when I hear the sound of his zipper going down it just about pushes me over the edge of excitement.

"No fair," I pout. "I want to see you naked too."

"Sure." Fletcher has the confidence of a man who knows his body is straight out of a male fitness magazine. "But if you're expecting me to do a little striptease for you, I don't think I could do it with this—"

It's dangerously hot the way he stands and shrugs out of his shirt. His torso is sculpted for the gods. His midriff is taut and well-defined with a six-pack of muscles. I can't wait to see more.

Watching the way he exposes his cock to me really turns me on even more. I think I gasp with delight, but I no longer know what sounds I am making because I am totally out of control.

Desperate to experience this man to the fullest, I suck his cock like a hungry animal, really giving it the business with my tongue and lips.

Fletcher groans, throwing his head back on the pillows and biting back the harsh, guttural sounds. "Fuck, Ivy, that feels amazing."

It all comes flooding back to me, how much he loves having me suck his cock. He even taught me how to do it the way he likes it, pumping my hand along the thick shaft and cradling his balls.

He hasn't changed. He's still as yummy as ever with his impressive girth and the throbbing veins in the shaft. I move so I can rub my breasts against him. It's only a tempting tickle, but I can tell from the way his cock jerks in my hand that he is sensitive to the way my breasts are affecting him.

Without removing my lips from the head of his penis, I ask him, "Do you want to come in my mouth?"

He moves quickly, flipping me onto my back and climbing on top. He is so strong. I can't help but give a little yelp of elation as he dominates me.

Yes, this is the man I remember from the yacht. Masterful, in charge, and ever-so-slightly bossy in the bedroom.

Holding my wrists above my head with one of his hands, he uses his other hand to touch me.

"After ten years, sweetheart, the first time I come, it better be inside that gorgeously tight, wet pussy of yours."

"I'm so excited, Fletcher," I say, fighting to get the bold words out. "I think I'm going to come the minute you slide into me."

"Then we're just going to have to delay it a bit longer."

"If you get any longer, I don't think I'll be able to fit you inside me."

There I go again, seeing the funny side of things. It's a mechanism I use to stop myself from coming.

"You're so wet, darling, I'm not going to have any problem penetrating you really deep...." He kisses me so erotically that my head spins.

I feel his hand move down my belly and stop at the soft mound. He caresses the hood of my clit lightly, and I just about go through the roof.

"Oh, Fletcher. Please, please let me come. I'm desperate."

"How bad do you want this?" His gruff voice turns me on. I can feel the rumble in his chest when he speaks.

Pulling his hand away from my clit, he demands I answer him.

He's doing this on purpose! Driving me mad with desperate longing.

"I want you so bad, Fletcher," I moan softly, tossing my head from one side to the other against the pillows. "But please, I need to come soon—I'm bursting."

Gripping my wrists tightly, I see him smirk. "Patience, darling. You've waited ten years for this—you can wait a bit longer. Tell me if you fantasize about us."

It's like he has a way of looking into my mind and seeing what is in there.

"Mmm," I murmur with pleasure as his thumb brushes lightly against the hood of my clit, I lose myself in my fantasy.

"Yes, yes. I fantasize about you fucking me all the time. I like to rub my nipples and finger my wet pussy, remembering how lovely it felt when you stuck your big cock inside me. Makes me come every time."

I can tell that he is totally enjoying my dirty talk. I never knew how to do it last time we were together, but I am all grown-up now.

"Do you masturbate like this?"

Fletcher massages my clit with his thumb while inserting his fingers inside my soaking wet slit.

"Or do you use a vibrator?"

This dirty talk is a big turn-on. I'm living for it as the excitement mounts steadily inside me.

"I use my fingers, Fletcher, but I miss the sensation of your big cock sliding inside me. It's the missing piece of my puzzle."

"Like this?" As he says it, Fletcher slowly enters me, letting go of my wrists so he can guide his cock into my pulsating vagina.

Then, he pulls it out again. "You like that? You want more?"

"Fuck me, please!" I can't help it, I almost scream the words. This seduction has driven me out of my head with anticipation.

Using the head of his penis, Fletcher rubs it over my clit and around my pussy. And when he pushes into me again, I start to come immediately.

It's not a short, sharp come, what I usually have when I need to sort myself out so that I can get back to other stuff. It's a long, languorous, slowly mounting orgasm, perfectly controlled and exquisite.

I lie back and let it happen. I don't need to work towards it or stress over maintaining it for the longest time. It just does.

Wave after wave of tender arousal increases in intensity as he thrusts into me. I don't need to move or grind myself against him. Fletcher hits all the right places without my help.

Once I have tilted my hips so that he can access my clit, I am free to ride my orgasm through to the end. The head of his cock must be throbbing too, because I can feel every stroke.

Fletcher gives a deep grunt as my pussy tries to milk him dry. "I'm not going to last much longer."

The thought that he is so turned on really excites me. Wrapping my legs around his slim waist, I rake my fingers lightly down the smooth skin of his back.

"Fuck me hard, Fletcher Banner. Give it to me real good."

Only then do I reach my peak. I feel his body shudder as he comes inside me. We are in sync.

It's as if the harmony of our first sexual encounter with each other never really went away.

I think I scream, but I can't be sure.

And then I remember how easy it is to fall in love with this man.

# Chapter 11 - Fletcher

The irony of Ivy being the first to wake up in the morning and preparing to leave is not lost on me. Lying on my back with one arm behind my head, I enjoy watching her dress in the pale pink light of the sunrise filtering through the windows.

"Can I at least see some ID before you go?" I want to tease her. It seems the best way to say goodbye.

She's leaning over the dresser, checking her reflection in the mirror. There is not a scrap of makeup on her face, but she's as beautiful as the first day I met her. Long black hair reaching halfway down her back. Tawny skin and deep brown eyes. Cheekbones that could cut glass.

Ivy looks at my reflection in the mirror as she asks, "ID? Why? Did I grift something from the restaurant?"

Trust Ivy to come back with a snappy reply. "Nope. I want to check that Ivy Woods is your real name. Jesus! Do you realize how many years we've wasted just because you lied about your name?"

That makes her turn around. Leaning with her arms crossed, she stares me up and down before answering.

"You might have been wasting the last few years, Jay, but I haven't."

Suddenly, I'm not sleepy anymore! Sitting up, I cross my arms too and start frowning with what Mary-Kay calls my "resting grump face."

"You were on a yacht surrounded by men and women who could have told you my real name in a heartbeat, Ivy. All you had to do was ask Kevin before you disembarked. 'What's Jay's surname?' He would have given you my life story, chapter, and verse."

The way she considers my explanation before speaking is a big plus in my book. Thoughtlessly spontaneous Ivy is most definitely not.

"I didn't speak to Kevin before disembarking, Fletcher. I told you. I did not get paid."

The significance of what she is saying to me registers slowly. It was ten years ago, so I have to think hard about what my gorgeous yacht girl, Forrest, told me.

The sex is etched in my mind like hieroglyphs, but our conversations have faded. If my first meeting with Ivy had not been so monumental, I would not be able to remember what we spoke about at all.

"Hang on. You said you were pressed for cash, weren't you? Weren't there tokens in the drawer? I'm sure Kevin told me that the girls get paid according to the number of tokens they could produce."

Ivy nods. She's looking serious as if the memories are not welcome to her.

"I found that offensive. A woman has to produce the equivalent of a blue ribbon award before she is deemed worthy of payment. Yuk!"

This is crazy. "I never thought of you like that, Ivy, I swear!"

Swinging my legs over the side of the bed, I start pulling on my briefs. Fuck! I thought we already managed to hash this out last night. Does she think I was ever the sort of man to exploit the financial circumstances of an eighteen-year-old girl?

"I know." When I hear Ivy say that, I relax and stop searching for my suit pants.

"Whew! You little minx. I thought you were upset with me for a moment. Right. If we're cool, my wanting to see your ID was just a joke. If you try to run away from me again, I'll just ask my sister."

Biting her lower lip, Ivy comes to stand next to me. The touch of her hand on my arm somehow manages to calm me down and heat me up at the same time.

"Oh, Banner, please tell your sister that we met here for the first time. I never told her about... about what happened to me on the yacht."

"If you're ashamed about it, I'm not. I'll stand on top of the tallest building in New York and shout it loud—'I banged a yacht girl.'"

The skin of her cheek is fragrant as she stands on tiptoe and kisses me lightly. Her smile is sad, her eyes downcast.

"I regret that yacht cruise so much. I was young and stupid—and broke. That can make a girl act all kinds of crazy."

The way she's talking makes sense. "I'm sorry you felt like that, sweetheart. If only you had been open with me, I could have helped you."

"I would have never told you my real name—or age! The only thing I liked about being a yacht girl, Banner, was the anonymity. Listen, it would affect my career negatively if anyone ever found out. And I think it would make any man look like a laughing stock if people discovered he had to pay for companionship—billionaire or not."

Running my hands through her hair and staring down at her pretty face, I murmur. "Sounds good. But I have yet to meet the man who has the balls to laugh about me to my face. I'm not ashamed of what I did, Ivy. Are you?"

That makes her take a step back and give a nervous laugh. "That review isn't going to write itself, Banner! I better go."

"What are you going to rate Sabine?" I'm half teasing, but I still want to know. Heck, I own a hotel chain and she is a critic.

Ivy shakes her head and moves to pick up her purse. That's not good enough for me. I grab her by the elbow.

"A little heads-up is all I'm asking for, Ivy. Please."

Her eyes go wide. "Oh my God. You said please. And I had you down as just another cocky one-night stand. Whoops! Did I say 'one-night stand'? I mean to say 'two one-night stands.'"

Ouch. Her words hurt. If she didn't look so damn gorgeous, I could get pissed real fast.

"Please. Please can you tell me the rating? And please can I have another one-night stand?"

Ivy's face lights up as she backs towards the door.

"Ten out of ten, Banner. You get ten out of ten and five gold stars—in bed."

And just like that, she's out the door.

Fuck it! Wearing only my briefs, I wait for the elevator to come back up and then get into it. The elevator is really fast because mine is the only floor it stops on. Stepping out into the private lobby, I see Ivy as she's telling the bellhop to fetch her a car.

"Ivy!" She turns, and her eyes get wide when she sees me standing there in my briefs. "Are you ashamed of me?"

We both burst out laughing. Ivy wipes the tears from her eyes and gives me one of her beaming smiles.

"You're crazy, you know that? No, I am not ashamed of us, but please can we keep this under our hats? For now."

I give her a wave and step back into the elevator. I am satisfied, but I know this happy glow will not last forever. I want more.

*** 

"Unca Flet!" Daniel is the one who answers the door after I ring the bell. "Mom! It's Fletcher!"

My nephew is growing up fast. There was a time when he couldn't wrap his speech around the name "Fletcher."

Ruffling his hair, I step into the Park Slope brownstone. "Where's your mom? Does she always allow you to open the door? What if it's a stranger?"

"I use my step to check through the spyhole first." Danny sounds kinda proud about this achievement, so I make a big deal out of it.

Mary-Kay comes out of the kitchen holding a towel. She's drying her hands. "Surprise, surprise. I didn't hear a helicopter landing on the lawn. That's why I'm surprised."

Motherhood has taken away none of Mary-Kay's wise-ass nature.

I have to play this cool so that my sister doesn't realize that I spent the whole of last night fucking her best friend.

"I don't fly everywhere, Mary-Kay. Sometimes it's fun to drive."

My sister makes a loud scoffing noise. "Ooh, yes. You flew that fancy private jet of yours all the way to Teterboro and then drove here. Big whoop."

I can see that Danny is not enjoying his mom's heavy sarcasm. I decide not to take the bait. Mary-Kay can be a bitter pill for me to swallow sometimes, but I would do anything to keep my nephew happy.

"Actually, my pilot flew. I haven't gotten around to renewing my jet license yet."

"Pfft!" My sister blows a raspberry at me and then points to a chair. "What do you want?"

Sitting down, I pat the place next to me for Danny. He clambers up, ready to show me his latest toy. I give him the perfect amount of quality time and attention and then send him back to his bedroom to play.

"Aren't you going to ask me about my weekend?"

Mary-Kay looks confused for a moment before the penny drops. "Did you actually go to Vegas to dine with Ivy? I'm impressed, Bro. Thank you."

"No, thank you." I don't bother telling my sister that Sabine at the Banderole is my establishment. "Why didn't you tell me your pal is a restaurant critic?"

"She's great, isn't she? Ivy. She was my rock in high school. Always there to get me out of trouble. And she also happens to be the best babysitter."

"How nice." I am playing my cards close to my chest. "I'm sore you didn't introduce us before."

Mary-Kay looks at me as if I just crawled out of something she was eating. "Why would I? You never paid the slightest bit of attention to me until I had Danny, so why would I think you'd be interested in my friends?"

I backtrack. "Yep, I see your point. But how did you end up with Ivy as your roommate?"

"Oh, Ivy was one of those gifted scholarship kids. She got some of her short stories published when she was still in junior high school! Won all the essay writing competitions and stuff. State and national. But her folks took all of her prize money, so she was heavily reliant on her sponsorship."

"Mm, really. How inspiring." I knew better than to make a big deal out of Ivy's talent. Mary-Kay can be very insecure when the mood takes her.

"Yeah. But her short stories weren't enough to pay her way through college... she struggled financially... a lot."

"How sad." Playing it low-key is the best way to keep my sister talking.

"The silly doofus could have had a massive payday after high school, but she fucked it up. That's how she got into restaurant reviews."

"Tell me more."

Kicking off her shoes and putting her feet up on the couch, Mary-Kay gives me all the details I need.

"She worked bussing tables and being a short-order cook. Got about four hours of sleep a night. Then she wrote an exposé piece about overworked kitchen staff for a famous cookery blog. It was picked up and syndicated. Her writing style about the culinary world was unique, and that's how she became a famous food writer."

I don't need my sister to tell me how famous and successful "Holly Forrest" is. My fingers are crossed that she liked the food as much as she loved the sex we had. I can't get Saturday night out of my head. It's like I'm living in that special moment over and over again....

"What's wrong?" Mary-Kay's voice goes all sharp.

I refocus quickly. "Nothing. Nothing is wrong. Why are you asking?"

She's staring at me with laser sharpness. "There's something different about you. You seem... I dunno... different."

Shit. Am I acting differently? "My hair. I've grown it out. I'm amazed that Danny recognized me. I must get it trimmed." I pull at the dark lock that has fallen across my forehead. "I must look like a pirate."

"Nuh-uh. That's not it." My sister is like a dog with a bone. "You seem relaxed, more chilled out."

I hold my breath. I don't want to break my promise to Ivy. She really wants me to keep our affair under wraps.

Mary-Kay passes judgment. "It's got to be LA. It's really mellowed you out, Bro. You should live there permanently. I won't mind. Just so long as you keep making those big deposits into my checking account!"

# Chapter 12 – Ivy

Rupert is on the phone.

"We need to publish that review for Sabine chop-chop, Ivy."

"I'm still mulling over it, Rupert. Don't rush perfection."

My agent chuckles. "It's not like you to be late, dearie. What happened?"

Oh God. The last thing I need is my publisher sussing out that I haven't got my head in the game. How could I be firing on all cylinders when all I can think about is Saturday night with Fletcher Banner?

But the memory of how good it felt when he parted my thighs and buried his face in my soaking wet pussy is too lovely for me to forget. I want more. I'm an addict.

I have never felt this way about anything before. Not caviar, not wagyu beef, not even that deliciously light and tasty blackened cod fish they serve at Nobu.

I might have even lost my appetite. The only thing I want to eat is Banner's enormous—

"I said it's not like you to be late. What happened? Is it a bad line?"

Rupert. Shit!

"Sabine is special, Rupert. I can't pull some random words out of my hat for a venue like that. Please try to understand."

"Mmkay, sweetie. Once you've finished, please upload the review right away—and don't forget to include images."

I could publish on my own website because I knew the password. Rupert's voice droned on about business.

"Now, to other matters. Le Creuset wants you to choose the color for their next limited-issue production run. Pastel, bold primaries, ombre—anything you like. And Japanese Damascus Steel Knives want you to do a spot about them on your next podcast. When can we crunch some numbers about your fee for that?"

For the first time since I clawed my way to the top of the restaurant critics food chain, I give Rupert the brush-off.

"Listen, I gotta go, Chief. I promise I'll check in soon once the review is live."

Immediately after disconnecting, I tap the contacts app on my phone. There it is.

Fletch the Wretch's phone number from Mary-Kay. She actually has him saved on her phone like that.

Why am I holding my breath? I know I'm going to do it. It's been five days. A perfectly acceptable amount of waiting time after the full-blown fuckfest session Banner and I had.

He's a busy man. I get that. But I also get that he must have hundreds of stone-cold babes running after him too. What to do?

My fingers are shaking as I try to hold my phone steady.

Come on, Ivy. You are a grown woman of twenty-eight. And the best thing is this—he can't hurt you two times in a row. Just do it.

I start texting.

Banner. Let me know when you come to the East Coast. I want to take you to one of my favorite restaurants. H. F.

Hardly a minute passes before my phone pings. My belly leaps when I see it's from Fletch the Wretch.

Howdy Miz Forrest. It sure is nice to git your message. This here cowboy's kinda lonesome and blue without you. Are you up for some sexting?

He's exaggerating. His Southern accent is not nearly as thick as that. Smiling to myself, I text back.

Naughty boy. I have to write a review. Rain check?

He texts back a couple of emojis. A thundercloud with the sun peeping out from behind it, a full sun... and a flaming heart.

The cowboy of the conference room knows how to pitch woo with emojis. You don't get any slicker than that in my book!

Inspired more than I can say, I pull my laptop towards me and begin typing.

Sabine at the Banderole - Food that almost forces you to fall in love.

One bite was all it took for me to look at Sabine through a loving lens. The amuse-bouche were delightful morsels, bursting with flavor and complex layers of salt and sweetness with just a hint of bitterness coming from the chocolate.

Yes, believe it or not, the expert hand at the helm of the Sabine kitchen started off the tasting menu with a bang. We were served an unexpected layer of sweet within the tempting savoriness.

To be fair, a tiny portion of my enjoyment of the meal might have had something to do with my dinner companion. Like the appetizers, he is ever-so-slightly bitter with a tiny amount of sweetness and plenty of salt!

Dearest readers and fellow foodie enthusiasts, I want to hear from you on this one. Is it possible for food to taste so good that you end up falling in love? Sabine at the Banderole has a tasting menu like no other and, just like I do with my delicious dinner companion, I want to carry on eating it until I pop.

I write another thousand words, totally inspired by the sexy shenanigans I had with Banner in the bedroom after my meal.

As for never getting a second chance to make a good first impression... all I can say is this—Sabine is likely to be fully booked in advance for the next few years as first-time customers rush to get a second helping. Just like me.

It's a daring review, but this is what my readers and subscribers want. They love getting a small peek into my life and experiencing it through me.

After copying and pasting the review and running it through an editing program, I drop it into my website. For one moment, I wonder if this article is a step too far. I've written about my dining companions before, but never like this!

I click to publish. It buffers for a second and then—it's live.

One hour later, Rupert is calling. He starts shouting when I slide to answer.

"Jesus! Ivy, what's up with the Valentine's Day style writing? And if I remember correctly, when I asked you to give me a great Valentine's Day article, you told me romance was lame!"

"It is lame." I'm acting cool, but I'm kinda stressed at publishing such an intimate review. "It's commercial bullshit, Rupert, and everyone knows that."

Rupert dithers. "Which one? Valentine's Day or romance?"

Darn. I stepped right into that one. "Never mind. What did you think about the article?"

Rupert is ruthless. "I need to know who the lover boy is, Ivy. I'm praying he's not some Vegas gigolo you picked up."

"Ugh! As if. He's connected to the hotel, so there's no danger of his identity leaking out. Keep your hair on."

The silence at the end of the line is ominous. I feel the panic rising up inside me and struggle to push it down.

"Staff connected to the hotel or upper management connected to the hotel? Don't lie, Ivy. This is important."

"Umm, I would describe him more as an investor. Rupert, I'm sorry, but it's a brilliant review and I won't change it. What could possibly go wrong?"

He's shouting into the phone now, making me glad I'm having the conversation on speaker so I can turn down the volume.

"If anyone found out that you dined at Sabine with someone who is invested in it turning a profit, Ivy, that spells the end for your credibility! You gave the fucking restaurant five stars!"

Rupert stops ranting long enough to draw breath, but then he's back with a vengeance. "Please tell me you didn't go upstairs with him afterward? Because that would be all the confirmation anyone needed to think that your good opinion can be bought. Please tell me you weren't that stupid?"

My silence gives me away. Rupert swears. He's such a polite, kind man, I'm kind of shocked when I hear him do that.

"Okay, I'll edit the review." It's been a long time since I have been this panicked. Sure my agent is stressing for nothing?

"It's too late." Rupert's voice is muffled as I hear him tapping on his keyboard. "The fucking review has already gone viral."

"How many shares, saves, and bookmarks?" I want to know. When website visitors do that it makes the search engine rank it even higher.

"I never thought it would depress me to say this, dearie, but the view counter is whirling around like a tornado. We can only pray that no one finds out who your sexy dinner companion was, Ivy. I hope he was worth it."

Rupert sounds bitter and worried before he disconnects from the call.

I'm not in the mood to go out for dinner after writing all day. Checking in the refrigerator, I whip out a microwave meal.

I've got Fletcher Banner on my mind, but not in a good way. How could I have been so stupid? Lucky for me, Mary-Kay doesn't follow my on-line reviews, but what if someone tells her what I wrote? She's going to know I have the hots for Fletch the Wretch!

After pouring myself a glass of red wine, I go out to the balcony to look at the traffic.

I stay on the Lower East Side. I use the word stay deliberately because I only ever use fur-nished apartment rentals. My job is all about hopping on a plane at the drop of a hat, so even a lock-up-and-go house would be too much.

When my phone rings, I don't think much of it. Then I see whose name comes on the screen. Fletch the Wretch.

Diving for the phone, I take a deep breath be-fore saying, "Hey you."

God, he has such a sexy voice. "Hey. It's raining."

I get it. Rain check. Raining. "What are you wearing?" I jump right into it. I have nothing to lose.

"Briefs. Not the same ones I was wearing when I last saw you, though."

That makes me chuckle. "That's good to know. Those briefs didn't leave much to the imagination. They were... snug fitting."

"This coming from the woman who wears white silk lingerie with lace cutouts."

"You don't like my lingerie?" I act surprised, but I know where this is going.

"I like the transparent lace cutouts," Banner confesses.

"Mm, but I know you like what's underneath better. Want to turn this into a video chat?"

"Do you use a VPN for privacy?" he asks.

For a moment, I want to tease him about being paranoid, but then I remember the restaurant review I just published. "No. Do you think I should get one?"

"Truth? I would rather we didn't do the long-distance thing too much, Ivy. I prefer you in the flesh."

I have to take a sip of wine to calm my racing nerves. "Phone sex is good. We can aim for doing it in the flesh at a later date." No reply. "Are you there?" I say, crossing my fingers that he is into my suggestion.

"I was busy removing my briefs," Banner lets me know in a teasing way. "Your turn. Tell me what you're doing."

Putting the glass down on my bedroom table, I lie down on the bed. "I'm lifting up my dress. It's a short summer frock, that barely covers my ass, but it gives me the freedom to do this."

"Do what?" Banner's voice is pitched low.

"I'm pushing my panty crotch to one side and touching myself. It feels so good. Gently stroking my clit, teasing it with my fingers. Do you like that?"

He gives a deep growl. "You're driving me crazy with this. But I can't stop now."

That pleases me. "Such a good boy," I'm really getting into this, stroking my sensitive lovebud until I feel it pout and harden. "Pump that thick cock of yours, Banner, but no rubbing the head. And no cheating."

"I'm imagining you sitting on top of me," he tells me gruffly, "lowering yourself down on me slowly. Taking me all the way up to the hilt."

He's making me miss his sex so much! Quickly, I begin to knead my clit with a deeper circling motion. "The thought of you jerking that lovely cock of yours is driving me wild. Are you rampant? Do you want to shove it into me and make me come?"

"I'm close, sweetheart." His breath is almost a gasp as his stroke gets faster. "Touch the pretty slit of yours. Slide your finger inside and tell me how wet you are."

I can tell from the heavy way he's panting that he's on the cusp of coming.

"I'm soaking wet, Banner. I wish you were here to fuck me good and hard. I'm close...."

We are desperate, in another world of sensual pleasure as we masturbate, tempting one another into experiencing the most awesome orgasm.

I've masturbated before. Of course, I have. But this is the first time it is so satisfying, so sensual. I reach a peak that is so amazing, that it takes my breath away.

But—"It's not the same without you." Fletcher Banner takes the words out of my mouth.

"I was just going to say that." I am trying to get my breathing back to normal. Gasping and giving little moans as my climax fades. "I miss you."

Banner says something back, but it's lost as my phone starts to ring.

"Damn! Text me later. I gotta go."

Disconnecting the call, I answer after getting my hectic panting under control.

"Hi. Is that Holly Forrest? This is Meg Stanley calling from Bon Cuisine. Do you have time to tell me a bit more about your Sabine restaurant review?"

# Chapter 13 - Fletcher

I know better than to call Ivy again. Like me, she seems to be very disciplined with her phone. The day after our incredible phone sex, I got a text from her thanking me and apologizing for having to take the call immediately after.

And then radio silence for another three days. If I was an insecure type of guy, I might think this was an emotional standoff. Seeing which one of us folds first.

I can't help worrying that she still holds our broken communication ten years ago against me. When a woman is as beautiful and confident as Ivy, I can understand her need to take things slowly.

She's in no rush. Ivy likes her sex the same way she eats her food. Small bites, savoring the enjoyment of each sensual moment. Eyes closed, lips slightly parted as she concentrates on what impression that first taste is giving her.

Damn, but she's so hot. I can't get her image out of my head. Gotta pump the brakes and focus.

I haven't exactly been sitting on my hands either as far as work goes. The Banderole is my flagship hotel and I want everything to be perfect.

It's not like me to take my eye off the prize, but my work comes first.

And then Ivy Woods comes storming back into my life in the most unexpected way.

"Mr. Banner, might I add my hearty congratulations on your great success."

Wow, this guy is really enthusiastic. "Er, thanks, buddy. The Banderole is doing well."

I'm sitting in the same wine bar with my journal in front of me. My parents raised me well, so I mark my place in the journal with the Montblanc and stand up to shake his hand.

"Sean Bowery, isn't it? You're one of Kevin Lewis's business associates?"

The middle-aged man is pleased I remember his name. "Yes, please call me Sean. Remember Kevin introduced us during that high-stakes poker game he holds every quarter on the East Coast? It's been a while, and then some."

I gesture for the man to sit down. "I remember. And please call me Jay."

Sean chuckles as the server places a glass of champagne in front of him. "The notorious Jesse James. Lines up the business deals and shoots 'em down. Ha-ha."

That's me in a nutshell. Making a gun with my finger and thumb, I pretend to pull the trigger and blow smoke off the imaginary muzzle. "Yep."

Sean says, "I haven't played poker on the East Coast for a long while. Kevin started letting in some hinky types. Wasn't sure the play was square there anymore."

I haven't hung out with Kevin since.... Well, let's just say that I haven't seen him for ten years.

"That's a pity. I used to enjoy those poker games back in the day. But Kev's in investing and I'm in hospitality, so our paths don't cross that much anymore."

"I hear you." Sean takes a sip of his drink. "But if I'm truthful, I wasn't talking about the success of the Banderole when I congratulated you, Jay."

My eyebrows shoot up. "No? Which hotel are you talking about?"

Sean shakes his head. "No one told you? I was talking about the Sabine review. And once again—a big congratulations."

His voice seems to be coming from far away. Sean carries on talking about how difficult it is to get a beneficial review from the public nowadays. "But that woman has them all eating out of her hand. She says 'Jump' and they ask 'How high?' That's how much power these young and pretty influencers have nowadays."

I pretend to be getting a phone call. Standing up, I apologize to Sean and tell him this won't take long.

Moving away from the table, I dial my assistant. The moment the call connects, I rasp out in anger. "What the fuck, Anton!?" I don't miss a beat waiting for him to reply. "Why the fuck didn't you tell me the review for Sabine was out?"

Anton is used to me being pissed. He takes it in his stride. "Which review? There have been quite a few. All positive. And I did tell you. A couple of nights ago, I called you to give you the good news, but you shut me down and told me not to bother you. I sent links to your email."

I remember that. Anton called me the day after my amazing call with Ivy. Every time the phone rang, I thought it would be her and when it wasn't, I got sort of grumpy.

"Fine. Good." Disconnecting the call, I flick over to my emails and scroll through them as I walk back to the table.

Sean taps the side of his nose. "You look pleased. Was it good news?"

"Yep, that was my assistant telling me about another review."

He chuckles again and then drains the remaining dregs of champagne. "My wife adores Holly Forrest's restaurant reviews. That's why I came over to say hi actually. I was hoping you could sort us out with a table?"

I'm dying to read what Ivy wrote. Standing up again, I shake Sean's hand and tell him to leave his details with the host. "I'll personally make sure you get a table within the next couple of weeks Sean. My regards to your wife."

Waiting for him to leave before I can sit back down and click on the link seems like a long time. Ignoring all the other reviews, I reach Ivy's article and begin to read.

The sensual language she uses in it makes my jaw almost drop to the floor. I reach a paragraph that makes me do a double take.

As the set meal progresses, I am filled with a craving for more. Eating here is more than an experience—it's almost life-changing. The food excites me. I can't wait to place it in my mouth and feel my taste buds explode with pleasure.

I'm not even aware of it when I let out a low-pitched whistle. That's some hot writing. It's steamier than the food was.

Just reading the article makes me relive our first dinner together. The pressure of her foot on my crotch. The sparks of anger in her dark eyes. The sexual anticipation ramping up with every bite.

Dropping my phone onto the table, I beckon over one of the waitstaff.

"Get Sami on the line, please. Tell him to bring my car to the private entrance."

"Yes, sir, Mr. Banner. Can I tell him the destination?"

"Vegas airport."

***

The thought of getting closer to Ivy is like the pull of a magnet.

I'm not fazed by the fact that I don't know where she lives. I can get those details from my sister.

Strange to say it, but I'm looking forward to seeing Danny again too. He's growing up to be a hell of a good kid.

Maybe Mary-Kay was born to be a mother all along. She sure didn't cotton on to doing anything else.

My money was always a safety net for her, but it never stopped her from misbehaving.

"Hey, MK. How's Danny?"

My sister launches into a long story about how she left the roof open in her car and left it out in the rain. Without missing a beat, she starts telling me about why she can't afford the insurance excess.

I'm in a good mood, so I don't get hung up about it. "That's okay. Flick the quote over to my email and I'll sort it out."

She pauses a beat. "There you go again not acting like your usual tightwad self. What's gotten into you, Bro?"

"I was never a tightwad, Mary-Kay. You were too extravagant. Someone had to pump the brakes for you."

I'm about to ask her for Ivy's address, but I pause. How the heck am I going to do that while Ivy wants to keep us a secret from my sister?

Mary-Kay interrupts my thoughts. "When are you coming to New York again? I want you to test out some bicycles for Danny. I don't know jack about durability and safety. And you promised him last time."

"I'm at the penthouse as we speak. I can be there in half an hour."

My stomach lurches as I hear Mary-Kay cover the mouthpiece and shout. "Hey, Ivy! Is it okay if Fletch comes over?"

A muffled reply makes me wait with bated breath. My sister doesn't keep me in suspense. "Ivy says that's cool. See you in a bit."

And just like that, I'm hooked up with Ivy again.

There's an edgy excitement in my belly as I drive to Park Slope. My sister's house was custom-built for her.

I bought two large brownstones and bulldozed the adjoining walls so that Danny could have a big garden to play in. I also added a side entrance so my sister had somewhere to park her vehicle off the road.

I find him playing in the garden as I park my Bentley behind Mary-Kay's waterlogged hatchback. He watches me unfold out of the driver's seat with an amused look.

"Hey, Unca Flet." Turning away from his truck, my nephew gives me a smile. "I hope I don't grow up to be as tall as you. You have to unfold like a Transformer when you get out of the car."

Hunkering down next to him, I give Danny a hug. "No flies on you. Do you have a Transformer? Which truck is your favorite?"

"I like them all, but they only go well on a flat surface." Daniel points to the grass.

"You look pretty lonely out here playing on your own, Dan," I say, rolling one of the trucks over the grass. "Haven't you got a friend to visit?"

"Yep." Danny looks proud. "My friend Luke is coming over with his mom. I think Mom and her are going out for drinks somewhere while Ivy sits with us."

Jumping to my feet, I'm suddenly full of smiles. "Really? Cool. I think I might stay and keep Ivy company."

"Woo!" Danny makes kissy-kissy sounds with his lips. "But please don't forget to find me a nice bike too, Unca Flet. Luke and me want to ride in Prospect Park."

Saluting my nephew as he goes back to playing with his trucks, I step inside. Ivy is in the sitting room, watching something on the flat-screen TV.

The sexy, secretive smile she gives me nearly drives me crazy. I'm close to hustling over and hugging her too, but I see her put her finger up to her lips and jerk her thumb towards the door.

Then she speaks in a loud, formal voice. "Oh, hey, Fletcher. How are you? Long time no see. MK is in the bedroom getting ready for a night out if you want to talk to her."

Replying in an equally loud, formal voice, I have to stifle my laughter.

"Gosh, Ivy. What a surprise. I'm visiting New York for business, but it's always nice to visit with my sister's friends."

That cracks her up. Ivy falls over, clutching her sides and wheezing with suppressed laughter.

Mary-Kay's voice comes from the bedroom upstairs. "That Fletcher? Make him comfortable, Ivy."

"You bet!" Ivy shouts back.

When our eyes connect across the room, it's electric. Wiping the tears of laughter away, she asks me in a normal voice.

"You want pizza? I've ordered for myself and the boys."

I'm a bit shocked to hear that Ivy eats pizza. I had her down for being one of those food snobs. "What kind of toppings?"

"Cheese for the boys, and ham and mushroom for me."

"Can I share your Regina?"

"Yes, Banner, you can share my Regina."

A woman steps through the open front door. "Coo-ee! Girls night out calling!"

When she sees me, her mouth drops open a fraction. I step into the breach. "Hey, I'm Fletcher Banner, Danny's uncle. MK's brother."

"Oh my...." The woman gives me a broad smile and moves to take the hand I'm holding out to her. "Mary-Kay never—I mean, she is not very complimentary about you. Oops, golly, I don't want to be nasty, but you don't look the way I imagined you to look at all."

"It's been that way since our folks died." I'm abrupt but polite. Giving her a tight smile, I try to explain. "It was up to me to be the disciplinarian."

Her son is my nephew's bestie, so I'm going to pull out all the stops to be nice.

My sister comes down the stairs, reeking of perfume with her face covered in makeup and her brunette hair straightened and flattened out.

"We good to go? Melanie, this is Fletcher, my grumpy brother. Flet, this is Luke's mom.

Come on, Melanie. Forget about him. He hates women. Let's go."

Melanie backs out of the room, smiling and giggling as she waves goodbye.

I move to the window to check if they are taking an Uber. Mary-Kay doesn't drink when she goes out because of Daniel, but I don't know about Melanie. They are in an Uber, so I can relax.

The pizza guy is walking up the path with Luke and Danny following close behind. I never expected this to be an intimate evening with the woman I am currently sleeping with, but I never expected to be looking forward to spending a quiet night at home as much as I am.

The two boys chatter as we eat pizza. Sports, school, latest movies—Ivy is up to date on all of it. The boys lap it up, going upstairs to change into their pajamas when she asks them to.

Finally, we are alone. I take her in my arms, but she wiggles out and backs away.

"Danny might see, Banner. Let's be on our best behavior." I might have been upset except for the tempting smile she gives me as she says it.

"I have always fantasized about fucking the cute babysitter, Ivy. Some braids and braces, and I'm there for it."

"Oh, ha-ha." She pats the seat next to her and turns the flat screen back on. "You're not fooling anyone, mister. Why are you here?"

Putting my arm around her shoulders, I shift closer. "I'm here to thank you for that glowing five-star review you gave Sabine, Ivy."

But when I try to kiss her, she scooches away from me with a shake of her head. "I was mad to publish that article, Banner. I regret it now… because I'm getting a lot of blowback that I just can't deal with."

My arms feel empty without her. "What are you trying to say?"

"I'm saying that we should have never… my career is important to me and I think what we did might have fucked it up!"

# Chapter 14 - Ivy

Banner looks hurt, but he's an amazingly understanding man when it comes to work issues.

"Was the engagement down on your site?" He shifts back, folds his arms, and gets serious.

Engagement is when a reader clicks on the website and how long they stay on it or share the link. Then Rupert shows those stats to advertisers when they want to know how many readers their ad is reaching.

Banner is looking particularly hunky this evening. Plaid shirt with a hint of white T-shirt underneath it and jeans that fit him snugly in all the right places.

The man has an ass you can bounce quarters off, but believe me when I say that his front parts are just as attractive.

He's built like someone who has never sat still for too long and enjoys some kind of hard activity. When I sneaked a peek at his online bio, I was interested to find out that Banner enjoys working on his own construction sites.

From what I know of the man—and from what I can see—that tracks as truth. His muscles are hard as nails and he is super fit.

I am so tempted to sink into his embrace, but I must be the strong, independent woman I've molded myself to be.

"The opposite. Engagement is off the charts. There is a rumor going around that my review crashed the internet. How can you not know this? Don't your staff keep you informed?"

He gives a rueful chuckle. "My staff are trained not to bother me unless it's an emergency. And—truth to tell—my head hasn't exactly been fully in the game lately...."

Oh, I am so tempted to kiss him right now. My entire body aches for his touch. I have to bite my lower lip hard to make me concentrate.

"Didn't you notice an upswing in bookings at Sabine? Apparently, table bookings are being auctioned off for thousands of dollars. Rupert told me the bookings for Valentine's Day are trading hands for half a million!"

That gets his attention. "I think you should take me to all your restaurant reviews, Ivy." I love his cocky smirk, but he just doesn't get it.

Then he gets all grumped out again. "Thanks for telling me that. I can't have Sabine's bookings taken over by scalpers. I'll tell the host to start asking for ID and put in on the website that scalping will not be tolerated."

I want to yell at Banner to stop making this all about him!

"Do you know how bad this could be for me if anyone finds out we're lovers? They will think a five-star Holly Forrest review can be bought!"

He still doesn't get it! I want to kick him for not taking this seriously!

"The food at Sabine is excellent. No one will suspect a thing. Chef Jean has run two five-star restaurants before this, you know."

Shifting sideways and putting one foot up on the couch so that I can look at him full-on, I try to explain.

"Banner, look at me. Pay attention. You are looking at the woman who gave Noma four and a half stars because I thought the foraging and locally sourced aspect of the restaurant was 'too contrived.'"

He winces and pretends to be scared of me by pulling a horrified face. "Oh no! That's unacceptable. How will they ever survive?"

His cheeky manner forces a laugh out of me, but I am quick to suppress it.

"I'm that girl—the one who's hard to please and very, very critical. My fans love it - they call me the 'boss lady' of the male-dominated world of chefs."

Running his hand up the inside of my thigh, he leans in. "I'm terrified, Ivy. But you can be my boss lady any day."

Of course, my body reacts to his hand. When he caresses my leg and slides his fingers lightly over the crotch of my jeans, I am instantly aroused.

But it only makes me mad. My career is everything to me. Does he even care?

Pushing him away, I stand up from the couch. "Listen. I'm glad you're here. You can keep an eye on the boys for me. I've got an early appointment tomorrow. I could do with a little extra sleep."

His face is a picture when I tell him that. Serves him right for not taking my problems more seriously.

"But, honey, I thought we could go back together. Mary-Kay is not going to be long. She sticks to her 11:00 p.m. curfew."

Walking to the hallway, I grab my purse and coat. "You presume waaay too much, Banner. No, don't follow me. I'm going to say good night to Danny and Luke."

Danny doesn't suspect a thing when I go up to his room to say goodbye. I get the boys settled for bed with the threat that their moms won't let them hang out again if they find them awake when they get home.

I call a cab while reading the boys a story. Tucking them into bed, I tell them to dream of riding new bicycles in Prospect Park before putting on the night light and going back downstairs.

Banner is waiting for me there, but he's no longer smirking.

"Please wait for MK to get back, Ivy. I'll drive you back. I want to show you my apartment."

"No," I am stubborn and insist on shooting straight. "You don't want to show me your apartment—you want us to fuck. How about you use tonight to try and find a way to help me?"

He's almost down on his knees, but he doesn't try to stop me other than holding my hand.

"My staff would never talk about us spending the night together, Ivy. Vegas is not the kind of town where employees tell secrets."

"You make double sure of that and I might think about visiting your apartment sometime. Rupert can't take down the review or change it, because it's getting millions of views a day."

Finally, I can see he understands.

"I never knew. I'm sorry. The knives will definitely be out to prove you wrong—and that puts pressure on both of us."

"Yes!" I can't resist stroking his arm. Those bulging biceps feel so good. "Thank you. You're finally seeing it for what it is. Viral articles are not always going to reach the lovers. There are a lot of haters out there too."

Banner doesn't have anything to say to that. I can see his mind ticking over.

"Would you have a problem if I used this to market a wedding package, Ivy? Reception catered by Sabine. Ballroom for the ceremony. The whole nine yards."

It saddens me that I might be forced to keep him at a distance until this review craziness has blown over.

"Can I get back to you on that?" My phone buzzes. My ride's here. Reaching up, I kiss his cheek. So delectable, so yummy. I want to gobble him up.

"Bye, Banner."

And I'm gone before he can change my mind.

\*\*\*

A call from Rupert wakes me up.

Groaning, I press accept. "What the fuck, Rupe? The meeting wasn't meant to be for another three hours."

"I know, darling, I know, but this is too good to wait. It's official. The bidding is in and we've been offered a hell of a lot for the syndication rights to your Sabine podcast."

Every month, I do a podcast to discuss my latest restaurant review and answer any questions the listeners might have sent in about it. When I hear how much is on the table for the rights to broadcast this month's podcast, I nearly fall out of bed.

"Jeepers! You're joking!"

Rupert chuckles. "I never make jokes about money. You know that. They want to boost their subscriber list and are willing to pay big."

"How many questions have come in?" I don't usually ask Rupert about details. He sends me a list of interesting questions, and I discuss them with my podcast guest.

But if I accept this offer, that means I get to be the guest on the Bon Cuisine podcast instead of hosting my own.

"Literally thousands. They all want to eat at Sabine at the Banderole and have a miniature orgasm as they put the food in their mouths. Ha-ha!"

"I guess I'm going to have to answer the biggest question of them all, then, aren't I? Can good food make you fall in love?"

Rupert quietens down. "Actually, I think the biggest question is going to be this: Who was your companion at dinner, Ivy?"

I clam up. "That's between me and the amuse-bouche, Rupe. I've never shared my private life with my followers."

"Heh. Don't you mean your bedroom secrets? That's because you don't have one. Never have. I'm not counting all those hookups you've had with cheeky chefs and saucy sommeliers."

"I... I don't think I should see him again." The words physically hurt me when I say them, but I have to consider it. I don't have time for a relationship, especially one that has the ability to mess with my success.

"Ooh, Ivy, I'm the last person you should be asking." Rupert is a confirmed bachelor and proud. "I had to dump my last man because he didn't like truffles!"

We laugh together, taking time to appreciate how difficult having a partner can be.

"Okay, Rupe. I'll do it. But please get a list of who their sponsors on the Bon Cuisine podcast are going to be first so I can research how their products are manufactured."

I don't support businesses that exploit minimum-wage workers.

"Already done, Ivy," Rupert tells me. "I sent it to your email."

We say our goodbyes.

I'm about to try for a bit more sleep, but then Mary-Kay sends a message.

Hey gf. Thanks for sitting with the boys last night. Melanie showed me your latest review. Please don't tell me you're in love with Fletch the Wretch. It would break my heart to know that not only did the bastard bulldoze our family home, but he stole my best friend too. Love, MK.

Shit. This could be a disaster. If Mary-Kay thinks I'm getting close to Banner, she might stop inviting me over.

I love Danny so much. He's a little ray of sunshine. Such a good kid and a credit to his doting mother.

I send a voice message.

"No way! I was only doing a bit. Rupe thought I should get folks in the mood for Valentine's Day next year, that's all. Speak soon. Love you."

With that out of the way, I turn my phone to silent and settle back down to—

Brrring! The fricking doorbell goes mad.

"Jesus Christ!" Jumping out of bed, I go to the intercom and glare at the screen. It's a delivery guy holding an enormous vase of flowers.

"Miss Forrest? Delivery."

I buzz him in and open the door. He holds a device out for me to sign. "Thank you." Taking the vase, I grab a ten-dollar bill from the jar I keep by the door and hand it to him.

Shutting the door with my foot, I carry the vase through to the dining room and place it on the table.

Oh, Banner. You certainly know how to sweeten the outcome. Roses are my favorite flower.

The flowers are arranged very old school. Lots of gypsophila sprays and white lilies mixed in with the red roses.

There's a card. After opening the envelope, I start to read.

Hi "Forrest,"

Remember me? I am so pleased to hear about your big success. Don't be a stranger.

Love, Julian Stratford

# Chapter 15 - Fletcher

"Hey, Boss." It's my head of security at the Banderole calling. I'm still sore after Ivy's rejection of me last night, so I'm not really in the mood to listen to a story about someone who tried to cheat at cards.

Fortunately, the staff are used to my grumpiness. "What?" I snap, taking a large sip of coffee as I think about what my next move with Ivy should be.

"A few complications have arisen, Mr. Banner. I know you like to be informed when something looks suss. Some of the staff brought this to my attention."

"Brought what to your attention?"

"It's complicated, sir. You might want to sit down with a few of the staff and get the facts in person...."

"I'll get back to you on that. Handle it for me and let Anton know when it's resolved." Disconnecting the call, I stare off into the middle of the room.

I can't get Ivy out of my mind! Picking up my phone again, I fire off a text.

When can I see you again? Straight up. You're right. I don't want to show you my apartment. I want to fuck you good and hard the way I know you like it. Is that something that you might be interested in?

After drumming my fingers on the table for a while, I manage to get some emails written. Waiting for Ivy to get back to me is killing me.

I'm not the world's most patient guy at the best of times. But I'm a hunter at heart and this is worth making the effort.

This being a work day, I answer my phone whenever it rings, hardly bothering to glance at the screen to see who it is first.

But then I see Ivy's name come up. "Hey, Ivy. Thanks for getting back to me."

Ivy gets straight to the point. "Banner. I'm scared. I'd love to have sex, but I also need a strong pair of arms to hold me. Is that something you think you can do?"

"Damn straight I can help you out there, sweetheart. What's wrong?"

She sighs. "It's a long story. And I'm not sure I'm ready to tell it yet. Drop me a pin and I'll come over."

"Or I can come to you." I want to be helpful because this woman is literally making my dreams come true.

"Call me paranoid, but I don't want anyone seeing you come over, Banner."

She gives me a time and I send her a pin to my location. Something is bugging me. For the first time in my life, I am not happy with making dates and living separately from a woman.

I want Ivy on tap, accessible to me any day or night.

I'm kind of hoping she feels the same way.

When the doorman calls to tell me I have a visitor I tell him to send her up. Going to the bathroom, I brush the taste of coffee out of my mouth.

Knowing that she's on her way up, I feel my penis getting tumescent. I have to adjust myself so that she doesn't see how excited I am.

I'm leaning nonchalantly against the doorframe as the elevator doors slide open. As always, Ivy is a sight for sore eyes.

She's dressed in her custom tight-fitting pencil skirt with a short slit on the side and silky blouse. Those red-soled stiletto shoes are on her feet, making her legs look elongated and shapely.

Her eyes are wide and slightly apprehensive. Running into my arms, she clings to me.

"Oh, Banner. I'm so scared. I don't want anyone to know we slept together in Vegas."

"If that's what's bugging you, sweetheart…." Pinching her chin, I tilt her face and kiss her.

"I'll go back there and make sure that doesn't happen. Okay?"

Melting into my arms, she returns my kiss with a fierce passion. "Thank you, thank you."

Picking her up, I carry her through to the bedroom. I'm hurting from wanting Ivy so much. Laying her down on the bed gently, I have to unzip.

Her eyes get big when she sees me haul out my cock. "You're getting straight to the point," she teases me, sitting up on the bed and pulling me closer. "I want this so bad, Banner. Your taste, your scent, your utterly gorgeous cock in my eager mouth."

The moment she begins to suck me, I feel orgasmic. But the expert way she uses her tongue and lips is tantalizing enough to keep me from shooting my load.

Ivy unbuckles me so she can access all of my lower body. I can't take my eyes off the way she is making a meal of my thick shaft and the head of my penis. She licks it, holding it in her fist so she can pump it hard.

"Mm," she murmurs, driving me wild from the vibration her mouth makes when she hums like that. "Your cock is addictive, Banner. When I suck it, I want to touch myself, finger my pussy, and tease my clit."

Biting back a groan, I growl, "That's my job. Because you're all I crave. I get hard just thinking about you naked."

"Well, there I can definitely help you out."

Ivy stands up and points to the bed. "Lie down. I want to ride my lovely cowboy." She starts to remove her blouse and she's got no bra underneath. Her skirt is hitched up her thighs, but she squirms out of it with a sexy little wiggle, leaving it on the floor.

All she has on are the shoes because she knows how crazy I am for them.

After rubbing her breasts and pinching her nipples, Ivy starts to crawl towards me from the foot of the bed.

"Rrr, Mr. Cowboy, I'm coming to eat you all up." Her throaty purr is such a turn-on as she prowls towards me.

Next thing I know, she's got me by the balls, her fingernails scratching lightly as her mouth fastens over the head of my penis again. "Talk dirty to me, stud. I want you to beg for me to sit on you."

"Fuck, Ivy. I'm ready to hit the roof. If I was wearing a Stetson, I would throw it in the air and shout 'Yee-haw.'"

She gives the side of my ass a little slap with the palm of her hand. "Ride 'em hard, cowboy. Only this time, I'm the one who's gonna be doing the riding."

Kneeling on the bed, Ivy straddles me. Lifting one leg, she twists to fit the length of my cock into the opening of her slit.

It gives me a flash of her glistening wet opening before she begins to lower herself onto me. It feels out of this world as, inch by inch, her pussy glides over me.

I grunt, physically overwhelmed by the surge of lust coursing through me. The urge to come is so strong, but my urge to dominate her is even stronger.

It's like Ivy can read my mind. "Oh, don't even think about it, Mr. Cowboy. I want to ride you until you sweat and then put you back into the stall wet."

Just to let me know who's boss, she gives my balls a kittenish scratch with her nails. Wow, she's so damn hot when she takes charge like this.

Leaning forward so that her breasts are a whisper away from my mouth, Ivy starts to ride me hard. Pumping her ass up and down my cock, her hand pushes against my chest as her pace gets faster.

The sensation of her pussy grinding down on me is super sensual. I'm loving this so much, that I can't hold back any longer.

I start to come, spurting my essence into her as I am lost in the thrill of the moment. Ivy knows that I stay rock hard for a long time after I come, but I think she's had her fun with me.

"Give it to me, Cowboy. Fuck me hard."

The spasming of her pussy makes me come even better. But when she's finished, Ivy rolls off me, almost leaving me hanging dry!

"It's a good thing I was finished," I say, pulling her into my arms and hugging her close. "You used me like I was a sex toy."

She smirks in that way she knows always gets me going. "Sometimes a girl's gotta be in charge, you know? It's empowering."

I totally get where she's coming from. "First the sex, now the hug. What got you scared?"

Ivy is quiet for a few minutes as she processes what just happened. Then she tells me.

"That review has got a few worms crawling out of the woodwork, Banner. I mean, I was famous before all this—but only in food circles. This is next level."

"Is any worm in particular giving you trouble, sweetheart?"

Pausing a beat, Ivy gives it some thought. "Nothing I can't handle... I think. But it would comfort me to know that you're on top of this.

You've got cameras everywhere in the Bande-role. Can you check for me?"

That makes me give a long whistle. "Woo, babe. It's a casino. There are cameras everywhere. Not just for security. For crime prevention too."

She shakes her head, biting her thumbnail. "I can't have any footage of us at the restaurant circulating, Banner. And I certainly can't have any of us going up to the suite."

I have to know the truth!

"Ivy, are you here to get me to put the lid on footage leaking out? Or are you here for me?"

When she lifts her face to kiss me, relief and happiness flood through me.

"I'm here for you, Banner." Then she gets that mischievous look on her face again. "For the hot sex, anyway!"

Her phone pings as we hit one another with pillows, shouting and laughing. Dammit, Ivy's got me acting like a teenager and I love it.

She glances at the screen and goes pale.

"Sweetheart, what's wrong?"

She holds the screen out for me to read.

Rupert: Clifford Braxton is publishing an article tomorrow, Ivy. He's doing an expose on restaurant critics who take bribes for good reviews!!!

I get really mad when I see the tears filming over Ivy's eyes. "So, what should we do about this? I'm ready to crack some heads!"

# Chapter 16 - Ivy

A feeling of dread creeps over me. Am I about to be exposed? Damn it! Sabine gave me a five-star dining experience, but my inability to rebuff the restaurant's luscious proprietor might prove to be my downfall!

The elation of being with a man I feel a special connection with seeps out of me. Is it too much to wish for a good man and a spotless reputation at the same time?

"You want me to get my lawyers onto it?" Banner asks me. "They could prise the Oscar winners out of the Academy before Oscar night if I told 'em too."

I smile a little bit at his joke, but I am way too highly strung to laugh about this. "I have a lawyer too, Banner! I'm not some flippant idiot playing at building a brand, I will thank you to remember."

He doesn't answer, but I can tell my petulant words have not offended him. He just gives me that sexy smirk of his, as if he's saying, "I get it—you're stressed and a small part of you wants to blame this on me."

What did I ever do to deserve such a lovely sex partner? He knows I'm feeling hella prickly and lets me work it out of my system on my own.

Banner only gets grouchy when I get up off the bed and start dressing. "Fuck it, Ivy, aren't you going to at least stay the night?"

He doesn't know that Julian Stratford is stalking me. The last thing I want to do is figure in Banner's mind as some damsel in distress. I'm a big girl now.

"Suck it up. What did you expect? For me to move in with you? I got places to go and things to do." I'm snapping like a bitch, but I don't care.

When he tells me what's on his mind, I nearly topple out of my five-inch heel Louboutins!

"Yep. I think you should move in with me—at least until we have this shit sorted out."

Does he know about Julian Stratford? I pray he doesn't. My short career as a yacht girl should not be defining this relationship!

"What shit?"

Holding up one finger for me to wait, Banner disappears into the bathroom. I want to scream with frustration as I hear the shower go on, but the more I think about it, the more the pros and cons of staying with him come to mind.

Pros: amazing sex on tap any time I want it, a safe base for me to live while I shake Julian Stratford off my back, and Mary-Kay always gets me to go to her, so there's no risk of her finding out my new living situation.

Cons: if we get caught out, the shit hits the fan in a big way. Can I really afford to jeopardize my friendship with MK, my career, and—most importantly of all—my heart by agreeing to this crazy scheme of Banner's?

It doesn't take me long to make up my mind. Collecting all my stuff, I tiptoe out of the bedroom and make a hasty exit. Only when I'm in the elevator do I text Banner from my phone.

Something came up. Thank you for a lovely time. Talk later. Ivy.

I've never been an exes and ohs type girl when I text. But if I was, the message would be row after row of lovely, lingering, long xxxx. Banner really is the most divine kisser.

Sticking my phone on silent mode, I prepare myself to brave this sticky problem on my own.

***

The photographers and film crew are waiting for me outside my apartment. Am I being paranoid or did they certainly get here real fast?

I try to get back into the cab, but they block me. Dozens of microphones and cameras are shoved in my face as I push my way to the door.

I can't shake the feeling that Julian Stratford has something to do with this.

"Miz Forrest! Miz Forrest! What do you have to say to the rumors that Fletcher Banner paid you to rate Sabine restaurant five stars!?"

"Holly! Tell your readers if your reviews can still be trusted?"

"How much did you charge Mr. Banner for the rating, Holly?"

Shit! Shit! It must be a slow news day. Reporters never bother with rubbish like this unless there's nothing else interesting for them to do.

I hate the way that every time I associate with fucking Fletcher Banner, everyone presumes I am selling myself to him!

Ducking my face down and holding my Louis Vuitton tote over my head, I shoulder on. The doorman steps out and shoos the pests away. "Get lost, you vultures. Miss Forrest will be making a statement later."

Bless his heart. Bert, the doorman, knows to call me by the right name in public. "Thanks, Bert," I say, letting my heavy tote drop. I inhale slowly, trying to calm myself down. "No one is allowed up until I say so."

Bert looks ashamed and starts to explain, and then I hear a voice I recognize. "Holly!" A short, plump woman moves from the lobby sitting area and walks towards me with her hand out-stretched. "I hope you don't mind me waiting for you inside. Meg Stanley, Bon Cuisine. Can we talk?"

If this nosy bitch thinks that she is getting an invite up to my apartment, she could not be more wrong. Moving her back to the lobby sit-ting area where no one can overhear us, I speak through clenched teeth.

"Well, seeing as you're here, what do you want, Ms. Stanley?"

Her eyes twinkle. "Call me, Meg, please. It looks like it's been a busy couple of weeks for you, don't you think?"

Barely suppressing an exasperated sigh, I make a circle with my hand. "Can we hurry this along, please? I'm not in the best mood."

Her eyes move to the double doors where the reporters are still crowding outside on the sidewalk. "I hear you. Sorry about all the furor, but I just want you to know that Bon Cuisine is standing behind you on this, Holly. We still want a partnership with you."

"Christ!" I can't help rolling my eyes. "Look outside, Meg. You can't possibly want all the controversy I'm having to deal with right now."

Giving me a wide smile, Meg Stanley shakes her head. "That's where you're wrong! We need a breath of fresh air like you, Holly. Bon Cuisine is stagnant. There are only so many rave reviews of good service and subtle ambiance we can do before readers get bored. You're right! We need to put the sex and romance back into fine dining!"

I can't believe what I am hearing. "You want to continue our partnership?"

"Yes, girl! I'm proud of you for wearing your heart on your sleeve like that. Most women are so afraid of telling a man that he is more desirable than a mouthful of ambrosia! Your writing is so bold."

"Well, if that's how you feel, Meg...." I can't stop grinning. "How about we take on Clifford Braxton together! Get him on the podcast tomorrow—especially now that he's published that fucking hit piece on me—and we can show his readers what a bitter, twisted sourpuss he really is!"

Meg gives me two thumbs-up. "Holly, I look forward to it." She turns to leave. "We'll be filming too, so make sure you come to the studio looking drop-dead gorgeous!"

When I get up to my apartment, a surge of triumph courses through me. I will fight this—and I will win! I never planned to dine with the Banderole's owner that night. And there is no way that I will let the silly mistake I made as a teenager define who I am today.

Stepping over to the vase of flowers, I pick it up and hurl it across the room with all my strength!

***

The next morning, I turn my phone's ringer back on and call Banner. I can tell from the background noise when he answers that he is on a construction site.

But he always seems to have time for me.

"Ivy. Everything okay? Anton tells me the paparazzi caught you entering your building."

"Who's Anton?"

"My assistant. He answers my phones so I don't have to."

"Cool. I guess we all need a little Anton in our lives."

He chuckles, but immediately gets serious again, allowing me to continue with my sad story.

"It's too soon to know yet, but our situation might get problematic. And that's not even taking Mary-Kay into consideration."

"Carry on." Banner's voice is gruff, but I know I have all of his attention.

"Rupert, my agent, filled me in on everything last night. You got some time on your hands to listen?"

"For you, I will always make time. Hang on while I get off this scaffolding."

I wait for a beat as he moves back to ground level, the noise of drilling and hammering going on all around him. "Right. Shoot."

"I don't want to go into too much detail, Banner, but there's a bit of a battle going on at the moment between the old-school restaurant critics and the new ones. Sponsors always want fresh and new influencers and that's putting the squeeze on the ones who haven't moved with the times."

"Yep, go on." I hear him take a sip of something and I get distracted for a moment. I can't help imagining whether he is wearing one of those plaid shirts or working shirtless. Or maybe he's got a white cotton sleeveless undershirt on?

Dressed in jeans and work boots, wearing a helmet, with a tool belt strapped below his waist. Those yummy iliac furrows making a sexy V-shape on his lower stomach as the jeans slip down when he takes a drink—

"You still there?"

I recollect myself. "Yes, as I was saying, I have a few enemies. And Clifford Braxton has to be the worst. He's a real Bitter Betty with an axe to grind. And somehow, he's gotten hold of something that ties us together. Do you have any idea what that might be?"

"My security reached out. They only caught it on video the other night. Someone recognized us when we were arguing on the sidewalk. They followed us inside and took pictures on their phone. Asshole took a whole lot of time and date-stamped images. Then he loitered outside and caught long-distance images of us the following morning coming out of the private suite elevator."

I remember how I left the elevator feeling like I was on top of the world. That would have looked normal, but....

"You ran after me in your briefs."

"Yep," Banner admits. "It was my fault. I'm sorry. I was indiscreet with your reputation, Ivy. Forgive me."

My lower lip trembles as I think about what my podcast with Clifford fucking Braxton is going to be like, knowing that he probably has those images. "It's not your fault. How were we to know some creep was going to be hanging around?"

Trying to cheer me up, Banner jokes with me. "Whatever happened to 'what happens in Vegas stays in Vegas'?"

"News feeds started paying big for stories, that's what." I can feel the anger building up inside me. "God, Banner, I have to find a way to squash this. I can't have Mary-Kay thinking I am the best friend equivalent of Mata Hari!"

"Leave this to me. I pay people to handle this kind of shit for me."

A blossom of hope blooms in my heart. "Do you think they can squash this in time for the interview?"

"When is it?"

I give Banner the time and place I have to be to record the podcast. He repeats the information, makes a mental note, and then says, "If I don't get back to you in time, tell security there that you're expecting someone to drop by. Tell them it's important."

"Tell them something like Holly Forrest plus one, you mean?"

He chuckles. I'm pissed he is taking this so lightly. I want to give him a piece of my mind! But before I can gear up to give him a good tongue-lashing, Banner warns me.

"I'm happy to be your plus one, sweetheart. But whatever happens, Ivy, remember to go along with it. I might have a solution, but you need to give me some extra rope to play with."

"Oh God," I moan softly, biting the end of my thumb. "I hope MK forgives me!"

"Mary-Kay is never going to believe any of this, Ivy. Relax."

I'm about to take his advice when my phone buzzes again. This better be good news!

# Chapter 17 - Ivy

"I see you took my advice. Sorry to send you a text, but it's important our guests dress up for the cameras because we don't have a makeup artist or wardrobe person on call!"

Meg Stanley greets me with a wink and a smile. "Bon Cuisine is trying to grow our online presence, so the footage is going onto YouTube, Spotify, iPhone podcasts—all the biggies."

Returning her smile, I shake hands with the team who are all there to welcome me.

"Holly Forrest! You're a legend, you know that? I'm Noah Blake. Pleased to meet you." The producer is my age—maybe a little younger—with one of those perfectly trimmed beards and long, light-brown hair tied back in a ponytail. "It's the first time I've read a restaurant review and gotten turned on!"

"Pleased to meet you, Noah. Are you going to be producing my podcast when I join the team?" I want to know who I will be working with in the future. Noah smiles and winks.

Rupert sent me the Bon Cuisine contract last night. It allows me to continue freelancing and I only have to do one podcast a month with them.

"We want to keep you exclusive," Meg tells me, propelling me into the studio by linking her arm through mine. "We want those listener figures to spike once a month so we have some comparative data to look at."

God! I can't believe I am actually here in the Bon Cuisine building! The travel and leisure department is on the floor above us, and the fashion department is below.

The whole enterprise is run by a publishing company that has been in business for over a hundred years. I wish my parents could see me now. They never believed in me the way I believed in myself.

Total vindication.

I have my Holly hat squarely on my head and my Forrest apron on. I enjoy hiding behind the anonymity my pseudonym gives me. And only a select few people know my true identity—just like a superhero!

All I have to do is sort out my problems with Clifford Braxton and Julian Stratford. Then I'll be truly free.

"Just checking that security knows to let my visitor in, Meg," I whisper to the host.

She whispers back, "All they have to do is sign in at the front desk and get a visitor's pass card, Holly. We're not that uptight about security here."

"How's the switchover from print media to audiovisual going?" I ask Noah as we sit in the sound booth. He helps make me comfortable with bottled water and a demonstration of how the cough button works.

"All the better because you're here." Noah gives my hand a quick squeeze as he helps me push the cough button under the desk. He takes the time to point out all three camera angles to me and helps me put on the headphones.

He's cute, I can't deny it. It's not often I go full-on with makeup and an outfit, but Bon Cuisine is associated with Bon Mode, the fashion magazine. I don't want them looking down their noses at me.

My long hair is down and I took the time to run it through a straightening iron this morning. A couple of spritzes of silicone gel and voilà! It's a shining crowning glory.

To match this stellar grooming effort, I have layered on the mascara and eyeliner, and dabbed bronze highlighter on my cheekbones.

I never use lip products; there's too much risk of it caking or getting on my teeth, and I'm not going to take that chance with the podcast being filmed.

A slick of Vaseline is the only lubrication I ever put on my lips. It's flavorless, so it doesn't get in the way of what I am tasting.

As always, I'm wearing my favorite brand of shoes—Louboutins—but this time, they are nude. My usual black pencil skirt fits tight on my waist, hips, and thighs, with two short slits up the side.

Instead of a lacy bra, I'm wearing a camisole under my transparent lawn blouse. Like all writers, my nails are short so that I can type better.

Flicking my hair back, I get chatting with Meg and Noah. We're laughing about the days when smoking was allowed in restaurants—something that I am almost too young to remember.

A commotion can be heard outside. A high-pitched voice is screeching.

"I did not agree to this! I will not enter into a debate with that woman on video! End of story!"

"I see Clifford Braxton has not let good manners get in the way of him making his opinion be known," I say dryly, but I'm actually quite mad.

Noah leaves to calm Braxton down, which gives me time to get my arguments in order in my head.

Fifteen minutes later, Clifford, Meg, and I are facing off on opposite sides of the desk. I can't help noticing that Noah didn't bother sorting out Clifford with bottled water or showing him where the cough button is.

The critic is shooting dagger-like looks at me from his chair, but I ignore him. I'm a professional and this isn't high school, but it seems Mr. Braxton didn't get the memo.

The light goes red to show us that the introduction music is ending, and Meg begins.

"Hello, and welcome to all you food and fine dining aficionados out there today. This is the Bon Cuisine podcast. I'm your host, Meg Stanley. I'm pleased to have two of the top restaurant critics in the studio with me today. The lovely Holly Forrest, who came first in the Top Restaurant Critic USA Awards last year—and the esteemed Clifford Braxton, a long-time contributor to the Sunday Herald newspaper. Hi, guys, thanks for being on the show."

Clifford says hello stiffly and I say hi, remembering to give a little wave because this is being videoed.

"Let's jump straight in. Clifford, you recently published a very pointed article about restaurant critics who accept bribes for good reviews. You claimed that you were about to expose the culprits and name names. Would you care to elaborate?"

Meg and I turn to listen to what Braxton chooses to spin.

I can see the critic is just loving being the center of attention. After licking his lips and adjusting his glasses, he says, "My lawyer has warned me not to be too specific, Meg. But I know every single one of the alleged sellouts, and they should be worried, very worried."

Meg turns to me. "Have you heard of this before, Holly? I'm confused. Aren't all the restaurant critics incognito?"

This is my chance and I take it. "Yes, Meg. Also, nowadays, we prefer to be called 'inspectors' or 'influencers.' Criticizing someone's efforts is kinda negative behavior."

Meg agrees with me. "When it's the chef's best effort? Definitely."

I carry on. "The restaurants are booked in advance under a fake company name. We go to great lengths to stay under the radar. We want to be treated just like any other guest. But having said that, social media has made all the main players easily recognizable—"

"Let me stop you right there," Braxton interrupts. "My thumbnail is used on every critique headline I have ever written for the Herald. You don't have to own a social media account for the staff to recognize you."

"Clifford has a point," I agree with him, "but I think his beef is with those people who visit restaurants with no qualifications in the hospitality and food service industry. Especially when they go on to trash the chef's reputation on Yelp. They have been known to ask for a free meal in exchange for a positive review—when they don't get it, they get mad."

Meg butts in when she sees Braxton getting ready to complain. "It happens more often than people think. Someone with eighty thousand social media followers called a hotel and demanded a free room! When they didn't get it, they did a hit piece on the place."

Clifford Braxton tries to move the conversation back to himself. "Excuse me, but we are here to talk about experts in the field, Meg, not those silly idiots who like to take photographs of the food and film everything! I've got better things to do than look at pictures of avocado toast!"

I can sense he is getting ready to drop the bomb. I brace myself.

Turning to me, he gives an oily-looking smile. "Holly, do you mind telling me how you got a table for the opening of Sabine?"

I have prepared for this. "Vegas hotels have hard and soft openings. The buzz around Sabine during the soft opening was enough for me to prioritize it. My agent books a table for two at every new fine-dining restaurant in every major US city before it opens. We decide which one sounds like the best eating experience for the readers, and that's the one I go to. The rest of the bookings are canceled in advance or they are postponed for a later date."

"Sounds very complicated," Braxton mutters under his breath, but the microphone picks it up.

"It's important to stay current," I explain. "My agent and I live, taste, and breathe exceptional dining experiences, Clifford. You gotta move fast because some places get booked up two years in advance."

The breath catches in my throat as Braxton opens his laptop on the desk.

"I couldn't help hearing you say you booked your table for two, Holly," Clifford Braxton's tone is triumphant because he thinks he has me trapped. "Do you mind me asking why that is?"

Meg fields the question for me. "Solo diners are the perfect way to stand out in a fine dining establishment, for all of you who are listening at home. It's like having a sign around your neck that reads 'I am here to review the food!'"

We all laugh. It gives me hope that I will be able to handle this.

After tinkering with his laptop keyboard, Braxton turns to Noah's booth and gives him the thumbs-up sign. The white screen on the wall next to the desk lights up—with a giant photo of Banner and me. We're canoodling at Sabine's entrance, talking to the host.

The audio on the video is turned up to full volume, loud enough for the whole world to hear Banner say, "Tear up the bill for table five." He gives my waist a tight squeeze as we stare enraptured into one another's eyes. Then Banner says, "This little lady is with me."

I want to slap Clifford Braxton's smug face when he gloats at me. "Do you mind explaining to all the Bon Cuisine listeners, Holly, how you came to spend the night with the developer and owner of Sabine restaurant and Banderole Hotel?!"

We're all shocked. The bastard has side-swiped me with this video footage. It's damning.

Meg butts in. "Err... the time and date stamp are the same as the night you reviewed Sabine, Holly. I know there must be a perfectly legitimate explanation behind this."

"Oh-ho! That's not all," Braxton continues rubbing it in. "Our source stuck around to see if Holly's bribe had an even nicer cherry on top and—boo-yah!"

An image of Banner in his sexy briefs standing in the VIP lobby entrance floods the screen. He's got his arms outstretched and his gorgeous eyes are laughing. And I am smiling back at him as if all my fucking Christmases have come at once.

Years of discipline keep me from showing my emotions. I have this under control.

"That's the night after your visit to Sabine, isn't it, Holly?"

I can hear Braxton's gloating voice speaking, but my brain is still scrambling for a comeback. Preferably one that explains how my review is not connected with the events on show.

Noah must be feeding Meg information from the booth. I see her start to read details off her laptop.

"Did you accept bribe money from Fletcher Banner, Holly? I mean, everyone in the hospitality industry knows he's a notoriously ruthless man. The archetypal hard-nosed hotel magnate. Did he force you?"

Clifford Braxton pretends to be scandalized. "These images were offered to the Sunday Herald's parent company for sale. That's how I got hold of them. I was shocked, Meg, shocked. Such unprofessional behavior!"

Meg carries on reading. "The elite billionaires he hangs out with call Mr. Banner the 'cowboy of the conference room' and 'Jesse James.' Not just because he was a sniper in the Marines, but because he likes to kill the competition."

Tears start to prick my eyes. My throat closes as I think of how lovely Banner has been to me.

They don't know him like I do. He's not some line 'em up and shoot 'em down cowboy. He's kind and patient and forgiving....

All my hard work and dreams are about to go up in smoke—and all because I had a blind date with my best friend's stunningly handsome, sexy, adorable brother. If only I had been able to say no to that meltingly lovely one-night stand in the hotel suite.

But I do not regret it one bit.

Noah opens the recording booth door. "Meg, Fletcher Banner is here—"

All three of us seated at the desk let out a gasp. We can't help it. It kinda feels like we're naughty school kids caught talking about a teacher behind his back.

Meg steps into the breach. "Listeners, you will be pleased to know that Mr. Fletcher Banner has stepped into the studio and is going to join our discussion."

Noah finishes setting up Banner with a microphone, headphones, and chair and then trots back to the recording desk. My heart flips when Banner reaches for my hand and gives it a squeeze.

We make eye contact briefly before he focuses on Meg.

"Thank you for having me, Ms. Stanley. I think I should be here. Especially if accusations are being thrown around with my name on it."

"Please call me 'Meg,' Mr. Banner. We were wondering if you could clear this up for us. Did you pay Holly Forrest to give Sabine a five-star review?"

I think everyone is holding their breath, waiting for Banner to answer.

"First up, Clifford Braxton doesn't need a lawyer to tell him not to make allegations—he needs a doctor."

"Wh-why?" Suddenly, Clifford Braxton isn't sounding so cocky anymore.

Banner almost snarls into the microphone. "Because I will break your face if you dare accuse my fiancée of receiving bribes again."

Oh my God! Banner looks so mad—I think he's going to punch the guy out!

# Chapter 18 - Ivy

There is silence for a beat until Noah reminds Meg that they have dead air. She fills in the gap with some challenging banter.

"Now, Fletcher, if you think that your engagement is going to save things, you might have it wrong. No restaurant inspector or reviewer is allowed to rate an establishment when it belongs to a family member or associate."

Leaning back in his chair and linking his hands behind his neck, Banner kinda grins in his irrepressible cocksure way.

"Why do you think Holly wrote that review, Meg? Have you even bothered reading it? We fell in love at first sight."

Clifford Braxton is hating this. I can tell from the way his lower lip is all pooched out. As for me, I'm just along for the ride.

No wait. Maybe I'm in shock! I know Banner said he had an ace up his sleeve, but this is ridiculous.

"Bullshit! You're just covering up your scam!" Clifford is outraged.

Moving quickly, Banner sits upright. The action scares old Clifford. He gives a little scream and shrinks away.

"For a man who paid bad money to gain access to images of a private moment on my property, Braxton, you sure do like to throw your weight around."

Is it my imagination, or is Banner's Southern accent more pronounced now?

Meg says quickly, "We would all love to hear what happened, Fletcher."

"It's simple. Holly asked a friend to set her up with a blind date for Sabine so she wouldn't stand out sitting alone. We met at the bar and then moved to the restaurant. She had no idea

I was the hotel's owner and I had no idea she was a critic."

Meg chuckles. "The date would not have gone down so well if you had known that."

Banner gives a lopsided smile. "Hey, full disclosure. I worked it out because Holly was making notes of everything. But the evening went so well I didn't want to bring it up."

"I call bullshit again!" Clifford does not want to lose this fight. "My source tells me that the two of you were arguing on the sidewalk outside the hotel. And Holly was hissing insults at you. That sounds like couple behavior to me."

Completely unfazed, Banner doesn't even bother looking at him.

"Yeah, I was a world-class asshole. I offered Holly money in exchange for a five-star review. She tore me a new one and then left. I chased after her and apologized. Then we spent the night together."

Meg sighs. "Oh my God. That's so romantic."

"Isn't it?" Banner smiles, takes hold of my hand, and kisses it. "And that bit in the lobby with me in my briefs, I was asking her to marry me. And she said yes."

"Have I fallen asleep and woken up in crazy land?" Clifford Braxton won't let go. "None of this matters. Holly Forrest gave Sabine a five-star review because she's in cahoots with the owner. End of story!"

Springing to my feet, I walk over to the Louis Vuitton tote I carry everywhere with me. Coming back to the desk, I throw my yellow legal pad in front of Braxton. "You know this as well as I do, Clifford, we always rate the restaurant onsite."

Sitting back down, I hold Banner's hand. "Go on, read my notes. I rated everything five stars. Room, decor, staff, food, presentation, and atmosphere. And I did all that before Mr. Banner and I spent the night together."

"Hey, you minx," Banner teases me, moving his hand to rub the back of my neck where I am the most tense. "You never told me that. You let me make a fool out of myself by offering you money."

Oh my God. I can't believe this. It looks like we're going to be able to pull this off.

Clifford tries one last time. "You should be ashamed of yourself, Mr. Banner. Bribery is corrupt."

Everyone laughs except Braxton. "I don't claim to be an angel, Cliff," Banner says clearly into the microphone, "but I was lucky enough to meet one that night at Sabine. And now we're engaged to be married."

Dabbing her eyes with a tissue, Meg sighs. "That is the most romantic thing I have ever heard. And that, dear listeners, is what great food can do. We love food, we adore falling in love. So doing the two things together is the perfect combination—and on that note, we have a quick word from our sponsors."

Noah signals for the commercial to start running, and we all sit back. But Banner pushes his chair away from the desk and stands up. "See you later?" he asks me. "My place or yours?"

"Yours. Mine is still crawling with reporters."

One final kiss and then Banner is gone as quickly as he came. Meg watches him go, all misty-eyed. "Holly, you are the luckiest woman in the world."

We have to carry on recording, but I am too excited and shocked to add much more to the story. When it's a wrap, I give old Cliff a cheery wave goodbye as he stomps to the elevators.

Meg and Noah invite me up to the publishing company's head office to be introduced to the team.

Is it my imagination, or is everyone being super-duper-friendly to me now? Is that because of Banner's billions?

"Where are you getting married?" Meg asks.

"Meg, I gotta go. The food market closes soon and I want to cook something nice for supper."

"Is he a 'high-protein diet' kind of guy?" Meg wants to know. "Or does he eat carbs? His body is amazing."

Waving and smiling, I walk away. "I have no idea. Bye, Meg."

***

Banner buzzes me into the apartment. I have a heavy feeling in my belly that is making me impatient and curious at the same time.

Are those my knees shaking? Where is the brave and feisty Holly Forrest when I need her?

But I'm not Holly Forrest. I'm Ivy Woods—and I think I'm in love with the man who saved my career, my life, and my hope.

My path might have gone in a completely different direction if that man on the yacht had been able to take advantage of me.

I might have given up and allowed myself to be sucked into that toxic lifestyle if Banner hadn't stepped in.

The second he opens the door, I fling myself into his arms.

"Thank you, thank you."

I don't make a list of all the times he's saved me, but I hope he knows.

Banner strokes my head. "It was my pleasure. It's always fun when we do things together, don't you agree?"

Suppressing my giggles so that I can kiss him, I murmur the most tempting words. "Darling, Banner. Can I please show you the funnest thing we can do together?"

He doesn't need me to ask him twice. Picking me up with absolutely no effort and carrying me to the bedroom, he lays me down on the bed gently.

"Show me," he says gruffly, removing his tie with one hand as his stare is riveted on my body.

"Oh, I am so going to show you," I promise him, "but first I must shower. That mean old food critic had me sweating in that booth this morning."

Clambering off the divinely comfortable bed, I go to the bathroom.

The more I think about it, the more I realize my knees are way too shaky for me to stand in the shower.

That's the thing about Banner. He manages to get me going with just one touch. I start running a bath, pouring in some scented bubble oil that's in the cabinet.

The room fills with the fragrance of patchouli and sandalwood—so delicious.

Undressing quickly and tying my hair in a knot on top, I slither under the scented foam, sighing as I lift up a handful of bubbles and rub my body with it.

When I get out of this bath, I am going to climb Fletcher Banner like a tree.

The door opens. "I'll be out in a jiff," I say without bothering to look at the door. "I deserve this bath. You can't believe how fucking stressful today was."

"Did you know that bath was specially designed for me?" I feel Banner slide into the bath behind me, his naked body cradles me gently. "Because I'm so tall."

Slipping my hand under the water, I grip his thick erection in my hand. "Because you're so big, I think you mean."

He doesn't answer and just enjoys me stroking him. Twisting around like a sexy mermaid, I glide my body against him, pressing my breasts against his cock and then wiggling slowly up to his chest.

"This bath oil feels so gooooood," I tease, "but how are you going to feel the wetness inside my pussy?"

The breath catches in his throat as he fights to control himself.

"Your pussy juice tastes way better than bath oil, Ivy. That's how I can tell the difference."

"Mm, you better show me." Sitting on the edge of the bath tiles after placing a towel down, I spread my legs wide open for him.

Banner laps at my slit, tonguing the hood and then sucking the hard nub of my lovebud. It doesn't take long for me to beg him to stop.

"Make it last," I tell him sweetly. "I want us to fuck all night long."

"Oh, believe me, that's going to happen whether you come now or not." Giving one last nuzzling suck to my pulsing clit, he pulls me back into the bath with a splash.

He's underneath me, so I lie back and enjoy the sensation of his rock-hard body covered in perfumed oil. When he begins caressing my breasts with his hands, I open my legs wider and glide my vagina down onto his rampant cock.

He slides inside me, impressively thick and erect. Banner is massaging my breasts, pinching and flicking the tips of my nipples. "Reverse cowgirl in the bath. I love it."

"You've got a new sheriff in town." Using my hands as leverage, I ride up and down his cock, rubbing my slick body against him. "And you are the biggest stallion I've ever had to handle."

I lean forward and press my most sensitive part on his balls. Instantly, I'm orgasmic.

"I'm close," I pant, biting my lip as I concentrate. "Don't you dare cum."

Banner must be getting a real eyeful of my ass as I twerk my pussy all over his balls while riding his big cock. I don't care. I'm swept away by my desire.

I think I scream when I come because my ears are ringing from the echoes as I fall back against him.

This is not the sort of man you want to give orders to in the bedroom—not when he's horny as a caged bull!

Flipping me onto my back, he grinds himself deep into me, growling his approval at my tight wetness.

When we are fully recovered, Banner shoots me one of his patented charming smiles. "What's in the bags you brought with you?"

"Supper for two."

"I love the sound of that, Ivy. This marriage is going to be a dream come true."

# Chapter 19 - Fletcher

When I say that, Ivy whips her head up, her brilliant brown eyes wide as she moves to sit opposite me in the bath. "What marriage? You said nothing about that fake engagement being real, Banner! It was a Hail Mary, wasn't it?"

Stepping out of the bath and strolling naked into the bedroom, I shoot a brief look at her over my shoulder.

She's sitting in the bath with her arms wrapped around her knees. Her hair is loose and wet, falling down her back with the ends waving like dark seaweed in the water.

I can see the pale triangles of a bikini tan outlining her pert breasts. I wonder where she was, and who she was with when she got them.

"Relax." I give a little smirk so she knows I'm teasing. "I would never want to jeopardize your friendship with my sister. Because that's what our relationship would do, you know."

I hear Ivy splashing in the bath as she washes herself. I can also hear the wheels turning in her mind.

"This sucks," she calls out. "It's... it's uncivilized! Why can't we all just be polite to one another and tell the truth? MK's a big girl. She can handle it."

"Let's wait to hear what Mary-Kay has to say about the podcast when it's been uploaded. I'm sure that friend of hers—Melanie—will have a few views on the subject too."

Stepping out of the bath, Ivy begins drying her hair. It muffles her voice, but I can still hear her.

"Should we give her a heads-up? How are we going to spin this?"

It's too tempting. She looks like a wet mermaid that has washed up on my beach. I grab her towel and start to pat the water off the curve of her back.

"Remember what I told you? We stick to telling her the whole thing was a fabrication. We did it to get publicity for Sabine. End of story."

Running the towel up her back, I dry the nape of her neck and then kiss it.

Immediately, her hands reach around and start to massage my cock. And just like that, I'm ready for sex again—rock hard and rampant.

This makes Ivy giggle. Turning around, she presses her body against me as she hugs me and kisses my chest.

"Oh, no you don't, Mr. Banner. I have some delicious ingredients for you to eat in the kitchen waiting for me to cook. Food first, then fucking. 'Kay?"

The sensation of her mouth moving against my chest as she talks really revs my engine, but the thought of eating my first home-cooked meal in the apartment is also attractive.

Going to the closet, I pull out a fresh tee. It's white cotton and custom-made to fit my torso. I have twenty of them on order each year from the designer in Italy.

"Here. Put this on." Passing it to Ivy, I sort through my sock drawer next. "You want something for your feet?"

When she pulls it over her head, the T-shirt reaches mid-thigh. "Your place is immaculate, Banner," Ivy tells me. "I can go barefoot, thanks."

It makes me smile when I see her lift the cotton to her nose and sniff it.

"Good?" I want to know.

"Lovely," she says. "Nothing like the smell of freshly laundered cotton."

We go through to the living area. Ivy opens some doors to look inside as she familiarizes herself with the penthouse.

"Ugh, this place is so boring, Banner. Books, files, and papers everywhere." She opens the door to the media room. "And viewing screens... and a conference room! What the hell! This is more like living in an office than a home. Don't you ever have visitors? Guests? Friends over for dinner?"

I am following her progress, an amused grin on my face as I watch Ivy critique the penthouse. "No. I mean, yes, I have friends." Hang on! I have to stop and think before I can answer fully. "I have associates and a few buddies from the construction side of my work. But if you think I'm going to invite a bunch of union men to drink beer and watch the game with me, you're crazy. We mostly hang out at the Vexillum Hotel downtown to do that."

Running her fingers through her hair to untangle it, Ivy gives up on inspecting the apartment and goes to the kitchen.

"The Vexillum Hotel is one of yours?"

Sitting down on one of the stools by the breakfast nook, I watch Ivy start opening the kitchen cupboards. "Vexillum is a banner flag from Roman Empire times, so yeah, it's one of mine."

Ivy pulls out a brand-new pot from the cupboard and holds it up to the light to inspect it. "How did this all start? Your own empire, I mean?"

Placing the pan on the stovetop, she begins opening drawers until she finds a wooden spoon. Then Ivy brings the bags closer and begins to unpack ingredients out of them.

I like watching her move around the kitchen. Her actions are economical and skillful. I can see her training shining through.

And then I remember how she was forced to work in a restaurant kitchen to pay for her studies.

Ivy made her own way in the world, the same as me. Actually, she started out with even less. When she was struggling, there was no ranch house equity to fall back on.

"I used my parents' insurance policy to fund construction on converting the ranch into luxury and budget accommodations. Luxury for tourists and budget for truckers. It took off."

Flicking on one of the hot plates, she places the pan over the flames to heat up before squirting in a thread of olive oil. Using the sideboard, she carefully halves four fat scallops, pats them dry, and then seasons them.

"Wasn't it dangerous aiming for the luxury market in a place like Texas? You were in a pretty remote location out there, weren't you?"

This little lady sure knows her stuff!

"I was a Marine, Ivy, not a hermit. In my spare time, I used SEO to promote the luxury accommodations as a spa retreat. The whole nine yards—health and wellness in the wild, get away from the city into the prairie desert, hot tub spa amidst the cacti—you name it."

"Get pampered in Pampa with the Pampas?" Ivy gives me a cheeky look as she puts the scallops into the hot oil carefully and then throws in a knob of butter.

That makes us crack up laughing. "Damn! That's a good one. I wish I'd had you with me back then."

Serving the scallops onto two plates with a light lemon butter sauce, she comes to sit next to me. "Me too. It must have been a nightmare losing your parents so young. I only got to hear

Mary-Kay's side of it—that was bad enough. She never stopped complaining about how your parents left you everything."

"As opposed to what? Them leaving it to MK?" Is my sardonic take on things.

"I see your point." Ivy chuckles.

I don't have much to say about family matters. I was all about God, Corps, and Country back then. The hotel was just a side hustle to get by.

After clinking our forks together, we start to eat. It doesn't take long for me to clean the plate. "That was delicious, Ivy. A food critic who knows how to cook. It doesn't get better than that."

After stacking our plates, she goes back to the kitchen. Her knife skills are impressive as she begins to peel and slice potatoes.

"Why did you leave the armed forces? Were you more interested in the accommodation and leisure sector?"

The memory that floods my brain makes me grumpy. "You know full well why I had to leave."

Ivy doesn't miss a beat. Her deft movements continue. "No. I don't know. Just answer the fucking question without giving me attitude, Banner! You should know by now that I don't waste my time asking for information about something I already know!"

"I had to leave because Mary-Kay got into trouble! She was running wild and no one could control her."

Ivy continues to fry potato slices and adjust the seasoning with a serene expression on her face.

"Must have been before Mary-Kay and me got to being friends. I knew she was a firecracker, but I admired her outrageousness. She wasn't one of the mean girls, even though she came from money. Most of the other girls at school ignored me because my parents were... low-income, middle-class. Father working on the boats and a stay-at-home mom. But that didn't matter to MK."

I have never heard my sister described like this. For me, Mary-Kay was always a major pain in my ass without the benefit of having an upside.

"MK was a mean girl to me! She has never apologized for dragging me out of my chosen profession and forcing me back into being a civilian."

Putting the potatoes into a dish in the proofing drawer, Ivy begins to unwrap two steaks. She pats them dry and seasons them with an expert flick of her wrist.

"It couldn't have been that bad. Don't create drama, Mr. Grumpy." She gives me a little glance from under her lashes. It's so cute, and it lets me know that she's enjoying our chat.

All I can do is give a low whistle and shake my head. Ivy really doesn't have a clue why MK and I have such a toxic dynamic.

"MK ran away from the hostel and hooked up with the head of a gang. By the time I found her, she was snorting meth and getting pimped."

That makes Ivy drop her wooden spoon in the pan.

"What!? She never told me any of this! When did that happen?"

The smell of grilling steak forces Ivy back to the stove. She turns on the extractor fan, so I raise my voice so she can hear me.

It hurts me to tell the truth, but I need to share this with someone because what happened next nearly killed me.

"She was thirteen. After I managed to track her down, I went ballistic. No deaths, I'm not stupid. But I broke some serious bones, I can tell you."

"How did you manage to take out a gang?"

"I'm a trained sniper with money, sweetheart." I manage to muster up a smile for her sake. "I knew the gang couldn't call the cops either. They were at the stash house. I waited on the roof of the opposite building with a silenced rifle, one with a telescopic lens and night vision. Leg shots and shoulder shots are difficult shots to make, but I was... motivated."

Ivy gives me a dazzling smile as she spoons melted butter and herbs over the steaks. "I just bet you were."

"The thugs who managed to survive my first assault were stupid enough to stay in the building. I went in and took out the rest of them—hand-to-hand combat."

Shaking her head, Ivy drops salad stuff into a bowl and mixes it with olive oil and balsamic vinaigrette. "So, you had them under surveillance for a few days—you knew how many were in there?"

Like I said, I love the way her mind works.

"Yep. They had guns, but most of them were so malnourished and untrained that they would have been better off with a bat. Or a knife. That's what I used when I entered the building to extract MK. All it takes is a stab wound in the thigh or groin to make someone drop out of a fight fast."

"I would never go up against a gun with a knife."

Smirking, I try explaining to her. "That's because you don't know how guns work in real life. A short barrel pistol or revolver is only accurate up to about five feet—and that's when someone has been properly trained to aim. Add drugs and stupidity to the equation and you've got a surefire miss."

Sliding the proofing drawer shut after putting in the steaks, Ivy comes around and gives me a hug.

"Poor big brother. But you did the right thing—getting her out of the city and into an academy for girls."

We cling together for a long time. When I am in her arms, all the repressed anger seems to melt away inside me.

"Let's eat," Ivy whispers in my ear.

"Let's go to Europe together," I murmur back.

I wait anxiously for her to reply because this woman is really keeping me on my toes. Will it be yes or no?

# Chapter 20 - Ivy

Sometimes being with Banner makes my head spin! One minute he's telling the world we're engaged to be married and the next minute he's saying we should go to Europe.

We eat our steaks as I mull over his spontaneous suggestion.

"Europe. Why?" Seeing the hurt look in his eyes, I quantify my response. "It sounds lovely, but why Europe?"

Moving back into the kitchen, I turn off the extractor fan and take a tub of vanilla ice cream out of the freezer. I might have to pop it in the microwave for a few seconds to soften.

Next, I empty the cream into a saucepan and start breaking squares of chocolate into it.

"I'm expanding into Europe," Banner explains. "I always check on the sites in person. I'm a hands-on kinda guy," he says as he walks around the breakfast booth and comes to stand behind me at the stove.

I feel his strong hands slide around my waist and wish that physical contact with Banner didn't make my legs go so delightfully wobbly all the time.

"You most definitely are a hands-on kinda guy." I love teasing him, but I have to be careful not to burn the chocolate, so I keep stirring.

"How about we take that dessert into the bedroom?" Banner's hands glide under the T-shirt and begin to fondle my ass. "I've always wanted to eat ice cream off your belly."

Pretending to be shocked, I hold the spoon up for him to lick.

Yes, I am definitely turned on again. This is crazy!

After turning off the gas flame, I spin around. "I will have you know that it's not the ice cream people lick off each other. It's the chocolate sauce."

"Both are very nice," he growls in a gruff voice, taking my spare hand and pressing it against the front of his jeans. "But isn't the licking the whole point, not the food you're eating?"

Giggling, I pretend to hit him with the wooden spoon. "Fine! I'll bring the dessert through to the bedroom. Now, go! I have to clean up in here."

But the moment I turn my back on him, I hear Banner unzipping. Pressing himself against me, he murmurs in a deep voice, "I'll stop if you want me to, but if you don't, then I'm going to bend you over this countertop and fuck you hard right now."

He knows I want him to. Sliding his fingers over my ass and feeling my slit, he probes my soaking wet pussy. One touch is all it takes for me to want more of him.

This is the fast food equivalent of sex. A quick bend over the kitchen countertop, and I'm loving it!

I brace myself against the surface. Banner is not a small man and I feel every inch as he slides into me. I push back onto him. All the way up to the hilt.

"Oof!" I gasp. "Take it easy, cowboy. That's a big gun you're brandishing there."

Banner gives me long, thrusting strokes at first, but his pace soon quickens as the urgent need to come mounts inside him.

Using my hand, I play with myself, enjoying my first quickie sex session. Sometimes a girl just needs a fast, frantic bang, you know?

Pounding into me from behind, Banner lets me know that he's close. I'm too focused on my own climax to care about that. I wish there was a mirror we could look into.

He plows into me real hard, and my feet nearly lift up off the floor as he releases into me. Being the best lover in the world ever, he waits for me to have my orgasm before pulling out.

"Whew. Thank you, sweetheart. That one crept up on me. Blame it on how short that T-shirt is. I kept getting flashes of your peachy ass underneath it." I hear the sound of him zipping up as Banner goes to the guest bathroom to wash. "So, what about Europe?" he shouts out to me.

I just lie there bent over the countertop as I wait for the waves of ecstasy to diminish. I can't think straight.

Banner tries to sweeten the deal when he comes out of the guest bathroom. "You can do your podcasts and vlogging from there. Take your reviews to the next level. Europe in the fall is much better than in summer. No bugs, no heat, and fewer tourists."

"Go wait for me in the bedroom," I snap back. "And don't fucking pressure me to do what you want, Banner. You know that shit doesn't fly with me."

Chuckling at my sassiness, he does as I ask. I'm left fuming in the kitchen as I throw things in the dishwasher after scraping stuff into the garbage disposal.

Spooning out ice cream into bowls and adding the chocolate sauce, I wonder where all this is going to end.

That's all the motivation I need! My God! I do not want to be anywhere close to Mary-Kay when her friends tell her about what was said on the Bon Cuisine podcast.

Carrying the two bowls to the bedroom, I place Banner's bowl on the table next to his side of the bed before going to sit down on mine.

This is bad. We already have chosen what side of the bed we're going to sleep on. Am I doing the right thing? This is a fake engagement, so why does Banner want to keep treating it like a real one?

"Okay. Tell me more."

"We'll be on the move, so don't think of this as a vacation. A couple of nights here and there at the most. I'll be gone during the day, so you'll be free to eat, drink, and be merry on your own. If you need restaurant bookings, I can arrange for most of the places. Gourmands who book two years in advance often don't live long enough to eat there, so the bookings become available."

I laugh and lick my spoon with relish. "You're joking, right?" But when I look into those sexy blue eyes of his, I can see he isn't.

"Rich people have the most expensive, danger-ous hobbies. We ski, fly jets and helicopters, use speedboats, and drive fast cars. Look it up—those activities kill wealthy individuals all the time."

Grabbing my phone, I use the search engine. The number of billionaires killed doing those things is insane!

Banner can't stop grinning, because he knows his statement has just been confirmed. "And that's the reason why booking tables two years into the future is optimistic at best and plain stupid at worst!"

That makes me thoughtful. I should seize the day and live my life now—damn the conse-quences!

"Honestly? Europe sounds perfect, Banner. The Bon Cuisine podcast comes out next week. Can we leave before that? And can I hang out here until then? To avoid talking to the press."

Banner plops a large spoonful of ice cream onto my belly. I scream, but I'm loving it as he begins to lick it off. "Sure thing, sweetheart," he says in between licks. "And now I'm going to eat you up just like one of those Transylvanian vampires."

***

Our first stop is Paris. I've been here before, but never like this. Never on a private jet, leaving from a private hangar outside of the city. And never with a man I've gotten into the habit of referring to as my "fiancé."

It makes me smile when I realize that I am living the life of a billionaire's girlfriend, exactly what Julian Stratford told me I would do if I agreed to go on his sleazy yacht cruise.

Before we left, Banner went to the safe in his apartment and took out a diamond ring set in white gold. Throwing it on the bed, he spoke to me over his shoulder.

"This was Momma's. You should have it—wear it for now, I mean. If it doesn't fit, we can have the size adjusted."

I didn't know what he was telling me by giving me the ring to wear. Banner wasn't facing me, so I couldn't read his expression.

Was he sad about his late momma? Could he care less?

"Thank you. I forgot that all this engagement crap involves wearing a ring."

"It's not 'crap,'" Banner replied. "It's tradition."

I didn't have a snappy comeback after he said that. I'm not a bitch, not unless I need to be, so I wore the ring—and I'm still wearing it.

I'm all alone in our hotel room now. I can't help looking at the ring on my finger as I sit on the penthouse suite balcony of the George V Hotel.

The Eiffel Tower is so close, it feels as if I can reach out my hand and touch it from where I am sitting.

The ring has been professionally cleaned. The stone is about one carat, a round blue-white diamond with a prong claw setting, the prongs gripping the stone securely like four little hands.

I don't know. I feel different. Could it be all the sex we're having?

It's almost like we're on our honeymoon. Lots of sex. Dining out at elegant restaurants every night. Squeezing in a visit to the Louvre museum one afternoon and then a slow walk through the Tuileries Gardens after some window shopping.

When Banner isn't buying me something luxurious from the divine Parisian stores, I am buying it for myself.

Perfume from Guerlain. Bags from Hermès. Shoes from my lovely Louboutin. And clothing from Chanel.

I tease Banner about not wearing any turquoise to celebrate his Southern roots. He teases me about not liking bananas.

"Shut up!" I fall about laughing when he asks for a banana to be added to our breakfast on the balcony. "I can't even with the bananas! The smell is so... pungent. Ugh!"

"What about the potassium?" he asks.

"Screw the potassium!" I tell Banner to go clean his teeth before allowing him to kiss me again!

I was never a fan of strong tastes—my palate is too delicate—but lately, my dislike has turned into straight-up hatred.

We watch the leaves fall and laugh about the cold nip in the air when we go out to the balcony in the morning.

This is what wonderful memories are made of.

And we're having lots and lots and lots of sex.

But here's the problem. I'm comfortable, but I'm not in my comfort zone.

I keep waiting for the other shoe to drop. It's been too easy, and now I'm suspicious.

Well, I'm soon going to find out, aren't I? The podcast comes out today.

Taking a deep breath, I call Rupert.

"Hello, darling. How's it going with that gorgeous man of yours?" Typical Rupert. He's always clued into what's happening in my life because of the food images I post on my social media feed.

"Hey, Rupe. It's going. Tell me the good news and then the bad news."

"There is no bad news, sweetie. Everyone is over the moon happy—everyone except that acid snake, Cliff Braxton, that is."

"What are the headlines?"

I hear Rupert pulling his laptop closer. "Mm, mm, mm. Let me see..., okay. Here's one on Page Six. 'Fabulous foodie, Holly Forrest, has nabbed billionaire bachelor of the century, Fletcher Banner, in her finger-licking good ten tacles.'"

That makes me huff. "Ugh! Why do they have to make such a big deal out of it?"

"Because it is a big deal, darling!" Rupert insists. "Here's another one. 'Hotel tycoon avoids the bimbo trap by getting engaged to top restaurant critic. The couple have left the States to get married at his French chateau. To continue story, please click'—yadda, yadda, yadda."

"Banner has a French chateau?"

Rupert chuckles. "Hell, girlfriend! You're meant to know that, not me!"

I'm still in a bad mood over all this. I don't want to overthink it either. A fake engagement to get me out of a bribery scandal suddenly doesn't seem like such a good idea.

The biggest headline I ever got before all this was after I uploaded a new top-fifty-restaurant list. It didn't include the most famous "from the farm, to the table" New York dining establishment, which totally shocked all the foodies and chefs!

And now my name is plastered everywhere.

What angers me the most is that all my complaints and concerns will just float out the window when Banner comes in! I will run into his arms with a smile on my face and in my heart.

He will ask me what I wrote about today and I will find out what he thought about the building site. And then we will eat, drink, and fuck in utter bliss....

"Thanks for the update, Rupe. Talk soon, 'kay?"

"Wait! Before you disconnect! I have to tell you something."

"What?" I am so not in the mood for Rupert's scandalizing right now.

"One of my pals told me that your fella's sister—she has some totally Southern name like Mary-Anne or something—is planning on making a press statement. Do you have any idea what that is about?"

This news gives me a real scare. "Dammit, Rupert! You should have led with that. MK is so unpredictable."

I wonder what the hell my best friend and fake fiancé's sister has to say about me?

# Chapter 21 - Fletcher

Ivy is pacing the room like a wild cat when I get back to the hotel.

"What's up?" I'm not in the mood for an argument. I've been doing that all day at work. These fucking union workers want to be treated like hothouse flowers!

"A 'hello, Ivy—how was your day' would be nice!" Ivy snarls at me.

Sighing, I go to the bar fridge and take out a beer. "Blah, blah, blah. Let's just pretend I said all that shit and then you can skip straight to the part where you tell me what's wrong."

Flouncing past me, Ivy goes into the guest bedroom and slams the door.

I leave her there. I am a firm believer in letting someone stew in their own bad mood instead of asking a whole heap of useless questions. Ivy will tell me what's bugging her when she's good and ready.

I knew that I would never end up with a woman who greets me at the door with a martini and asks me how my day was. Blame that on the Corps.

Existing for eight years without someone who gives a fuck suited me just fine. The most I ever had to do when I felt like sharing something was file a report listing casualties and kills.

I've never been a touchy-feely sort of guy.

Then I think about Ivy sitting alone in that room. Maybe she's crying? Shit.

"Sweetheart?" I can't believe I'm doing this—knocking on the door. "Are you okay in there?" Feeling like a real asshole, I swallow my pride. "I'm sorry I snapped. Crap day at work, and all that."

The door opens. Whenever I see Ivy, it seems like all my Christmases come at once.

It was like that from the first time we met. When I saw her on the yacht, my God! Her long black hair was middle parted, shining and straight, bright like her smile. Her dark brown eyes were like liquid pools of molten chocolate.

Pretty, so young and pretty. I wanted to rescue her—fly her far away from all her problems. The primal instinct to protect her was as powerful as my need to fuck her, hunt her down, and dominate her.

Because deep down inside, I wanted this—a perfect partner. Someone who stands up to me—while standing firmly by my side.

I was pussy-struck when I saw Ivy for the first time. And now I'm stuck because I have deep feelings for her.

I know I will never let anyone hurt this woman.

We hug it out. She feels fragile in my arms. Then she pulls away.

"Banner, I've been pushing this to the back of my mind, hoping it will go away. That was wrong. I should have given MK a heads-up."

I curse long and loud. "Son of a bitch! It completely slipped my mind. Is she mad?"

"I don't know," Ivy says, shrugging her shoulders. "Like I said, I pushed it to the back of my mind. She's hooked up with Clifford Braxton's news agency—they say she'll make a public statement really soon."

That makes me laugh. "Don't worry. I'll throw some money at her and she'll go away."

Ivy gets so mad with me, that her eyes go black with rage.

"You see? Right there—that's the problem. You and Mary-Kay have a toxic relationship. When are you going to realize that MK came first!"

Gripping Ivy's arms, I growl. "Does she still come first? I'm not going to get into a territorial dispute over you with my sister, Ivy!"

Shaking herself loose from me and shooting me an acid look, Ivy goes to sit down.

"A man can never understand how important girlfriends are to a woman. I was never that popular at school, Banner. Mary-Kay was my rock."

I have to scoff. "Huh! Your 'rock' got you into a shitload of trouble over the years, Ivy. Please don't try to sugarcoat things."

Going to the fridge, I take out a beer and wave it at her. Ivy looks at the beer bottle like it's kitty litter.

"I-I'm not in the mood for a beer, thanks. Please pass me a ginger ale."

I bring the drink over, pop the tab, and pour it for her. The sugary spicy flavor of ginger tickles my nose as the bubbles fizz.

Ivy takes a small sip and seems to feel better. She allows me to put my arm around her.

"My work takes me all over the country 365 days in the year, Banner." Giggling a bit, Ivy snuggles closer. "That's why I love being based in New York—it's so easy to find a dinner date there. But there's a huge difference between a date and a girlfriend—there are just some things you can't talk about with a man."

I give the "I surrender" sign with my hands. "Fine! I get it. So, call Mary-Kay and find out what's going on."

Ivy gets weepy again. "I can't. She's blocked me."

Swearing under my breath, I stride into our bedroom and get one of the burners from my bag.

"Here, use this."

Ivy shoots me one of her looks. "What are you? James bloody Bond? Why've you got a burner phone?"

Smirking, I give her a wink. "Never you mind, Miss Nosy. Use the damn phone—let's find out what's bugging my sister."

Holding up her finger, Ivy lets me know it's ringing on Mary-Kay's side. She keeps the phone pressed close to her ear so I can't hear my sister's voice.

"MK, it's me—please don't disconnect! I'm begging you!"

I can hear the shrill tone of my sister's voice blaring out of the receiver. It's so loud, that Ivy has to pull the phone away from her ear. I can hear everything.

"You fucking traitor, Ivy! You hook up with Fletch the Wretch? What's wrong with you?"

"I can't tell you the truth, Mary-Kay, because you'll just go blabbing to Clifford Braxton. You know how much he hates me. And I would never choose your brother over you and Danny. I love you both so much."

Mary-Kay huffs. "Huh! You have a sick way of showing it. But you better tell me the truth or else I really will spill the beans at the press interview."

"What beans?" Ivy laughs. "I never did anything bean-worthy."

"Not on you," Mary-Kay splutters with anger, "on that no-good tightwad brother of mine. He's done some shit that would make your hair curl."

I whisper, "She's talking about all the pimps and dealers I took out."

Ivy nods to show me she understands. "Listen, MK. It's all a hoax. I'm not engaged to Fletcher. We just said that to get Clifford Braxton off my back."

"Then why did you give his shitty restaurant five stars and write that article? And the podcast with the happy couple—vomit. Melanie showed me everything. She says you're a liar and a snake. She contacted Clifford and told him about how you stabbed me in the back."

"Let Melanie say that to my face, Mary-Kay! She wouldn't dare! I promise you the engagement is fake. Ask Fletcher, why don't you?"

"That creep? Ugh. No way. I never want to hear from him again—except if it's money."

I get up and leave the room. I've heard enough. Why is my sister not able to let it go? It's like her hatred of me has become part of her personality.

Suddenly, Paris doesn't seem so dreamy anymore. I lie on the bed, staring at the ceiling.

Ten minutes later, Ivy comes back into the bedroom to return the phone.

"Sorry you had to hear that, Banner. Mary-Kay says she'll cancel the press release." She gives me a little kiss on the cheek. "Want to come with me to Spère tonight? French-Asian fusion—yum."

"Don't you mean 'Fletch the Wretch'?"

Am I pissed over and beyond my default factory settings? Hell yeah!

Crawling onto the bed with me, Ivy gives me a hug from behind. "Give her time, Banner. She'll come around. And don't forget that Daniel loves you."

It's been twenty-five years. I guess I'm over letting my sister's grudge upset me.

Turning over to face Ivy, we snuggle together. Pressing her ear against my chest, Ivy says she loves listening to my heartbeat.

"Tell me more about this restaurant we're going to this evening, sweetheart?"

***

I start to notice little things happening at Spère. If it was just one thing I might have let it slide, but it's not.

Everything Ivy puts into her mouth seems to be making her sick. She's wrinkling her nose and swallowing quickly. The food is absolutely delicious and I know we ordered her favorite dishes—so why is she revolted by it?

She quickly covers her glass when the server tries to give her some champagne. Shaking her head, Ivy gives no explanation for preferring water.

"Did you eat seafood for lunch?" I want to know. This is not like Ivy. She lives for good food.

"Why?" she snaps back. "Do I smell like it?"

That makes me chuckle. "No, you little fire-cracker. You seem to be a bit nauseous, that's all."

When she doesn't answer and keeps staring at her plate, I call for the check. For the first time since Vegas, Ivy doesn't put up a fight when I pay.

Usually, she's always saying, "No, let me pay, please. Then it's tax-deductible because it's work." But it seems like Ivy can't wait to get back to the hotel.

Flopping onto the passenger seat when I hold the door open for her, Ivy slumps down. She's pale and shivering. She doesn't say anything, but I know it's seafood poisoning.

By the time we reach the George V, I've made up my mind as I hand the car over to the valet to park. "Are you okay to go up to the room alone? I'm going to reception to get a doctor."

"No!" Ivy revives long enough to object. "Come upstairs with me, please Banner. It... it's not an emergency."

Back in the suite, I try to cheer her up by making a joke. "Is this your way of telling me you don't want to have sex tonight?"

Ivy tries to smile, but her lips twist with discomfort.

"Ha-ha, Mr. Comedian. If you want to know the truth, I've been longing for us to have one of those sleeps when all we do is lie in each other's arms."

"Turns out I can help you out there, missy."

But I can't rest easy when I see Ivy leave to use the guest bathroom instead of the one in our room. She takes her toothbrush with her—a sure sign she's sick.

We fall asleep with our legs and arms intertwined. Ivy presses her head against my chest, listening to my heartbeat. It's sweet and innocent, just like Ivy herself.

*** 

I wake her with a kiss. "Breakfast on the patio?"

"Mff." Ivy groans. "No. Go away."

I don't take the hint. Sliding my hand between her thighs, I start to kiss her neck, moving my mouth down to her shoulder and breast.

"No breakfast? Okay. I'm hungry for something else anyway." Using my tongue, I lick the dark skin around her puckering nipple.

Shifting her peachy ass away from me and lying on her stomach, Ivy makes it clear. "No!"

I've never lived with a woman before, but I've had enough relationships to know when women are not in the mood.

That's what I like about being with Ivy—we snuggle as much as we make love. I guess snuggling will be okay until she's better.

"I'm off to shower and then head out to work. Text me when you feel better. We'll do lunch."

No answer. Shrugging, I use the guest bedroom and bathroom to get ready. I'm wearing a black Italian-made suit.

It's more casual with a single vent and notch lapel, a light silk wool blend, every stitch handmade. White shirt and dark plaid tie—I don't wear silk ties because they are too shiny—and I'm ready.

My day passes in a whirl of meetings, cost estimates, and visits to the construction site. I forget to call Ivy to find out how she is.

That reminds me. Double parking on the side of the road, I dash into the florist and buy Ivy a bunch of red roses.

Red like the bikini she was wearing when I first met her....

I can't wait to tell her about the project—I finally made progress with the workers on the site.

"Hey, sweetheart! You feeling better?"

Throwing the key and room card onto the side table, I walk into our bedroom.

It's empty. Not just empty of Ivy, but empty of all her stuff too.

"Ivy?" I walk around the penthouse, calling her name, but I can tell I'm alone. I picked up a sixth sense about shit like that when I was in the Corps.

Sitting down heavily on the couch, I throw the roses next to me.

And then I see it.

My mother's engagement ring on the coffee table.

What happened between this morning and now that made Ivy hate me?

# Chapter 22 - Ivy

I don't know what to say to Banner, so I don't take his calls.

The flight back to New York was the worst of my life! It's kinda like I was living in a nightmare of uncertainty and endless questions.

The nausea got really bad after Banner left for work in the morning. Somehow, I managed to haul my ass out of bed and find the nearest pharmacy.

It was actually easier than I thought it would be. Every pharmacy in Paris has an enormous illuminated green cross outside, so I didn't even have to use my search engine to find one. I was too embarrassed to ask the hotel staff.

"Er... j'ai besoin de une—" I can hardly say the word to the pharmacist who is waiting patiently for me to blurt out the damn words! "Pregnancy test!"

The French don't say "I need." They say, "I have a need for—"

The pharmacist understands what I am saying. She hands me a pregnancy test box with a joyful smile.

I have a need for an emergency exit! Help! If this test comes back positive, I don't know what I am going to do!

But being pregnant is the only explanation for the crazy shit that is happening to my body right now. Since when did I not like food? The fragrant aroma of truffles, sushi, chocolate, and caviar gives me life!

That's no longer the case. The smell of food makes me sick and the thought of drinking alcohol turns my stomach.

Of course, the test came back positive. I've never been a weepy girl, but tears of excitement

filled my eyes. A warm glow of tender loving-
ness filled my heart.

A baby! My very own creation baked in my very
own lovin' oven!

Wasting no time going goo-goo over this
life-changing moment, I acted instinctively.

I had to get home fast. I knew what the optics of
my pregnancy would look like to my billionaire
boyfriend. Banner will think that I want to turn
our fake engagement into a real one!

I needed some time alone to think about letting
Banner into our baby's life short term and long
term.

Yes, I'm an independent woman with a wild-
ly successful life. Yes, I promised myself that I
would never leave the city.

I love the vibe and the rush. The shops and the
endless cycle of places to eat. And I used to
enjoy the constant crowd of men who formed
my dating pool.

But is that what I wanted for my baby?

Fleeing France and its wonderful food might not make sense to anyone with an appetite, but I can't stand the thought of food without my belly churning.

The moment my flight lands, I have my phone out. I give the driver the address of the medical suite. I made a doctor's appointment yesterday in Paris before I left.

Before I left Banner's engagement ring on the sitting room table. Before I never left a note because I had no words I could use to explain things to him.

The OBGYN doesn't make me wait, bless her. Maybe the diagnosis won't be so bad after all—I managed to eat some crackers and keep them down on the plane.

"Hey, Ivy. What brings you here today? And so early in the morning."

"Thank you for squeezing me in, Dr. Renee. I took a pregnancy test and it turned out positive."

My lovely and kind doctor wastes no time ushering me through to the examination room with comforting murmurs that reflect my excitement. The assistant nurse helps me undress and put on a robe. The process and the room are very calming—professional and reassuring.

When I am settled on the examination bed, in comes Dr. Renee, snapping on gloves and pulling a sonar machine arm over my stomach.

"Okay, let's see what we have here."

After warming the gel with her hands, she rubs it on my belly just above the pubic mound. "You been on vacation?" Pointing to my near-naked bikini wax, Dr. Renee makes polite conversation as she moves the wand over my skin.

"Europe, but I'm in a relationship now, so I get waxed as often as I can."

"Okay, well it looks like your relationship is moving to the next level, Ivy," the doctor says, smiling before taking a few still images of what is showing on the screen. "See here? That's the amniotic sac. And see that little black shape? That's your baby."

Dr. Renee takes a measurement and calculates. "Baby is the perfect size for a five- or six-week-old fetus. You sure caught your pregnancy early."

I can't believe I fell pregnant that first night Banner and I spent together in Vegas!

She tells me to wipe off the gel and join her in the surgery.

"What's the matter, Ivy?" Dr. Renee wants to know. "I can see you're happy, but something is bothering you."

"I don't seem to want to eat much anymore, Doctor. Sometimes, these crazy urges to eat something get inside my head. Slush Puppies, chili cashews, slices of lime—junk! The urge to eat it almost takes over. But when I'm back home with the food, the idea of me eating it makes me sick again."

Dr. Renee shakes her head. "Welcome to the frustrating world of morning sickness, Ivy. I'm going to book you in for some tests in two weeks, 'kay? But it's not urgent, because you got a full body scan and blood test three months ago for your health insurance." The doctor checks my file. "You're going to have a healthy baby, so don't stress about that. Your folic acid is good, so I'm not worried there."

"That must be from all the iron-rich foods I eat at restaurants. Pâté is full of chicken livers."

"Lucky you," the assistant nurse tells me. "We've gone vegan at our house, but there are some things I really crave."

"Try making pâté with black mushrooms," I suggest, "you'd be shocked how yummy it is."

By the time the nurse has left to throw my gown in the basket, all I want to do is get back home and sleep.

Dr. Renee's last words to me as she shakes my hand goodbye are not all sunshine and roses. She gives me a pamphlet.

"Ivy, please start eating responsibly. No more pâté. No sushi. No processed meats. And please tell me you didn't eat any unpasteurized cheese in Paris?"

I take a look at the pamphlet that lists all the foods I am no longer allowed to eat.

Fish (because of possible mercury poisoning), seafood.

Caffeine. But no caffeine-free stuff either because of the chemicals they use to make it!

No homemade mayonnaise. No undercooked meats. No store-bought salads or sandwiches.

The list goes on.

No herbal teas or unknown herbs.

No alcohol or low-alcohol beer.

No high-sugar drinks or sodas (chemicals and additives).

Use only face creams and body creams recommended for use during pregnancy.

Stop using hair dye.

No over-the-counter medications except mild antacids.

The last prohibition catches my eye and makes me smile.

No kinky sex, like heavy S&M, bondage, and whipping.

"I guess kinky couples like to fall pregnant too," I joke to Dr. Renee.

"Actually, we don't know the effects of choking and blood restriction during kinbaku, so we suggest couples stop doing it for the duration of the pregnancy."

"Kinbaku?"

"The Japanese art of rope bondage. Apparently, a master knotter can tie the silk ropes around a woman in such a way that the clitoris is continuously stimulated. You can imagine what a never-ending orgasm might do to a woman's lower stomach muscles! The contractions would be bad for the baby."

I toss the idea around in my head for a moment.

When I'm with Banner, my orgasms last long enough, thank you very much. And I love snuggling and cuddling afterward too much to want my orgasms to last longer.

And then I worry about how I left things in Paris.

Ugh. This pregnancy is making me act crazy!

Dr. Renee is still lecturing me.

"The foods might be fine for someone to eat in small amounts, but no long-term studies have been done to gauge the effects some ingredients and additives might have on the baby. But don't be fooled—a few of those foods on the list can be highly problematic for a pregnant mother."

Ouch! Half the foods on that list are what they serve in restaurants!

After giving me the name of a supplement I should start taking, Dr. Renee has one more thing to tell me. "Ivy, please eat a healthy diet. It's the number one best thing you can do for your baby. Organic, whole foods if you can. If you have to review a place, give them your dietary restrictions up front."

I promise the doctor that I will do as she says. This is my first baby and I am determined to do my best.

I love you, my little beanie. We're going to get healthy together.

\*\*\*

Oh, my God! I feel so sick!

I wake up, and this time I know my morning sickness is worse. I couldn't face eating much last night. A couple of nibbles of dry toast, that was it.

Late at night, I got a weird craving for peach cobbler and spent hours trying to track one down online. I couldn't sleep unless I had it!

Finally, Bert did the unthinkable. He left his post in the lobby and ran to a diner where he knew it was on the menu.

I thanked Bert and gave him a big tip, but I only managed to eat a few spoonfuls of the peach cobbler before the sickening nausea rose up in my stomach again.

Drinking a glass of water to fill me, I stare at my face in the mirror.

I don't think I can do this on my own.

Turning on my phone, I look at the screen blankly before pressing Banner's number.

He picks up after two rings. "What the fuck did I do wrong this time, Ivy! You know how paranoid I get when you go missing after what happened to us on the yacht! What if we had been in Albania? I might have thought you'd been taken by the fucking mafia!"

I cut him off. "I'm sorry, Banner! Please shut up. I'm sick. I wanted some 'me alone' time. That's all."

Several seconds pass as he makes up his mind about the information I just gave him. When he speaks, he sounds calmer.

"Okay, I can understand that. Nothing worse than having an upset stomach when you're trying to be romantic with someone."

That makes me laugh. "Banner, you have no idea. But it's not that kind of sickness. And besides, that penthouse suite was so massive, I could have murdered someone in the other rooms and you would've probably never known about it—so I wasn't worried about you hearing me be sick."

"Can I send you anything? My doctor makes house calls."

No way! The last thing I need is for Banner's doctor to be sticking their nose up in my private business.

"I'm...." I can't tell him I'm fine. I feel so nauseous all the time. I'm so hungry, but I can't think of anything I want to eat. "If I need something, I'll reach out to Mary-Kay. It's time I hooked up with my best friend again."

"Have I been hogging you?"

God, but I love it when his voice gets all gruff and deep like that.

"No, but you have been hugging me! Mary-Kay came first. We need to remember that."

Banner doesn't reply immediately, but he does eventually.

"Sweetheart, maybe it's time for you to move on from your high school buddies. No, don't say anything—please hear me out. What has Mary-Kay done for you lately? You babysit Daniel when she needs you to. But Mary-Kay never invites you to those lady lunches she goes to with all her mommy buddies. You don't shop together or go out for coffee. You're not a member of her book club or the school carpool. It seems pretty one-sided to me."

He doesn't know that I am going to be relying on Mary-Kay a lot soon! He doesn't know that I will be one of those mommies grabbing lunch together in a year's time!

"I love Daniel, you forget."

"That makes two of us," Banner says, "but I'm kinda envious of Danny now."

"Why? Because he's in New York and you're not?"

"No, because you love him."

"Aw, Banner. We're one big happy family. You, me, Mary-Kay, and Danny. Speak soon. Bye."

"Get better soon, Ivy Woods."

And then he's gone.

Miserable beyond any description, I haul my shivering body over to the bathroom and start to vomit.

All I am bringing up is the acid from my stomach. There is nothing more in my belly except
saliva and bile.

This is bad.

Could there be something seriously wrong with
me?

# Chapter 23 - Fletcher

My work takes me from Paris to Rome to Athens. I've shifted my focus from construction to renovations—buying up old buildings and turning them into hotels.

It was the only thing I could do to keep my sanity. European bureaucracy is a nightmare on a local, national, and international level. As soon as I cut through one layer of red tape, another one would raise its head.

I call Anton, trying to ignore the empty spot beside me in the bed. The place where Ivy is meant to be, reading a book off her device or painting her cute toenails. All those girly things I love watching her do.

"Hey, make a note of this. I want you to set up a meeting with Rick Thomson. Find out where he is and connect us. Call me when it's done."

Anton is only allowed to send me texts in an emergency.

"Wait, Boss! Don't disconnect. Mary-Kay contacted me. Said your phone was switched off. I tried to tell her about time zones, but she didn't care."

Typical Mary-Kay. "Yep. What did she want?"

"She said a whole lot of stuff about you messing with her friend. She went on to say that they were going to pay her for an interview, but she canceled it for your sake...."

Honestly, at this point, I'm not even listening anymore. Mary-Kay and I have always clashed. Besides the fact that we come from two completely different mindsets and values, our generations are incompatible too.

She doesn't make me feel old, even though there's a ten-year age gap between us. My sister can make me even more grouchy than I usually am.

I wait for Anton to finish. "So, how much does she want?"

"She wants a new house in Manhattan. Says she doesn't vibe with Brooklyn anymore. And she also wants a new car."

And the fillings out of my back teeth too?

I have to play nice with Mary-Kay because she did Ivy a solid. At this stage of my Ivy obsession, I would buy my sister a rocket ship if it meant Ivy was safe and happy.

"Fine. Start looking at places in Gramercy Park and the Lower East Side. Easy access to the park at least, or preferably a private garden. And only vehicles with the highest safety rating. Send me a link to all the private schools within walking distance of the property too."

From the sounds Anton is making, he is typing this down. "Got that. And there is one other thing Mary-Kay wants to know, Boss."

I wait for the hammer to fall.

"She wants to know who inherits all your money if you die."

"What is this!?" I can't help raising my voice. "A fucking Agatha Christie movie!"

Anton doesn't say anything back to me. He just waits for me to calm down and give him my final answer.

That's the problem with being a private enterprise. Banks, lenders, and business partners always want to know what happens to their investment if I die.

This is a typical Mary-Kay move. She's terrified I might meet some sexy man-trap and leave all my money to the man-trap instead.

"Tell her that my legal team is authorized to liquidate all my assets if such an occasion arises. Explain to her that means selling everything, settling any outstanding loans, and then splitting the money between the beneficiaries in my will."

"Yes, I already told her that. But she wants to know the names of the beneficiaries."

So much for Mary-Kay's "friendship" with Ivy. My sister is already worried that Ivy might take preference over her in my will.

Jumping the gun much? Ivy is so fiery and challenging, I don't think she would ever want to settle down—never mind doing it with a grump like me.

A woman who has no desire to gain access to my money. Someone who actually wants to keep our relationship on the down-low instead of showing me off around town like some kind of a show pony.

A woman who has made it clear that she loves having sex with me, but doesn't want the boring domestic side of being in a partnership to take over.

And yet I cherish that meal she cooked for me. It was like Ivy gave me a taste of what my life could be like with her—and then she goes and whisks the domestic bliss plate off the table!

"Tell Mary-Kay to fuck off," I snap back and disconnect the call.

I am lost, stuck looking at the empty space next to me on the bed. Damn, but it kinda hurts knowing that an ocean stands between Ivy and me.

Reaching for my phone, I check the time and then call her.

Ivy picks up. I can hear from the huskiness in her voice that she was asleep.

"Hey, Banner. What's up?"

"You go out last night? You sound like you tied one-off."

She chuckles. "Oh yeah. Big time. Rolling with the homies, getting down and boogying, shaking my ass. All the New York clichés."

"Coolio was West Coast, not East Coast." I'm really enjoying our chats as usual. It helps me forget the king-size bed with only one person lying in it.

"Hey, I love all dance music. It reminds me of when Mary-Kay and I used to sneak out of the hostel and go clubbing."

"Speaking of MK, how did it go with her? You girls made up?"

"Yes. I told her the engagement was a lie to get Clifford off my back, and she accepted my apology."

I can feel myself getting madder. "What do you have to be sorry about, Ivy? Did Mary-Kay say something about you being a gold digger?"

Silence, but I can hear Ivy taking deep breaths. Finally, she speaks. "When have I ever shown an interest in taking money from you, Banner? Answer me!"

I backtrack. "No, I never said that, but I wouldn't put it past Mary-Kay to suggest something along those lines. Shit! Please don't overreact. It's fucking irritating when you go off the deep end. You give me no chance to explain."

"I gotta go." Ivy retreats away from me again. "I'm not feeling well."

"Still?" How many days has it been now? "I want to send my doctor to—"

"No! Shove your doctor up your ass! I don't want your money and I don't want your fancy medical personnel up in my business, Banner! Goodbye!"

"Wait!" Jesus, this broken way Ivy and I have of communicating with each other has got to stop.

"Please don't trust Mary-Kay, sweetheart. She looks after herself first. Remember that."

"And why shouldn't she do that? She has a son. You remember that. Buh-bye!"

The line goes dead, leaving me feeling half-dead inside.

\*\*\*

Anton calls to let me know the meeting is set up with Richard Thomson in London. I take the jet to Luton Airport where a driver is waiting to take me into the Chelsea and Kensington Borough.

We have a table booked for two at Scalini. The restaurant serves the best Italian food in England, hands down.

Ivy would love eating here. The food is outstanding—deep-fried courgette flowers stuffed with cream cheese, spaghetti, and black truffle butter, veal cutlets—and the decor looks like the manager's grandmother did it.

I like the place immediately because the tables are spaced well apart. The bustle and chatter of happy diners drown out the discussion I am having with Rick.

"I refuse to fucking deal with that European red tape, Rick," I say, getting straight down to business. "I've formed a company that specializes in renovations. Screw this building from scratch bullshit."

I can see that Rick is loving the food, but his hands are fiddling around his pockets as the amazing waitstaff brings us espressos. He's a smoker.

"I've heard the same thing from other hotel chains, Jay," Rick agrees. "Too many bribes needed upfront, and that's not even a guarantee things will go smoothly."

"Yep. So, I'm buying up a whole lot of pensions and converting them into accommodation. That's where you come in."

"What's a pension? You getting into the money management markets?"

"Not retirement pensions. Pensions are the European equivalent of a boarding house or guesthouse. Most of them are really run-down lodges whose owners were not able to keep up with maintenance. That's where you come in."

Rick leans closer. I am poised to make a deal with him. I know he will agree just so he can go outside and have a cigarette.

"You have all those travel websites. They're excellent. I've had a look at your figures. Thomson's is the number one choice when it comes to Americans booking accommodations overseas."

"And you want us to partner up?"

I nod. "Yes. I renovate the pensions and you book travelers into them. Package deals. Tours. The whole nine yards. I'm prepared to offer you five points more on the booking fees than you get from all the other accommodation facilities, but only if you promote the Insignia rooms above everyone else's."

For some weird reason, Rick looks relieved. He can't want a cigarette that bad, can he?

"Sure thing, Jay. You got a deal! This is really good news for me, buddy. I'm in a real jam at the moment and need all the collateral I can lay my hands on."

Let the record reflect that my face showed I was interested in hearing more!

Rick continues. "Someone has got the screws on me, Jay. And they're tightening them. Have you heard about yacht girls?"

I nod slowly, keeping my face neutral.

"Shit! Jay, I wish I had never heard of fucking yacht girls. That's what got me into all this trouble."

Somehow, I manage to keep my shit together as Richard Thomson tells me more.

# Chapter 24 - Ivy

Bert bellows into the intercom.

"That lady from the magazine—Meg Stanley—is here again, Miss Holly! Please, please let her in."

Damn. It's Meg. She's a sweetheart, but I knew my story about having the flu would only work for ten days max.

She wants to know when I am coming in to record the next podcast.

"Let her come up, Bert—and thanks."

I'm almost too weak to get up from my bed and answer the door. I have to go and sit on the couch because my legs aren't strong enough to let me stand.

Meg steps inside the apartment and doesn't even notice me slumped on the couch.

"Yoo-hoo! Holly. Why are you being such a stranger?"

"I'm over here, Meg." My voice is weak and raspy. Meg jumps when she hears me behind her. Her eyes dart around the room until finally, she sees me.

"Jesus jumping Christ!"

Meg's mouth drops open and her eyes get wide. "I didn't... I mean... I'm so sorry, Holly." Meg bursts into tears and lets her Louis Vuitton bag fall to the floor. "Is it... oh God, please don't let it be cancer...."

Patting the seat next to me, I whisper, "Don't cry, Meg. It only feels like I'm dying. I'm not actually dying."

Coming to sit down beside me, Meg hugs me hard. "Oh thank God. My dad passed from cancer and... and you look just like he did. So, I thought...."

Taking hold of her hand, I give it a small squeeze. "Sorry about the podcasts. I've been really sick."

Jumping up, Meg glares down at me. "Been sick? Are you kidding me? You're at death's door, for fuck's sake! What have you got?"

Now, it's my turn to cry.

I can't. I just can't. This is all too much for me.

Picking up her bag off the floor, Meg takes out her phone. "I'm calling an ambulance, Holly. It's been two weeks. Whatever you have is clearly killing you."

I need someone to talk to. I need a friend!

"I'm pregnant!"

Meg is the first person I've told. I can't tell Banner or Mary-Kay, because they will think I want money. I haven't told poor Rupert, because I've been hoping the morning sickness would go away.

Dropping her phone on the couch, Meg goes from zero to one hundred in a split second.

"Oh my God, girl! Congratulations!"

She hugs me, but quickly pulls back. Hauling me off the couch, she drags me to the bathroom. "Get on those scales, Missy. I want to check your weight. When was your last doctor's appointment?"

Drying my tears, I go to stand on the scales all wobbly and weak.

Meg bends down to read the numbers. She stands up again quickly and escorts me to the bed. "I am calling the ambulance, Holly. You have to be admitted."

"Why?" I rasp, closing my eyes because it's too much effort to keep them open. "Don't need an ambulance."

"You're about five-six? Five six and a half? You weigh less than a hundred pounds, Holly. That means you must have lost about fifteen, twenty pounds over the last couple of weeks."

"But Dr. Renee says I mustn't take antinausea meds, Meg. She says it can harm the baby's development."

"Is that what's doing this?" Meg sounds astonished. "Morning sickness? That's crazy."

I'm too exhausted to say anything back. My mind is in a whirl as I hear Meg giving her credit card details to the ambulance service.

When I try to stop her, she shushes me. "Bon Cuisine has medical coverage, Holly. We can sort it out later."

As we wait for the ambulance to come, Meg goes through my fridge and cupboards, tut-tutting as she sees expired food and bare shelves. The garbage can has not been emptied and is full of smelly, uneaten food I chucked out.

Bert and Meg let the EMTs in. I am hardly aware of everything that's happening.

"She's pregnant, but it looks like she hasn't been able to keep anything down for at least two weeks," Meg explains to the medics.

A man prises my eyelids open and shines a light at me. "Ma'am? Can you hear me? What have you eaten?"

Licking my dry lips, I croak. "Water. Some lime slices...."

"Shit," I hear Meg say as she paces around the room.

"Ma'am? Stay with us, please. Do you have any medical conditions we should know about? Allergies? Asthma? Ongoing treatments?"

I manage to shake my head. "No medicine that will harm our baby. P-please."

"You do not want to know who the baby daddy is," Meg tries to crack a joke. "Just imagine one of the most powerful men in Manhattan—that's him."

The medics tell me that they are going to lift me onto a stretcher after they set up my drip.

A wave of nausea hits me as they lift me up. I retch and spit. The room spins around as I fall back to sleep, lulled by the rolling stretcher as it gets wheeled out of the building.

***

Dr. Renee is waiting for me in the ward. She puts a rush order on my blood tests and stabilizes me by injecting about three syringes into my drip.

I feel peaceful immediately, drifting in and out of consciousness. For the first time in what seems like ages, I am no longer nauseous or hungry.

Meg stays by my side, answering any of the questions that she can.

"No, she hasn't eaten anything fancy or exotic for work, Doctor. Holly has been off work for half the month. The doorman at her building says that Holly has been having serious cravings, but nothing seems to have stayed down except water."

Dr. Renee knows to protect my secret identity. Because she reads my blog, my doctor knows I work under the name of Holly Forrest.

"That's because Holly has a severe type of nausea and vomiting during pregnancy called hyperemesis gravidarum. It's a dangerous, interactable type of nausea. There have been cases of it killing the mother if it goes untreated because toxins in the body can build up quickly when the body malfunctions like this."

"Holy shit." Meg is shocked. "Like food poisoning?"

Dr. Renee explains, "A small fraction of pregnant women get the condition. No one knows why it occurs. The problem is this. Medicines that were developed to treat nausea during pregnancy have an appalling track record! There is a real risk of it harming the baby's development. All we can do for Holly is monitor the ketone levels in her kidneys and blood and feed her intravenously. If she doesn't respond to the medications, we'll have to move to enteral feeding."

"Er... enteral feeding?"

"A feeding tube inserted into her intestine to deliver nutritional content to bypass her stomach."

I feel Meg grip my hand. "Holly, when is Fletcher coming? He should be here with you."

I shake my head. "He's in Europe. I can't drag him back here for this. It's... it's trivial."

Dr. Renee quickly butts in. "Pregnancy is a delicate time for a mother. She might feel depressed or alienated from her partner. She might feel undesirable. Miss Stanley, can I speak to you outside, please?"

The door of my private ward slides shut, blocking out their conversation.

A nurse comes in to take my blood pressure. I can hear what Meg and my doctor are talking about in the corridor.

"The father must be informed. It's her fiancé, isn't it? I listened to the podcast. Fletcher Banner."

"Yes. But he's in Europe. I don't want to overstep my boundaries. Mr. Banner advertises a lot in our sister magazine, Bon Voyage."

"Who's her next of kin?"

"I think Holly's parents are up in Maine. Didn't she write about her family connection to Maine lobster once?"

"Hang on," Dr. Renee says. "I'll call my office. Every patient has to give a next of kin name and contact number on their form."

A long pause. The nurse is busy reading my file and making notes in it.

"Got it. I'll get my receptionist to call them. They should know." Dr. Renee sounds pleased.

"Please, can your staff give the hospital her medical insurance details too, Doctor? However, I must tell you that Bon Cuisine will be more than happy to pay. We want Holly back at work as soon as possible. She's like a magnet when it comes to readers, and the podcast listeners love her. She has that magic touch when it comes to making food sound wonderful, and—"

"Miss Stanley," Dr. Renee says, "we're not talking about a weekend in the hospital here. Holly is seriously ill. The pregnancy is taking everything it can from her, leaving her in an extremely weakened and vulnerable position. There is no way she can go back to work."

The nurse asks me if I need to use the bedpan and then starts showing me how to use the call button.

Meg whispers loudly, "You mean Holly won't be able to dine out for the next eight months!"

"Show me a restaurant that wants to be critiqued by an inspector who keeps vomiting up their food, Miss Stanley, and then sure, Holly can go back to work!"

The nurse injects something else into my drip.

Before the blackness takes me, I want to scream out loud.

Leave me and my baby alone! Who are you contacting as my next of kin? I must know!

# Chapter 25 – Fletcher

"Hoy, wake up, you slacker!"

Opening my eyes is not as easy as I thought it would be. They feel leaden.

"Ugh, my eyes are all crusty, Mary-Kay. Please pass me a wet towel."

I hear my friend going to the bathroom and the sound of a faucet being turned on. An ice-cold damp towel gets shoved into my hand.

"Th-thanks." It's refreshing. I'm shocked to feel what an effort it is to do something as simple as wipe down my face. My arms are like limp noodles!

To be honest, I use the time I have with my face covered to muster the strength to deal with Mary-Kay.

Putting the towel on the side table, I force myself to smile. "Hey, girl. How did you know I'm in the hospital?"

Hopping up onto the end of my bed, Mary-Kay inspects me closely. Her eyes move from my face down to my hands.

"You never told me about the fake engagement, Ivy. And now you don't tell me about your pregnancy. What's up? Don't you want to be friends anymore?"

I can feel the blood draining out of my face. This confrontation is not what I need right now.

One of the nursing staff slides the door open and sticks their head in.

"We okay in here, Miss Forrest? Your monitor showed a spike."

Lifting my hand, I make a "stop" and then a "thumbs-up" gesture to let the nurse know I'm fine.

"Okay, Miss Forrest, but please take it easy. We allowed your visitor to come in because they are listed as your emergency contact."

As soon as the nurse leaves, Mary-Kay giggles. "Oh my God, Ivy. Who do they think you are? Someone in witness protection? Why don't they just post a fucking police person outside your door?"

"Thank you for coming, MK. I've been too sick to overthink things, you know. And these meds make me so tired."

Reaching over to the trolley tray, I take a sip of the iced water. Joy floods through me as I relish the liquid instead of it making me nauseous.

Maybe I can still make this work? Perhaps I can keep on reviewing restaurants?

Mary-Kay continues speaking.

"How do you think I feel, Ivy? First, I find out that you have this suspicious underhanded shit going on with my pig of a brother. And now the hospital is calling me to find out how to contact your parents. Why? Because you're pregnant! What the fuck?!"

I take another sip of water. "Did you give them my folks' contact details, MK?"

"That's not the fucking point!" Mary-Kay punches the mattress next to my feet. "The point is that you're trying to steal Daniel's inheritance!"

That gets my attention! "How the fuck did you reach that conclusion, Mary-Kay? Please tell me how you got from me being pregnant to me trying to steal Daniel's inheritance. I don't want a brownstone in Brooklyn, for Christ's sake. I want to get better and travel the world eating in the best restaurants!"

Mary-Kay scoffs. "Huh! Don't give me that 'Little Miss Innocent' shit. You know full well what I mean. Daniel must inherit all of Fletch's money. But now suddenly you're miraculously pregnant with his baby—despite you saying the engagement was fake and telling me you had no feelings for my fucking brother!"

My mind is blank. This is so not like me. I'm meant to have a quick answer for everything.

And what is going on with Mary-Kay? She's not that happy-go-lucky young mom who loved being my best friend not so long ago.

"Cat got your tongue?" Mary-Kay sounds pissed. "Melanie told me that the first night she saw you and Fletch together she could see you had your claws dug into him. Melanie says you got one sniff of my brother's money and decided to make a play for him. I can't believe I fell for your shit about needing a dinner date for Vegas. You are such a bitch, Ivy."

Melanie. Sounds like Mary-Kay has got herself a new best friend. Banner warned me about this, but I didn't listen.

There is only one thing I can think of doing to fix this.

"Please settle down, MK, or else the nurse will come back in here." This is it. It's the only thing I can think of doing to make things right. "What I have to tell you must stay between us, okay? No telling Melanie and no telling your brother. Promise?"

This catches Mary-Kay's attention. Folding her arms, she agrees. "Fine, but don't fucking spin lies to me. I'm Fletcher's only living relative, Ivy. When he dies, his money has got to come to me!"

"I met Fletcher before. On the yacht. When I was eighteen. I didn't tell you because being on that yacht is not something I'm proud of."

"Fletcher was on the yacht! B-but you never made any money from that trip," Mary-Kay reminds me. "I remember that much! I wanted to borrow some of that cash and you went and screwed it up. Coming back with nada."

"That's because I didn't do anything on the yacht worth being paid for, MK! I am not, nor was I ever, a girl who wants to factor the exchange of money into her sex life!

"What are you trying to say? Spit it out."

It takes me so much to say this, but it's the only way.

"I am not pregnant with Fletcher Banner's baby."

\*\*\*

Fletcher

Sami is waiting for me at the hangar.

"Good trip, Boss?"

"Started out well, then not so much." I carry my own bag to the car and throw it in the truck.

"I'm sorry to hear that, Boss. Where to?"

I sigh, but this has to be done. I can't run the risk of Mary-Kay getting upset with me again in the future and doing something irrational.

"Park Slope, Brooklyn. MK."

"Gotcha." Sami points the car towards the 95. After checking my messages one last time in the hope that there is something from Ivy, I leave my phone alone. Loading the financial reports onto a retractable screen, I check the markets during the drive.

We pull up outside the brownstone less than an hour later.

"This shouldn't take long, Sami, but you can drive around the block if needs be."

Touching his cap, my driver settles down to wait.

That woman my sister is hanging out with now answers the door.

"Hey there, Fletcher. How was Europe?"

Fuck, I am so not in the mood for this shit.

"Fine. Where's my sister?"

"MK is upstairs. We're going to La Trattoria for lunch. I'm going to blog about it afterward and write it up on Yelp. I'm passionate about good food, you know. Do you want to join us?"

"Er... that would be a hard pass from me. What's your name again?"

"Melanie." She looks shocked. "Don't you remember the last time we met? I'm your sister's bestie."

"I wouldn't get too comfortable calling myself that if I were you, Melanie. MK calls a lot of people her best friend."

Mary-Kay comes in. "What's that you're saying?"

I shoot Melanie a killer look when she opens her mouth. She shuts it quickly and then changes what she was going to say.

"We're just passing the time, girlfriend," Melanie says with a nervous giggle. "But I think Fletcher is feeling a bit grumpy today."

"Nope," Mary-Kay says, flouncing past me and slumping onto one of the couches. "That's him being normal. My brother was born to be the biggest grump in the world. What do you want, Fletch?"

I want to tell her I wasn't born with the weight of the world on my shoulders. I want to tell her that being left as guardian to a miserable teenage girl who continuously acted out was the reason for my bad temper.

But I don't. I'm not big on oversharing.

"I want to know why you're not happy with a nine-million-dollar house in Park Slope anymore, Mary-Kay?"

My sister seems to take my question like it's some kind of an insult.

"Don't use that snippy tone with me, bro! I want a luxury property in Manhattan! You're a fucking billionaire. Suck it up!"

Mary-Kay has never shown a blind bit of notice in my net worth before. I see Melanie sidling to the other couch, trying to look nonchalant.

"Did you start this?" I say to Melanie with a snarl, pointing at my sulking sister.

"Don't growl at my best friend, Fletcher," Mary-Kay snaps back, replying on behalf of her friend. "And if you want to know, yes. Melanie was kind enough to show me how much money you're making. Now I want my share."

I just want this over with. "Fine. Anton will send you links and set up viewings for you. But Daniel's needs must come first, so it must be close to schools, gardens, and playgrounds, you know."

"And I want the car and property to be put in my name."

Somehow managing to keep calm, I try to explain. "No, that's not how it works. For tax reasons alone, I can't do that, MK. The new house will stay as part of Insignia's property portfolio."

Sitting up straight, Mary-Kay shouts at the top of her voice. "So that you can leave all your money to some bimbo and cut me out of it? I don't think so!"

"You have never filed a tax form in your life, MK! What do you think the IRS is going to do to you when you get gifted a fifty-million-dollar house in Manhattan?"

Jumping to her feet, my sister gets in my face. "So! You don't deny it! You are going to marry some bimbo! If you do, don't you think every-one will want to know about all those yacht trips you went on ten years ago?"

My blood runs cold.

"What the fuck are you saying?" I can hardly get the words out.

"I'm saying," Mary-Kay says, looking triumphant, "things are going to be a little different around here, bro. I knew something was hinky about your dynamic with Ivy. She told me how the two of you met. Ha! She is under the impression that we are still best friends—as if I would ever be besties with that ho."

"If you think I am the sort of man you can black-mail, Mary-Kay, then you don't know me."

I head for the door.

Melanie runs after me. "Wait! Don't leave, Fletcher. This isn't blackmail. MK just wants what is owed to her."

The selfishness astonishes me. "I owe my sister nothing. I'm tired of her using Daniel as a pawn to get money out of me. And now she's doing the same thing with Ivy."

Melanie sneers. "I really like you, Fletcher, but you're blind. Ivy Woods is a ho."

Backing away from her, I open the door, but Melanie follows me, hissing her warped opinions.

"Ivy Woods is pregnant, Fletcher, and you are not the baby's father. I want to help you rip that Band-Aid off, right now!"

I am blinded by rage as I storm back to the car. Sami doesn't say anything to me—he can read all the warning signs by now.

Who am I dating? Ivy Woods or Holly Forrest? And which one of them is after my money?

# Chapter 26 - Ivy

"You have to get out of that hospital, girl," Rupert warns me. "Audiences are fickle. I need another review to publish."

I've been on a drip for two days. It is supplying me with the perfect balance of nutrients for the baby, but my stomach and appetite are still shot.

I've stopped checking my reflection in the bathroom mirror because it's too depressing. Even with my dark hair and olive skin tone, I look haggard and pale.

I love Rupert, but I'm scared to burden him with the truth. I have enough self-respect not to be seen out in public like this.

If I were honest with myself, I think I might have more of an appetite if things had gone better with Mary-Kay. I don't know if I can trust her to keep my secrets anymore. My work friends and my old school friends seem to be pulling me in opposite directions.

"Please, Ivy, give me something."

"You're starting to sound like a broken record, Rupe," I say in a teasing way. "Don't you think I'm getting this flack from Meg Stanley as well?"

Actually, Meg is definitely not bugging me to host another podcast with her. She is very supportive, visiting every day and bringing flowers from the Bon Cuisine team. There was a huge bunch of yellow roses and daisies from Noah with a note telling me to get better soon.

The announcement of my fake engagement to Banner obviously didn't put off our sound engineer; Noah signed the card with three large exes and ohs.

Rupert heaves a sigh. "I've put out a press release in tandem with Bon Cuisine actually. You are indisposed and will be back at work soon.

End of story. But c'mon! You have to give me something to work with here!"

"I hope 'indisposed' doesn't read as 'food poisoning,'" I can't help saying.

It's so frustrating being stuck in bed. Meg has my apartment keys and brought me my laptop. Tapping the metal frame around the keyboard, I think hard.

"No details were given out, Ivy. People hear 'sick' nowadays, they don't jump to conclusions."

"How about we do a few articles to promote our advertisers? 'Ten Essential Kitchen Tools a Chef Won't Leave Home Without'? Or 'Cheap Kitchen Appliances versus Expensive Ones'?"

"Hmm...." I can hear Rupert thinking. "That could fly. You're going to be a bride soon. Why not write an article about ten items a bride-to-be should add to her bridal gift list?"

"I love the way you think, Rupe." My ear is starting to get warm because my earbud extension is back at the apartment. I'm not allowed to use the speakerphone in case the noise of my conversation leaks into the corridor. "I'll type it up and flick it over to you ASAP. Please can you add the shop links?"

Rupert agrees, tells me to get better soon, and hangs up.

I'm left staring at my laptop. I can't seem to work up the energy to start typing.

Banner, where are you? No texting, no sexting, and no call? I feel kind of cheated. I had a whole list of excuses lined up to give to him about why I had gone radio silent.

A nasty bout of food poisoning.

An important deadline for work.

Or maybe I should be on a new fruit juice-only detox cleanse? I know those make someone feel wretched. I never want to have such nasty caffeine withdrawal again!

The cold, hard truth is this—he hasn't bothered getting in contact with me since I told him good-bye. I know I should blame myself, but I can't. I was in shock and didn't know how to break the news to him.

Mary-Kay is right. It looks like I fell pregnant on purpose so that I could scam darling Daniel out of his inheritance.

Sighing again, my fingers fly over the keyboard as I ask the question that has been keeping me awake in those moments when the meds allow me to: What foods can make the pill stop working?

It's a long list! Lots of things can make the pill ineffective. Why didn't someone ever tell me about this before?

Antibiotics.

Detox tea.

Laxatives.

Charcoal ice cream, charcoal bread, and any edible charcoal.

Heavily chargrilled meats.

Saw palmetto.

Garlic pills.

Flaxseeds.

Herbal remedies containing St. John's Wort.

Grapefruit juice, grapefruit segments, and grapefruit sorbet...

Foods I eat all the time as part of my job!

I really wish I could write an article about this, but it might be a little bit too much on the nose.

Hmm.

This is crazy, but falling pregnant feels like fate. I signed up for a juice cleanse a couple of months ago. It's something we restaurant reviewers do all the time.

Fasting on juice is the best way to freshen the taste buds and flush out the toxins. I try to do it at least two times a year. It really revives my appetite, and makes me look forward to eating high-quality food—and by that, I mean the decadently rich ingredients served in restaurants—again.

The effect of eating rich foodstuffs was recorded in seventeenth-century London. Oysters were considered peasant food and served to servants daily. Eventually, the servants rebelled, forcing their masters to give them something else to eat.

I guess you can have too much of a good thing....

Because I chose to do the grapefruit juice cleanse—one month before I dined with Banner at Sabine!

That's the best example of fate I have ever experienced. At any stage of our meeting, I could have walked away from Banner and never looked back.

But then I would have missed out on the best sex of my life. My hands itch to pick up the phone, but I don't.

I give a little jump as my phone vibrates.

Banner. Talk of the devil. I've never been one of those "let it ring five times before answering" kind of girls, so I pounce.

"Hello?" It's the only thing I can think to say, considering my last word to him was buh-bye.

"Where are you?" Typical Banner, abrupt and to the point.

Pregnancy has changed me. Before this, I would have been all sassy. I would have said something like, "Aren't you going to say hi first?" Or, "Where the fuck have you been?"

But I don't, because I can't be a smart mouth to this man anymore. Banner is the baby daddy, and he deserves my respect for that alone.

"I'm in the hospital. The one closest to my apartment. I think Bert must have done one of those 'hospital closest to me' online searches."

My phone vibrates again, shaking against my ear. "Please hold on, Banner. A message has just come through."

All I get as a response is stony silence. I swipe on the message box with shaking fingers.

I don't know what's wrong, but I can hear that something is off about Banner.

In a flash, I imagine what my life would be like if this is the call that every woman dreads. The call from a man to tell her the relationship is off.

Then I read the message:

You're a pain in my ass, Ivy, but you are still Daniel's favorite person in the world (his words, not mine). A quick heads-up - I let it slip to Melanie about your pregnancy. And about you being a yacht girl. She's a friendly ear for me to talk to, so please don't blame me. Any-hoo, Melanie told Fletch the Wretch. Just thought you should know. MK.

How is it possible that I am feeling both hot and cold at the same time? I was right. Banner is calling to break it off.

The phone lies on my lap like an accusation. He's still waiting for me to say something. I am so tempted to break it off with him first.

If I pick up, Banner is going to ask me who the baby daddy is.

I've never been a coward since the day I chose to leave home and attend school in New York. I'm not going to start chickening out now.

"Hey, thank you for waiting. That was Mary-Kay. She texted to tell me that her best bud, Melanie, gave you my news."

There, I've said it. Now all I have to do is wait for the hammer to fall.

"Who's the baby's father?"

"I don't have to answer that, Banner. It's private."

He's shooting questions at me like a machine gun.

"Are you in the hospital to have an abortion? Or are there pregnancy-related complications? How many weeks are you? When did you find out? Was it while we were in Paris?"

"Terminating anything is not in my vocabulary, buster! You should know that right now!"

Taking a deep breath because I don't want the nurse to come in, I manage to speak more normally.

"I don't know where to begin, Banner. We haven't known one another long enough for me to feel comfortable discussing—"

"Try starting at the beginning and we go from there?" he snarls so effectively the phone shakes in my hand.

I don't know what to say.

"Okay. All out of cute comebacks? All I want to know is this, Ivy: Do you love me?"

Oh shit.

The only integrity I have left is to tell my truth. "Yes, but now that I've gone and fucked it up, what's the point?"

Fuck. Tears are starting to leak out of the corners of my eyes. I give a doleful sniff.

"That's all I needed to know."

Banner disconnects the call, leaving me holding the dead device in my hand.

"Knock! Knock! The nurse said I could come in. I hope I haven't caught you at a bad time?"

It's Noah. I'm torn between being grateful for the distraction and pissed that he chooses this time to visit. I look crap. I feel crap. And I have a lump in my throat the size of a tennis ball.

"Oh, hey, Noah. Please come in." My voice is all raspy and strangled because of the lump.

Noah has brought more flowers. Lilies and ferns. After giving my hand a quick squeeze, he messes about finding a vase for the flowers and emptying the longevity sachets into the flower water. Then he perches on the edge of my bed, even though there's a chair and a bench for visitors.

Giving my foot a joking pinch, Noah settles down to tell me why he's here.

"Holly, there's some online chatter that has got us worried at Bon Cuisine."

I don't say anything. After Mary-Kay's text, I think I know what's coming—Melanie and her loud mouth.

"Rumors are going around that your engagement to Fletcher Banner is fake. And that you might have done things in your past that you have not been open about."

"Who is saying that? Is it a real person, or are these blind items?"

Blind items are bitter little pieces of information online that mention no names, but hint at who the person might be. They are hideous scandal fodder, but there is nothing that can be done about them. Most of them are published with an "anonymous" source.

"Blind items. That's why Meg sent me to tell you. She's having a home day with the kids or else she would have come here herself. But I-I was happy to step up, you know." He gives my foot another squeeze.

"Thanks for letting me know, Noah."

"I can't help noticing that you haven't denied it." Noah is looking at me intently. "To be fair, it would be completely understandable. You wanted to twist the knife into Clifford Braxton and Fletcher Banner wanted to show that sneaky photog who's boss."

I'm not going to rise to the bait. All Noah gets out of me is a wan smile.

He continues, looking down at the bed sheets. "I was kinda hoping your engagement was fake, Holly. You're not wearing a ring. That's hardly likely to happen with a fiancé who could afford to buy up the whole of downtown Manhattan."

"Not even Fort Knox could buy up the real es-
tate downtown, Noah. It's worth trillions."

"I know that," he chuckles, "but I'm glad to be
here anyway—I just want you to know that I'll
always be around to help you out. Now, or after
the baby is born. I... I really like you, Holly. You're
one in a million."

"Actually, she's one in a billion, buddy. Do you
mind telling me why you're sitting on my fiancée's bed, cuddling her feet?"

Both Noah and I give high-pitched shrieks of
surprise as Banner steps into the private hospital ward.

"Banner!" I cry out, flustered beyond belief that
he is seeing me at my very worst. Forgetting
about poor Noah, I lunge for the makeup pouch
on the side table. I accidentally pull at the drip
needle stuck in the top of my hand. It makes me
cry out.

Noah jumps up, facing Banner. "H-hi, Mr. Banner. I was just here to give Holly these flowers—"

Banner is holding an enormous bunch of exotic orchids sitting in an antique Oriental jade pot. He takes one look at Noah's flowers and smirks. "Never get into a bouquet war with a billionaire, Noah. Now scoot before my patience runs out."

Noah says a hasty goodbye and scoots. A quick slick of Elizabeth Arden eight-hour cream on my cheeks and lips is the best I can do before Banner demands my attention.

"You don't have to get into a dick-measuring contest with poor Noah, Banner. He's not the baby's daddy."

Banner is not in the mood for my cheeky attitude. "Okay, so who is?"

Now I'm stuck! Should I tell Banner the truth or not?

# Chapter 27 - Fletcher

"I'm not ready to make a claim on the father yet." Ivy swallows hard as if her emotions want to get the better of her. "Announcing my pregnancy is the least of my worries."

"You don't think I can use my connections to find out how many weeks you are?" I remind Ivy. "If you push your drip wheel into the corridor and go stand in the lobby, you'll see there's a Basil and Roberta Banner Wing in this hospital. I built it."

A wicked spark lights in her gorgeous dark eyes. "Wow. That must have taken you ages, Banner—building an entire hospital wing."

"I paid for it to be built, you sassy little thing."

She giggles and smooths the shiny balm over her lips using the baby finger of her right hand. Very sexy, even if she looks pale and thin.

"Fine. Keep your secrets for now. Tell me why you're here." I want to know.

Why am I deflecting from finding out the baby's daddy? Is it because of what Richard Thompson told me? It got me really worried, but I have a bit of digging to do first.

Ivy explains what's wrong with her. "They call it HG, Banner. Hyperemesis gravidarum. Uncontrollable vomiting, extreme weight loss, and dehydration."

"And those are not the ideal symptoms to have when you must be trying to eat for two."

Ivy looks so fragile lying in bed. It's time for me to step up.

"I think you should come and stay with me. The medical team told me you let things get so bad you were too sick to think straight, so let me do the thinking for you. At least until you feel better."

"Dr. Renee has put me on these really strong meds," Ivy explains. "I can keep stuff down now, but my appetite is shot."

We both pause for a beat.

"No more restaurant reviews for a while?" I hazard a guess at the new problem in Ivy's life.

She shakes her head. "Nope. I don't know what to do. I'm scared."

Suddenly, Ivy seems to shake off her sadness and uncertainty. That's what I like about her. She never lets a bad situation get her down.

"I usually write about high dining and cutting-edge cuisine. But it's time I expand my brand to include other things. I was thinking about getting into hotel reviews. I'll use my lack of appetite to segue into accommodation. What do you think?"

"I think it's time you got out of here." Selecting a number from my list of contacts, I press to connect. "Hey, Ben. Please can someone get a doctor up to Miss Forrest's private room? We want to know if she may be discharged."

Ivy shakes her head, marveling at my audacity. "You say 'jump' and everyone asks 'how high.'"

Lifting her hand to my mouth, I kiss it. "Not everyone, Ivy...."

I find myself searching her face, looking for some sign that Ivy might be playing me. I'm not the most trusting man at the best of times, but what I heard from Richard got me spooked.

"Aren't you going to pester me about the baby daddy?" Ivy looks at me speculatively. "I mean, you asked me if I love you, and I said yes. After a declaration like that, isn't it normal for us to have a conversation?'

I have no concerns on that score. When I want to know how many weeks pregnant Ivy is, I'll find out.

"A hospital isn't the right place to have that conversation," I say. "When I tell you I love you, Ivy, it won't be inside a fucking private hospital room that smells of antiseptic!"

"Aren't you even the slightest bit concerned about the baby's father?" I can tell from the way

Ivy is insisting on getting an answer that she is feeling very vulnerable.

"When we rekindled our relationship, Ivy, I take that as our starting point. I don't give a flying fuck about what you did before that."

If Ivy is guilty of anything, I know me saying that will make her embarrassed. I want her to know that I don't care about her yacht-girl origins... but does she?

She looks at me with those adorable dewy dark eyes. Ivy has nothing to hide as far as I can see. "That is the most romantic thing I have ever heard, Banner."

Grinning, I consolidate my stance. "It's not really romantic. It's just that I'm confident enough in my own skin to genuinely not give a fuck about ex-boyfriends."

Giving me a wink, Ivy chuckles. "You are so cocky, Banner, but I love it."

A doctor comes in.

"Miss Forrest. We're a bit confused about billing. Is the account for Woods or Forrest?"

"It's for Banner," I say, passing my card to the doctor. "Please tell accounting I will pay for all my fiancée's bills."

The doctor spends the next half an hour fussing over Ivy's chart and taking her blood pressure.

"I'll discharge you, Miss Forrest," the doctor says, "but you must keep your appointment with Dr. Renee Spargo tomorrow. As your primary doctor, she'll be in charge of dispensing your meds and charting your weight gain."

Telling Ivy that I'll be waiting for her outside, I leave the doctor to remove her drip. Half an hour later, we are sitting in the back of my town car and Sami is asking Ivy how she is.

"Hey, I thought we were going to your apartment." Ivy looks out of the window. "Sami, did you forget?

"No, Miss Woods. Mr. Banner thought you might need some stuff from your apartment."

"Genius!" Ivy is pleased as we pull up outside her building. "Thank you. I won't be more than a few minutes...."

"If you think I'm going to wait in the car for you like a pet dog, Ivy, you're wrong." Getting out of my side of the car, I follow her inside. Turning to Sami, I ask him to go back to the hospital, collect the flowers, and deliver the bouquets to my apartment.

Bert is happy to see Ivy and shoots me a curious glance. "This is Banner, Bert. And before I forget, I want to thank you for calling that ambulance."

"No problem, Miss." Bert is all smiles now that he knows I'm with Ivy. "I signed for all your bouquets."

I can see that Ivy is anxious to get inside. I don't blame her. She's an elegant woman wearing baggy sweats with no makeup. She must be dying to have a shower and change.

"Here. I'll help you carry up the bouquets, Bert." I offer to carry the biggest bunch of flowers. Let's hope there are no thorns hidden in the roses.

Knowing that she'll be in the bathroom, Ivy has left the front door open for us. Hefting the flowers onto the counter, I start looking around for some scissors and vases. Bert says he'll pick up the stem cuttings for composting if I leave them outside the door. Then he leaves.

"I'm not arranging these flowers, Ivy!" I shout through the bathroom door. "You want to know what kind of man I am? I'm the guy who will never fucking ever be caught dead arranging flowers."

A burst of giggles can be heard on the other side of the door. "Okay. Fine! Just unwrap them and leave them in the kitchen."

That I can do.

A large card catches my eye. It's pinned to the cellophane wrapper of that big bunch of roses. The message given to the florist to put on the card faces outward.

Hi Holly.

I hear yacht cruises are really good for your health.

Missed you on the podcast.

Get better soon.

Julian Stratford

As I read the message, it's like a red mist explodes behind my eyes. Going to the bathroom door, I raise my voice to be heard above the jets of water. "Ivy, I'm going out. Sami will be waiting for you at the curb."

She burbles something that sounds like "Where are you going?" but I'm already halfway out the door.

That's the problem with being a man of action. I never stick around long enough to debate my actions in advance!

My blood is boiling and I am headed to the best place where I know I can get answers.

It's been a long time since I was in this building, but it still holds bitter memories for me.

Shouldering my way through the doors like a running back rushing the ball downfield, I ignore the astonished girls sitting in the waiting room and go straight to the reception desk.

"Hey, Janet. Remember me?"

"No. And you have to have an appointment. Mr. Stratford's time is very important."

I can see the uptight bitch is getting ready to give me the bum's rush, so I preempt it. "If you look at your appointment book very carefully, Janet, you'll see my name right there between 'who cares?' and 'I don't give a fuck.' Got that?"

Striding to the doors to Stratford's office, I growl over my shoulder. "Don't bother announcing me. I know my way."

Julian Stratford looks up when I burst in. He's got some sweet little thing standing in her underwear in front of his desk. She looks just as shocked as Stratford does at my entrance.

Bending down, I pick up her clothes. "Get dressed and go back to your mother, kid," I tell her. "Do you want to ruin the rest of your life?"

Hurriedly, she hops back into her dress and shoes and runs out, leaving me alone with Stratford.

"You're still a sleazeball, Julian."

He tries to get up out of his chair, but I walk around his desk and push him back down. "We're going to have a little chat, just you and me."

"If you lay one finger on me, Mr. Banner, I'll sue!"

My smile can look dangerous when I want it to. "Nope, that's not going to happen. Your little scam is too valuable for you to risk involving the police. I hear you like podcasts?"

He is alarmed. "So, it's true. You did hook up with Holly Forrest again?"

Ignoring him, I grip his shoulder. My thumb presses into the pressure point above the collarbone. Julian winces in pain.

"You are going to forget all about Holly Forrest, got that? And then you are going to forget all about me. If I so much as dream that you have contact with Holly again, I'll come back here, Julian, and you don't want that." My words are clipped, vicious, as I rein back my anger.

"Yes, yes, whatever you want. I'm sorry. Holly and I are old friends. That's all."

"Shut up," I scoff, digging my thumb in deeper. "You. Are. To. Forget. About. Holly."

I press into the nerve every time I say a word.

"Yes—" Julian is close to passing out from pain. All the blood has drained out of his face. Removing my hand from his shoulder, I grip the back of his neck instead.

"Right." Hauling Julian up, I jerk him from one side of the room to the other. "Where's the secret panel hiding the video camera?"

"I never—!" Julian tries to deny it. I give his neck another squeeze.

"Okay! Okay! I'll show you," he groans.

Julian pulls a piece of wood paneling and a board slides back. Pushing him away so he sprawls on the carpet, I grab the camera and then smash the panel door with a vicious punch.

Janet opens the door. "Mr. Stratford! Should I call the cops?"

Waving the camera at her, I say to Julian. "I don't know, Janet. Should you?"

Groaning, Stratford stays down on the floor. "For fuck's sake, let him go, Janet."

As I am going out the doors, Julian Stratford has a parting shot. "She's not the nice girl you think she is, Banner, but it's your funeral."

"It'll be your funeral if I ever have to come back here."

But I can't help thinking—what if Julian Stratford knows something I don't? I am starting to hate the fact that I met my fake fiancée on a pleasure cruise.

# Chapter 28 – Ivy

Banner is acting weird when he comes back. I'm feeling frisky after showering, shaving my legs, and rubbing scented cream all over my body, so I ignore his ferocious scowl.

The more I am with this man, the more I am starting to realize that Mary-Kay might have been right. Her brother is a real grizzly bear!

I packed a small case full of my prettiest casual wear and the items of clothing I know I look great in. Black Lycra yoga pants, crop top tanks, and off-the-shoulder T-shirts. Banner's apartment is temperature-controlled, so as far as I'm concerned it feels like sunshine in here.

The balmy temperature gives me the chance to slip into some cute lace pajama shorts and a satin camisole. If I have to spend time in bed, I might as well look pretty while I'm doing it.

One look in the mirror tells me that I am border-line skinny. My hip bones stick out and my legs and butt have lost the sexy roundness I used to have around my ass and thighs.

But on the plus side, my boobs look amazing! The nipples have filled out and gotten lush. When I pinch them, my nipples are definitely more sensitive.

Padding through to the living room, I check out the kitchen.

Banner's fridge is stocked with some really tempting foodstuffs. After checking what my body craves to eat, I make myself two massive peanut butter and jelly sandwiches.

High-class dining this most definitely ain't! But I have to listen to what my body wants now. Forcing it to eat meat and two servings of vegetables isn't going to work anymore.

But there are other things here that tempt me more....

"Ta-dah!" I say when Banner comes in. "I've arranged all the flowers from the hospital! D'you think Sami can collect the ones I left at my place and bring them here?"

"Who are these flowers from?" Banner looks like a thundercloud as he prowls from vase to vase, inspecting the 'Get Well Soon' cards. "Or are they all from that lovestruck idiot from the podcast?"

"No, Mr. Grumpy, they are not all from Noah. He brought the lilies, remember?"

Muttering curses under his breath, Banner barges into the bedroom. I hear him in the shower.

"You were gone for a while. Nothing bad at work, I hope?"

I find it interesting how easily Banner and I slip back into being partners without any preamble.

"I can't hear you" is all he says as he lathers shampoo on his scalp.

This is not how I planned our reunion. And now that one of my appetites is sorted out—and as I watch Banner standing naked in the shower—my other appetite rears its head.

Stripping off my clothes, I open the shower door and go to stand behind him. Snaking my hands around his waist, I caress his cock gently.

"That's the funny thing about appetites, Banner." My voice is a throaty purr as I lick the water falling down his back. "The moment one appetite is satisfied, the other one becomes desperate for some attention."

Pressing my breasts against him, I slide my hardening nipples across his skin. He's already completely rampant in my hand. Massaging the head of his penis, I move my grip up the thick shaft.

Banner kind of grunts as he forces himself to regain control over his body. He turns around and finds an extremely excited dripping wet mermaid standing behind him.

He is even more impressive from the front. No words can do him justice. My perfectly scrumptious, delicious, yummy man.

Dropping to my knees, I push his hands away and start to suck his cock hard. Like I'm really hungry, starving for him to fuck me good and hard right now.

"You're still so fragile, Ivy. I don't want to hurt you."

Banner can hardly get the words out! He is completely wrapped up in what's happening to him right now.

"Shut up!" I move my mouth away just long enough to show him I mean business. "For once in your life, Banner, let me be the boss."

It's so hot when he spreads his arms wide and presses his hands against the glass wall. Tilting his head down, Banner watches me giving him head.

"You're a hungry girl this evening, aren't you?" The corner of his mouth lifts in a gorgeous lop-sided smile as I lick his shaft and then go back to gobbling as much of him as I can fit into my mouth.

"Mmm." That's all I can say. It feels like I'm melting because my pussy is so inflamed with desire. That is why I find myself always coming back to this man. He makes me feel like no one ever has.

From the first time we met, Fletcher Banner somehow managed to ensnare my sexuality. Since I was eighteen years old, images of his face flash across my mind whenever I come.

I only ever want to have this man fucking me, because he is literally the best.

It is so thrilling when I feel his hand guiding my head. I can feel he's close, and he doesn't want me to miss a stroke. It's gone from me sucking his cock to him basically thrusting himself into me.

I can't help it—I gag a little bit when his rigid shaft drills deeper into my mouth. The back of my throat has become more sensitive.

Banner pulls out, holding himself so his thick girth can't slap my face. "Are you okay?"

When I look up, the shower water splashes in my eyes. My mascara must be a real mess.

"Maybe that's a sign telling me it's my turn."

Banner doesn't need me to say it again. Sure, he would love to come, but he totally gets off on stimulating me too.

Helping me stand up, we stumble out of the shower and into his bedroom. We're both slick with wetness and slippery from the sandal-wood shower cream he uses instead of soap.

Pushing me onto the bed, Banner pulls my legs apart. The next thing I know, he's eating me out as if he is ravenous!

I guess my chance at being a boss bitch is over. Banner is way too much of a dominant man to handle that for too long.

Staring at the ceiling and trying hard to hold back my moans of pleasure, I let him take control. His mouth is sucking and lapping at my clit, teasing me into utter delight.

He knows how to do it right, keeping the hood over the most sensitive part so that I last longer. Dipping the tip of his tongue into my slit and rubbing his face over my mound.

His touch sends me over the edge as his fingers probe my sopping wet pussy.

"I'm at that point where I would love you to stick that delicious cock into me," I gasp as his tongue makes me writhe and lift my mound up toward him.

Don't you dare stop sucking and fucking me now, Mister! I am so turned on—my orgasm is mounting inside me like an ecstatic wave.

"Your wish is my command, sweetheart," Banner murmurs, crawling to join me on the bed, spreading my legs open even wider with his knee as he positions me for his penetration.

When it happens, I almost lose my mind from how turned on I am. This is the best part—when I can feel his stiffness cleaving deep into my pussy, gliding against the dripping wetness of my soft, tight walls.

My orgasm purrs, rubbing inside me as my clit swells and pouts.

I start to pant and moan. "Banner, I'm so close. I can't stop."

His growl vibrates against my lips as he kisses me. "Don't come yet. I want to fuck you so hard."

Flipping me around after pulling out, Banner uses some pillows to raise my ass up. He gives my ass a little smack. It tingles but somehow manages to arouse my clit at the same time.

This has never happened to me before. I am loving it as Banner takes charge. Burying his face between my thighs, he passes his tongue over my thick, juicy lips and even up my crack. Feeling helpless against this tide of arousal sweeping over me, I bury my face in the pillow and bite the corner.

Finally, after exquisite sensations mount higher and higher in my tingling lovebud, Banner slides his cock back into my pussy. The tight walls begin spasming right away as my wet vagina tries to milk him dry.

"God, you feel amazing," Banner grunts like a wild animal as he thrusts deep and fast. "I'm coming."

"Mmm, yes, fuck me hard. I want you so bad." My face is buried in the pillow, but it kind of helps me concentrate on the climax shuddering through my body. Pushing my ass back against him, I scream with pleasure as he moves his finger around to my clit, making my orgasm a million times more intense.

My knees give out and I collapse against the pile of pillows.

"The next time we make love," Banner says, "I want you to tell me you love me while you're coming."

"That, Mr. Banner, is something I can most definitely do!" When he comes to lie beside me, I kiss him.

Oh my God, I should tell Banner about the creepy bunch of roses that was waiting for me at my apartment! I flushed the card down the toilet, but the sender's name is still etched into my mind.

Thank goodness Banner hates arranging flowers or else he might have seen the card!

Get better soon. Julian Stratford.

But I can't confess—because now that I have admitted my love, I don't want to lose Banner—ever.

# Chapter 29 – Fletcher

I'm still not sure if Julian Stratford got the message. Especially after I view the USB card from the video camera that was concealed behind the panel in his office.

I've locked the door to my office even though I know Ivy is asleep. Inserting the flash drive into my laptop, I put on headphones and click play.

The camera must have been placed at the perfect angle to capture every sleazy moment. Julian Stratford seems to think that a hair transplant, perma-tan, and facelift make him look young and desirable.

He could not be more wrong.

"Hey, sweetie. Thank you for coming in." He looks down at the clipboard on the desk in front of him. "Jade. Cute name. Listen, I hate to be the bearer of bad news, but you're eighteen. Don't you think that's a little old for you to start thinking about modeling?"

"B-but, Mr. Stratford, your website says 'eighteen and over'? I don't understand."

Julian clicks his tongue. "Well, sweetie, I have to put that on there. Can't have all those killjoys calling me a pervert, can I?"

The young girl looks confused. I can feel myself getting angry as I watch the video helplessly. Using a destress technique I learned in Japan, I breathe in green and exhale red before continuing.

"I tell you what. I'll put you on my books because I think you are very pretty. And…." Julian looks really pleased with himself as he says it. "I'll give you your first booking, but only if you have a younger friend you can get to join the agency as well."

The young girl cheers up. "My sister is fifteen! She was really jealous when she heard I was coming here. Can I bring her too?"

The greasy grin on Julian Stratford's face gets wider. "That's perfect! But let's keep it a secret from your parents. When you two girls book your first gig, you can surprise your folks—think of all that money you'll be making!"

"I don't know if I can get Polly to come here without Mom knowing," Jade says, "but maybe we can wait until we stay at Dad's for the weekend. He works all day on Saturdays—leaves us to do our own thing."

Julian cheers right up when he hears that. "That sounds ideal, Jane."

"I'm Jade."

"Jade. Jade. Yes. In the meantime, I want you to go get tested. We have a strict no-drugs policy here at Stratfords. Just making sure."

"But, Mr. Stratford, all the kids in my class smoke a little weed! It's no big deal. I'm not a stoner."

"Yes, sure. But we have to check you don't do that hard stuff. Get Janet to book you an appointment at the clinic—and remember, keep this between us for now. You don't want to look stupid when you never get booked. Then all your friends and family will laugh at you."

Jade gets up to leave. She's all smiles, the light of hope shining in her eyes. "Thank you, Mr. Stratford. I won't let you down."

"Oh, Jade…, before you go. I have to check your breasts and buttocks for stretch marks. Our clients don't want to waste their valuable time having to airbrush your bikini photos."

I've heard enough. Clicking stop, I spend the next few moments centering my calm. If I don't, I am so close to storming back to the modeling agency and beating the crap out of that sleaze-ball.

Then an idea hits me. Clicking play again, I skip to the part in the video where Jade has gone. The receptionist, Janet, enters with the next clipboard.

"There's one born every minute, Jannie," Julian Stratford says, his confident grin back.

"You shouldn't be celebrating, Julian," she snaps, "Only Fans is taking a large chunk of our business. Those men can find what they're looking for without getting on a yacht!"

"They can't find virgins on Only Fans," Julian says. "Business has picked up since we added them to our menu."

"That billionaire boys club you like so much, Julian, some of the men have started to warn the others. I think it's time for us to cash in our chips and get out."

"The big fish and whales will always be tempted by tight young pussy they're free to fuck without condoms. Those 'vitamin' shots we give to the virgins were a brilliant idea! The girls think they're getting a booster. They're too stupid to know it's a contraceptive."

Janet collects the old clipboards from the desk and then clasps them to her chest. "Think about getting out while we're ahead, Julian. You're going to mess with the wrong billionaire one of these days."

Clicking on the screen, I eject the flash drive.

You're fucking right about that, Janet. You didn't just mess with the wrong billionaire, you messed with his fake fiancée too.

Am I thinking about turning this fake engagement into a real one? You bet! But I can't risk having someone saying that my future wife is a yacht girl.

Putting my angry mood to good use, I order my favorite restaurant to bring up some brunch for Ivy and me.

When the doorman asks if he can let the delivery man up, I say yes. Dipping my hand into the jar for tips, I pull out a twenty.

"Hey, Fletcher," the delivery guy says when I open the door. "Are you just hungry or have you got company?"

What the hell. I may as well embrace the inevitable. "I'm engaged, Marty. You can expect to be bringing us a lot more breakfasts in the future."

Thanking me for the tip, Marty says congratulations and leaves. I could get used to the warm glow of happiness that filled me up when I con-firmed our engagement.

Maybe I won't have to order brunch anymore. Ivy can scramble the eggs while I butter the toast. That unused kitchen of mine would smell of breakfast grill food....

First things first; I have to find out more about these billionaire blackmail rumors.

Is it okay for me to carry the bag of food into the bedroom? Or will Ivy expect me to plate it for her? Shit. I haven't got a clue. All of my previous relationships never got to the sleepover stage.

Ivy is not the sort of woman I want to piss off when it comes to serving food. She is my equal when it comes to demanding perfect service.

That cute smile of hers can go from pleased to pissed if she does not like what she's eating! How did I fall in love with such a demanding little lady?

I think it's because of the way she goes from a helpless damsel in distress to a woman in charge with one blink of her liquid, choco-late-brown eyes.

And while I'm more than capable of serving her sexual needs, I'm lost when it comes to flatware and silverware.

"What are you doing, Banner?" She's standing in the bedroom doorway, looking ultra-adorable in her lace pajamas. "I smell something real good."

Moving to kiss her, I push the video flash drive to the back of my mind. "That would be me. And I smell so good because I slept with you in my arms all night."

She smiles, twinkling her eyes at me. I can tell she's washed and brushed her teeth. Ivy is im-maculate with her hygiene.

"I got my favorite deli to deliver brunch." Push-ing the bag over to the breakfast nook, I point for her to look inside while I get plates out of the cupboard.

Ivy starts pulling boxes of cheesecake and stacked bagels out of the bag. I get orange juice and glasses and put them on the counter.

This eating-at-home stuff isn't so difficult after all!

"I need some fattening up," Ivy tells me. She's commandeered both slices of cheesecake. "But you can have a forkful if you're a good boy."

Swallowing my mouthful of bagel, I reply, "Good is not an adjective I am often associated with, Ivy. Could you spare a forkful for a bad boy?"

"Mm," she whispers, holding the fork to my mouth. "I like the sound of that. And I'm hungry for more of what we did last night."

Brunch has never been this much fun before.

"How about I eat the rest of this cheesecake of those rock-hard abs of yours, Banner?" Tracing her fingernail down my arm, Ivy smiles enticingly. "I'd rather suck that tasty cock of yours than eat a bagel."

The sun pouring through the sliding doors leading out to the patio turns her clothes transparent. The dark skin around her nipples makes my cock stiffen as I imagine myself sucking them....

Forcing myself to pay attention, I say what I need to say.

"I have to work. We're breaking ground on the new hotel downtown today and I need to be there for the press junket."

Typical Ivy, she doesn't let this get her down. "Sounds boring. What time are you coming back?"

I shrug, racking my brains for a way to change the conversation. "Speaking of boring, my buddy contacted me about something you might be interested in."

Ivy looks up from her plate, giving me all of her attention.

"Yeah, remember what happened to us on the yacht? Well, the same thing happened to my buddy. He asked me if I knew anyone who could help him out."

Ivy's eyes narrow. She takes a small sip of juice and licks her lips. "How the fuck could I possibly help, Banner?"

Shit. "Can you remember any of the yacht girls' names?"

"No. I can't...." Ivy looks at me with a mix of suspicion and doubt. "But my heart goes out to your buddy."

"That's a shame." It's a shame for me because it's going to make everything a lot harder. Ivy interrupts me as I reach for my juice.

"But I recognized one of the girls when I was scrolling through social media a couple of months back. She's working under the name of Emerald de Vine now. She was definitely on the yacht with me."

Leaning over, I kiss her. "Thanks. You've made him a very happy man. Maybe Miz de Vine knows how my buddy can contact his sweetheart."

"Maybe."

From the way she says it, I know Ivy isn't happy.

I'm so worried that I'll return to an empty apartment when I come home again!

# Chapter 30 - Ivy

I knew one look at my skinny body might send Banner running into another woman's arms. It's so unfair. And he doesn't even bother trying to hide it.

His lame excuse when he asks me to do a solid for his "buddy." It's so obvious he wants another yacht girl to fuck.

Is he worried I'll get all unattractive as the pregnancy progresses?

For a moment, I'm torn about whether to give him the information he needs or not.

Making up my mind, I tell him about Emerald de Vine. She's definitely not his type, so I feel a bit more secure.

Ever since I was young, I could sense when a man has a "type"—that ideal fantasy woman he can't get enough of.

I know from the way he touches certain parts of my body—and how he gazes at me with longing clear in his possessive eyes. Banner is enslaved by the way I look.

How did I get so confident? Because Banner always comes back. He's not the only one who can be cocky in this relationship!

"We cool?" Banner checks that I am happy with what he just said. "I don't want you thinking this is for me."

Snap! "Can I come with you, then?" It couldn't hurt for me to ask. "I wouldn't mind seeing Emerald again. I can't remember the name she used on the yacht, but her face on social media is the same."

"Don't prostitutes change their names all the time?" Banner asks. "I mean, most guys probably don't even remember an escort's name or face. Why would they?"

Is he deliberately trying to piss me off? He's twisting the knife about my Forrest persona.

"Thanks for that update, Banner, but you still haven't answered my question."

He shifts on the bar stool like it's suddenly uncomfortable for him—or maybe his big brass balls are getting in the way!

"That's a hard no, Ivy. It's going to be dangerous enough for me to visit an escort on my own without having to drag you along with me. We were photographed once before. Let's not push our luck."

Offering to stack the dishwasher, I move away from him.

My hands are shaking. I thought we were doing so good, and now this.

"Cat got your tongue?" I can't believe he's trying to tease me about this!

Coming to stand behind me, he wraps his arms over my shoulders and nuzzles my neck.

"The last thing I need is for someone to start selling the story that Fletcher Banner and his beautiful fiancée are shopping around for a threesome." His warm mouth presses against my shoulder. I can feel the whole length of his rigid penis rubbing on me. "You're more than enough woman for me, Ivy."

Frustrated, I pull away from him. I'm angry with myself for getting turned on when I have other things on my mind. He is acting like a player.

If that's how he wants this to go down, fuck him! I'm a big girl. Two can play this game. I can't believe he's being so blatant about it.

"No, the cat has not got my tongue, Banner!" I snap at him. I can't help it, even though I know it will only make things worse. "I think you're using secrecy as your camouflage, and that makes you a coward!"

Pivoting and stalking out of the kitchen, Banner grabs his jacket and heads for the door.

"All I've ever wanted to do since Vegas, Ivy," he growls, "is look after you. Try keeping that in mind."

Guilt pricks my conscience the minute the door slams shut.

You really shouldn't talk about cowardly behavior when you're hiding more than enough secrets of your own, Ivy!

I am so tempted to call that wretched man, Julian Stratford. He was the one who started all this. He knows that I am in a very vulnerable position now that I am with Banner.

If Julian says anything about me to the press, I might take Banner down with me.

Damn it. I have to find a way to protect the man I love.

Heaving a heavy sigh, I start to pack my case. Turns out you can get too much of a good thing, especially when that good thing is in danger of being sucked down into the swamp with me.

***

Feeling a million times better with that lovely brunch food in my tummy, I start to strategize.

I need to find myself a yacht girl of my own!

Where do I start and what do I do?

Only one thing for it. I call Rupert.

"Your latest article about essential kitchen gadgets for a new bride is going gangbusters, darling!" Rupert sounds so happy. "When can we get the next one?"

"Soon. Rupert, you're a cosmopolitan gay gentleman. Which of the five-star hotels are the best places to hook up—with an escort."

Rupert is completely unfazed by the question. Like I said, he's a typical New Yorker. Hard to shock and really clued in.

"I'll text you a list. But I don't need to. Every luxury hotel pretends that they don't tolerate such shenanigans, but they're all lying. Part of a concierge's job is to get tickets for the hottest shows on Broadway, book tables at all the best restaurants, and find an escort for the guests if they ask for one. Ditto with drug dealers."

"Thanks, Rupe! I'll send a new article soon."

Disconnecting, I find a luxury hotel where I have eaten several times, enter the number, and ask to be put through to Mr. Symons, the concierge.

"Concierge desk, how may we help?"

"Good morning, Mr. Symons, it's me, Holly Forrest."

"Why, Miz Forrest, how lovely to hear from you. Ivan is so pleased with the review you published. He said you must come back and give him his fifth star."

"I might just do that."

The concierge goes on to congratulate me on the news of my engagement, making this next thing I need a very awkward conversation.

"Thank you, Mr. Symons. On a completely unrelated note, I was wondering if... if you could introduce me to an escort."

Silence for a beat and then the concierge regains control over himself.

"I can do that, Miz Forrest, yes."

"Cool!" I jump straight in. "You might have to ask around, but I need a yacht girl. An older yacht girl, so she might not be operating on the yachts anymore. I need her to have been active on the yacht girl circuit ten years ago. Is that possible?"

I can tell that Mr. Symons is jotting down notes on a pad. Old school. So he can dispose of the note afterward.

"That is possible, Miz Forrest. Please give me a few hours. Can I get back to you on your usual number?"

After saying yes, I disconnect the call. Staring at the phone in my hand, I start to laugh hysterically.

I can't believe I am about to do this! But it has to be done.

***

My pencil skirt is a bit loose around my waist, but I smile because I know it won't stay like that for long. In two or three months, my darling baby will have grown so much bigger.

It's not so warm today, so I slip a fitted jacket over my blouse before walking down to my car service. Waving by to Bert, I tell him to chuck the roses I left outside my door onto the compost pile.

Good riddance to bad rubbish!

Piece by piece, I'm cutting Julian Stratford out of my life like a cancer.

Mr. Symons is waiting for me in the hotel foyer. He greets me and hands me a room key card.

"She's already waiting for you, Miz Forrest."

Thanking him, I walk to the elevators.

The hotel corridor is dark and soothingly quiet as I go up. There is something very serene about luxury hotel spaces.

The woman sitting on the end of the bed looks up as I come in.

"Wow!" she says, standing up and moving to hug me. "This is my lucky day. You're gorgeous!"

I step back.

The woman is dressed elegantly, but I can see her clothes are not luxe. The thick pancake makeup is doing her skin no favors. The subtle pink lipstick is starting to bleed into the thin, vertical lines above her upper lip.

Her face is kind and optimistic like she's breathing a sigh of relief that it's me and not some random man.

"Before I confirm the booking, I need to know you're a yacht girl."

She looks at me funny. "I was, but I'm 'too mature' for that crowd now. That's a nice way of saying that I aged out. Do you mind me asking why you want a yacht girl?"

Fishing an envelope out of my purse, I hand it to her. "This is one thousand dollars. Please count it. Then we need to talk."

Her eyes get large. There's a slick layer of sweat where she has unbuttoned her blouse to show the deep cleavage her fake breasts make.

"Thank you!" she squeaks. "But you don't have to pay before. I trust you. The concierge says he knows you."

Pointing to the minibar, I tell her to help herself. "What's your name?"

"I'm Maxine," she tells me while unscrewing a bottle of white wine. I hold up my hand to show her I don't want any. She pours herself a big glass.

"So, what do you want to know about yacht girls?"

"Everything. How you got into it and what's the deal."

Maxine looks at my designer outfit and Louboutins. "Have they gotten their claws into your husband?"

I shake my head, so Maxine continues.

"Yacht girls.... About ten years ago I answered a job posting for 'print models.' I was too short for catwalks, but I was a cheerleader and all my friends said I was pretty, so I went to see this man at the Stratford agency."

I nod to let her know I'm listening.

"The man told me I was hired, but I had to take a blood test to prove I wasn't on drugs.

Apparently, I had a vitamin deficiency, so they gave me a booster shot."

That didn't happen to me. I wonder why?

"It was shockingly easy for me to con my mom into thinking I was at my friend's house for the weekend. But I was really on the yacht." Maxine shudders. "It was awful. An old man dragged me into one of the cabins and forced himself on me. I was told all I had to do was sunbathe topless in front of them—that was all! Some flirting, maybe some under-the-top stuff. I was so naive."

She shakes her head and wipes her eyes. "The man who took my virginity gave me a red wristband type of thing. He told me to show it to the yacht host before disembarking. He said I wouldn't be allowed to get off the boat if I didn't have one!"

I feel so grubby and grim listening to this poor woman's story.

"I wish I could say I didn't do it again, but like I said, I was so naive. When I told the agency that I got my fifty thousand dollars and I was tapping out, they said they had videos of what I did! They threatened to tell my family if I didn't do what they said."

Sniffing, poor Maxine drains down the last of the wine. "It got so bad, that I dropped out of college. I... I was manipulated into doing some pretty hardcore stuff. Every time I tried to get out, they would threaten me again. Telling my landlord! Telling my grandparents! Posting on-line what a whore I was. Eventually, I just gave up—it only stopped when I turned twenty-five. I guess I got too old for their warped taste."

A poisonous numbness is coursing through my body as I listen to Maxine.

"Thank you so much for this money. It gives me the chance to pay my rent and not worry for a couple of weeks. After those people have finished playing with you, they don't care. It's like I'm disposable, you know."

That could have been me!

But now a burning question is in my mind. How many more people know about the yachts?

Mary-Kay, Melanie, and the Stratford crowd. Which one of them is going to be the one to turn around and bite me on the ass?

And why didn't Julian Stratford try to blackmail me? Or maybe he just hasn't gotten around to doing it yet!

# Chapter 31 - Fletcher

I'm kinda shocked at how easy it is for me to get some face-to-face time with Emerald de Vine.

All I have to do is create a fake social media account, download the app, and stick her name into the search engine.

After some tantalizing DMs go back and forth between us, she agrees to meet me.

She sends me her bank deets—I deposit five thousand dollars into it—and the next thing I know, Emerald is telling me to meet her at a hotel.

Time for me to flex my wealth and get her hooked good and proper.

No. I'm not meeting you in a shitty four-star hotel chain like that. Go to the Ensign on Fifth and ask Maurice the concierge for the penthouse suite. I'll meet you there.

I pause for a beat, waiting for her to reply.

It comes through just as I predicted.

The Ensign? Ooh-la-la. Now I'm really looking forward to meeting you! See you there. P. S. Any kinks I have to cater for are extras on top. All my hot sticky love, Emerald xxx

I call the private line at my flagship hotel on Fifth.

The manager picks up.

"Hey, Maurice. How are you? How's the family?"

It might surprise people to know that I am never a prick to my staff. I'm definitely not one of those "You're all part of the Ensign Family" bullshit bosses either. Everyone in upper management is a friend. End of story.

"Pas mal, merci, Monsieur Banner. Comment ça va?"

Most of my hotel staff at the luxury branches are French. Not too shabby, thanks, Mr. Banner. And how are you?

Once I knew my goal was hotel chain world domination, I learned the language. Hell, there wasn't much else to do in my spare time whenever the Corps was told to stand down.

"I'm engaged to be married, Maurice. It doesn't get much better than that." I remain upbeat, even though the security at my building called to tell me that Ivy had packed up and left. "Someone is coming to collect a key card for the penthouse suite. Please can you show her how to use it so that the elevator goes straight up to the entrance?"

"Felicitations on your engagement, Monsieur Banner. I will escort the lady to the penthouse suite entrance myself."

We say goodbye politely. Poor Maurice. He's going to be really confused when Emerald de Vine arrives at reception.

I have some time on my hands as I wait for Emerald to reach the hotel. Clicking the remote,

I get the drapes to shut and the screen to turn on.

Moving my eyes from one trade to the next, I analyze the stock market and mergers carefully.

After half an hour of flicking over the charts and finance news, I find what I want.

Borkum & Associates liquidate their assets as the company prepares to sell. The headlines are large because the news is shocking.

B & A has been one of the leading securities brokerages for nearly eighty years. There is no reason why they would be turning the company over for cash.

Glancing at my watch, I check it's time for me to leave the office.

"Shall I call your car for you, Mr. Banner?" Anton asks.

"Nope, thanks. It's not far. I'll walk." And I also don't want anyone clocking me arriving at the main entrance of the Ensign on Fifth!

Maurice knows what to expect. Using my pass key, I enter the staff elevator via the underground parking lot. I knew where all the security cameras were placed, so I had no problem circumventing them by going up the fire escape stairs.

On the floor below the penthouse suite, a security guard is about to bar my way. One flash of my card and he steps back saluting.

At the guest elevator, I swipe my card one last time. The doors slide open onto the penthouse suite floor. I don't expect Emerald to be waiting for me in the entrance hall.

I check my reflection in the mirror and go to the master suite door.

Miss Emerald de Vine is sitting on the edge of the bed waiting for me.

Her mouth drops open like a trap door when she sees me.

"Jesus Christ! I should be paying you! Well, aren't you just the sexiest tall drink of water on a hot summer day!"

She's removed the clothes she arrived in. Her lingerie is a well-known luxury brand. Very expensive and so flimsy it's only good for one or two wears before it has to be chucked out.

Her long slim legs are smooth and suntanned, her feet encased in what can only be described as "fuck me" shoes. In stilettos with five-inch heels and lots of toe cleavage—her toenails are painted red.

Everything about this woman screams "high-class escort." I know she probably thinks she passes as some high society New York lady, but she could not be more wrong.

A few things are off. No upper-class Manhattan matron would be caught dead with those long, fake almond-shaped fingernails.

Emerald's perfume hits me in the face like a punch. Dolce & Gabbana something. Italian. The privileged and wealthy only buy their perfumes in Paris. French, and usually Guerlain.

The elite classes are not big when it comes to supporting brands. They prefer to patronize the same businesses their great-grandparents did. Anything with "House of" or "Maison" in the name is where the stealth wealth drops their cash.

Everything Emerald brought with her is covered in labels and logos. That alone would have her clocked as an escort the moment she walks into an exclusive hotel.

Hair extensions make her bleached blonde hair reach down her back. No Swiss limited edition watch on her wrist. But the final kicker that gives her away are her breasts. They are cartoon-size big.

You can't pass as classy in New York if you base your image on what they think is beautiful in Los Angeles.

"Howdy, Miss de Vine. Thank you for meeting me." I'm laying on my Southern accent real thick. Not because I know the ladies love it, but because I want to cover up my identity.

"Ooh, you're lovely. Oh my God! I wish you were wearing a Stetson or something, but the suit works for me too."

She pats the bed invitingly. "Come on over here, Cowboy, and let's get to know one another."

Shaking my head firmly, I go sit on the couch. Leaning with my arms spread out on the back of the couch on either side, I make it clear from my body language that I want Emerald to keep sitting right where she is.

"Emerald, I didn't ask you to come here to fuck me. I need some information."

Standing up, Emerald struts to the massive tote bag she brought with her. Slowly and seductively, she begins to remove her lingerie. Her breasts look like two large balloons as she removes her bra.

"I'll save my La Perla panties for some other time, then, shall I?" She bats her lashes and gives a little smile. "Don't mind me. Go ahead and ask your questions."

She's completely naked. Bending over with her back to me, she digs deep in her purse for some plain white cotton knickers, giving me an eyeful of her pussy. The hood of her clit is pierced with some dangly bauble made to look like a zipper puller. Cute.

"Tell me more about the yacht cruise you went on ten years ago—the one Kevin Hastings hosted. Here are a few more names you might recognize. Amir, Brent, and a young girl called Forrest."

That makes Emerald stand up and turn around pronto. She looks at me closely, but there is no way she would recognize me. I spent all my time in the media room or the cabin with Ivy.

"How did you—?"

I stop her right there. "I figure five thousand dollars buys me the right to ask the questions, Emerald, not answer them." Sticking my hand in the inner pocket of my jacket, I bring out a stiff white envelope. "I have another five thousand here in cash." Flicking open the flap, I show her the wad. "Please answer."

Pulling a white cotton tank over her breasts, Emerald finally realizes that I'm not here to play games.

"Start at the beginning. Take it from the top."

"Look, I want you to promise me first that I'm not going to get into any trouble. That's why I became a freelancer, you know. I couldn't take the deception anymore."

I indicate for her to continue.

"I worked for Stratford Modeling Agency since I was fifteen. That receptionist, Janet, spotted me in the mall and gave me her card. Told me to come to the agency without my parents if I wanted to make some serious cash. You have to understand, Clint, that is the most exciting thing you can say to a teenager."

I bet it is.

"Julian Stratford put me on his books after I passed the drug test. They knew all the best ways I could get away for the weekend without my parents knowing. They told me it would be easier if I could get one of my friends to join with me."

I see Emerald's eyes dart to the minibar in the corner, but she quickly turns her gaze away from it. "Look, I guessed I wasn't chosen to be a model, but they made it sound so sophisticated and exciting to be a 'paid companion.' Go on a yacht, and chat with rich men who are looking for girlfriends. Spend the rest of your life in complete luxury. I was actually looking forward to it! Flirt with billionaires and get paid fifty thousand? Hell, yeah!"

"What was the catch?" I ask.

Emerald rolls her eyes to the ceiling. "Oh boy, you don't want to know. I was so gullible. It was fifty thousand per fuck. More if you were a virgin. No such thing as a free lunch, hey?"

I nod to show her I'm following.

"They only wanted young girls on the yachts... no, wait. They also wanted famous girls. B-list actresses and real catwalk models. If a girl had booked an advertising campaign or appeared in a movie, she could get up to a million dollars a night."

She sighs. "You would think that fifty thousand dollars would be enough to last me a long time, wouldn't you? But they forced me to go back, and I got hooked on the lifestyle. First-class flights, shopping trips in Milan, luxury hotels, and designer clothing. Then came the drugs and booze. I knew I was being pimped out, but I couldn't say no."

"How did you get out?"

"After I had been fucked every which way until Sunday, they cut me loose. No more blackmail, no more parties. But there was definitely no sign of any billionaire wanting me to be his girl-friend either. They just used me. When I heard what was happening to them, I didn't give a shit, you know. They all deserve it."

This is what I really want to know.

"What was happening to them?"

With her sordid story out of the way, Emerald begins to relax a bit. She looks triumphant.

"Clint, I read your bio. I see that you're a rancher from Texas. You should thank your lucky stars that you're not a billionaire in New York. If you were, you might have reason to be very, very worried."

"Why would I feel the need to be worried if I lived in New York?"

When Emerald tells me, I begin to take her seriously.

Holy shit! I was on one of those fucking yachts! Am I going to be the next East Coast billionaire to be targeted?

# Chapter 32 - Ivy

It looks like it's going to be another long, lonely night for me in my furnished apartment.

Why do I keep thinking about how wonderful it would be to sleep over at Banner's penthouse this evening?

There's no chance of that happening. I have no doubt he's off banging Emerald de Vine somewhere.

Trying so hard to not gnash my teeth, I want to be Zen about it. My suspicions are going to stay under control this time! But having said that, there is no smoke without fire.

I have enough on my mind to be able to block it out. Beautiful Maxine gave me so much information. I can't believe Stratford has been running his scheme for so long!

When I got out of the shower this evening, I went to the full-length mirror and looked at myself sideways. There's still no baby bump, but I want one.

What do I want for supper?

Peanut butter and jelly sandwich? Lemon drizzle pound cake?

The answer comes whizzing into my brain. Cherry clafouti. You want cherry clafouti. Now!

Shit. Why can't baby want normal things from the kitchen cupboards? I don't feel like baking right now.

How about if we have cherries and cream instead? Would you like that?

That is an acceptable substitute.

Smiling to myself as I pat my belly, I take a can of cherries off the shelf and pull the tab on a carton of cream.

The intercom buzzes. Bert is off duty, so it must be the night-shift doorman.

"Miz Woods? Mr. Banner is down here for you."

"Thank you, Juan. Please send Mr. Banner up."

Running to the mirror in the bathroom, I check my face. Are those my eyes alight with happiness I see staring back at me?

Yes. Yippee-yee-ki-yay, yes! Banner is back! He wasn't lying about wanting Emerald's contact details for his buddy!

A surge of some other emotion spreads over me, warming me from my head to my toes.

I think this is what love must feel like.

I'm leaning against the door waiting for him when the elevator slides open.

"You're just in time to eat cherries and cream with me." My smile even feels wide on my face, I'm that happy.

"Why did you leave the penthouse?" Banner wants to know as he comes in, shrugging out of his jacket and hanging it on a hook.

I pretend to be a little girl caught out being naughty. Sticking one finger in my mouth and biting the tip, I flutter my lashes and scuff the floor with my toe. "Sorry, Mr. Banner. I was a bad girl."

That makes him smile. He comes close enough to kiss me. When his mouth lingers on my cheek and then moves to my lips, I know he's here to fuck my brains out. That excites me so much.

"Maybe I should give you a little spank, Ivy Woods."

Rubbing myself against him, I whisper, "Cherries and cream first, 'kay?"

He laughs, following me through the bedroom as he unbuttons his collar and loosens his tie.

"Are those from a can?" he asks, looking at the bowl.

"Mm-huh. But it's what I feel like, so there! Since my appetite went walkabout, I am not such a foodie snob anymore."

Hooking off his socks and pulling off his pants, Banner comes to lie next to me on the bed.

Does he look stunningly sexy in his tight briefs? Yes. Double damn, yes!

He shifts closer and opens his mouth. I give him a spoonful of cherries and cream to eat. It makes him lick his lips like a jungle cat.

"You have cream on your lips, Ivy. You want me to lick it off?"

I can't put the bowl on the end table fast enough!

When our mouths connect, it starts off sweet. A light brush of lips against each other.

"Why do you keep running away from me, Ivy?" he murmurs, his deep voice making my toes curl with delight.

"I guess I'm scared of getting hurt." When Banner and I are like this, it's as if we have an open line of communication where we can be truthful with each other.

"So am I, Ivy," he says. Giving a little growl, he moves his tongue over the sensitive philtrum of my upper lip. "But I trust you to never hurt me. And I want you to know I'll do the same for you."

"Why?" I'm breathless with desire, over-whelmed with rapture as his tongue traces my lips.

"Because I want this fake engagement of ours to get real."

Oh my God....

What did I do to deserve such an amazing man in my life?

He's waiting for me to reply.

"Yes, Banner. That's a hard yes from me."

"You want hard?" Taking my hand, he guides it down to his briefs. He's rock hard, his tumescent penis strains against the confines of the pouch.

Hooking my finger into the waistband, I free his cock. It stands erect and proud, so thick with veins that I know that girth is going to make me feel every inch when he penetrates me.

Scraping my fingernails over his balls, I release his entire package from the briefs. Stroking his shaft and the head of the penis while I kiss him is so thrilling. The power I hold over his passion is undeniable.

I give the shaft of his cock a tight pump with my hand. That really wakes Banner up.

"Whoa, little lady. You better rein this stallion in if you want a nice, long ride."

Even the way he talks can make my pussy melt.

Pulling my hand away, I help him take off his briefs.

"Your turn." Banner looks so gorgeous as he leans on the pillows and watches me undress. I can't wait to get back on that bed.

The sensation when we intertwine our bodies together will never lose its magic. I melt into his arms, surrendering myself to the inevitability of our sexual union. His kisses, his touch arouse me in such a special way.

Banner growls a command, running his fingers through my hair and giving my scalp a small tug. "I still haven't forgotten that you were a naughty little girl to run away from me."

I am so up for some roleplay. The memory of him bending me over and fucking me hard doggy style is still one of my favorite fantasies.

"How do you want to punish me?" I ask, playing along, knowing that our sex games make us both so hot.

His hand slides down my belly and makes slow erotic circles on my mound. "I'm going to make you beg for it, Ivy. If you want this"—grabbing my hand, he places it on his stiff cock—"to fuck you real good, you gotta beg."

Shoot. When he says it, I immediately want him to insert that throbbing erection into my yearning slit.

His kisses get deeper. Then Banner moves his mouth down my body, lapping at my nipples with predatory mouthfuls. I get turned on when his mouth almost devours my breast, sucking the entire nipple, while his dark blue eyes watch my reaction.

"You like that, don't you? Are you ready for my cock now?"

When he says that, his fingers give the hood of my clit a quick rubbing up and down. I can't help it. I squeal with pleasure as my body's excitement level mounts higher.

"Yes, yes! Please fuck me, Banner. I'm begging you."

I can't wait for his long shaft to split my pussy lips wide open. That's all I can think about.

Am I obsessed? Banner's sexual mind games are next level.

Smirking, he shakes his head. "Nah, I want you so wet that you squirt when I stick it in you."

"I'm wet, I'm wet," I promise him. "I'm ready for you. I want you to fuck me now. Please."

Banner inserts one finger inside me. "Mm, you weren't lying. You are dripping wet. Such a good girl. Remember what you promised me?"

Straining my memory, I try to recall. "You want me to tell you I love you when I come?"

"Yes." I'm kinda thrilled that my answer pleases him. I want to please this man so much.

Moving his mouth down my belly while holding my wrists so that I can't control his head, he gives my clit a rough lick. Then he does it again and again, slowly increasing the rhythm. The steady stroke of his tongue on my clit makes me orgasmic.

It gets even better when he pushes two fingers into my slit and begins to slide them in and out of my tight pussy.

I can't help tossing my head from one side of the pillow to the other as the ecstasy mounts inside me.

"Uhh, uh, yes." I urge him to continue because I am so close to coming.

"No." Banner stops. "Not yet."

Now I'm desperate! "Please, Banner. Don't stop. I need to come."

"Promise you'll say it?"

"Yes, I love you. You know I do. Now, fuck me hard. I need to come over that big cock of yours."

He can tell that I'm serious. My eyes almost roll back as he guides himself into me, making sure to rub his shaft against my clit during the long, leisurely penetration.

I start to come spectacularly. My pleasure mounts higher and higher as Banner grinds himself into me, pushing his cock in deep.

My legs are splayed wide as I welcome all of his girth inside me.

We start to come together, but I don't forget what to say—because it's true.

"God, Banner, I love you! I love you so much."

That makes him really pound his cock into me, ramming my pussy as he groans and releases.

"I love you, Ivy."

When he says that, I feel myself get next-level happy. As our rapturous spasms subside, I am totally lost for words.

But the next words that come out of his mouth shock me to my core.

"You want to help me catch a blackmailer, sweetheart?"

# Chapter 33 - Fletcher

Ivy's hair is always so delightfully tangled and mussy after we make love. So when she pushes me off her and sits up, she looks like a mysterious witch about to cast a spell.

Her dark eyes sparkle with interest—and a little bit of petulance too.

"I hope you're not planning on going after your sister's bestie, Banner! Because I've got that under control."

Falling back on the pillows with a lazy sigh, I lace my hands behind my head and look at her.

"I thought you were my sister's bestie?"

Coming to snuggle beside me, Ivy lays her head on my chest. "Not anymore. You were right. Mary-Kay has moved on. The only person we have in common is Daniel. Melanie is the new kid on the block."

"Why would you have to control the two of them? Is my sister's big mouth getting you into trouble?"

I watch as the corners of her mouth tilt up in a smile. "Mary-Kay is being indiscreet, yes. But I know at the bottom of her heart that she loves me. It's got to be hard on her with no outside interests or hobbies."

"Mary-Kay has got a hobby—obsessing over what might go wrong with her elite and privileged lifestyle!"

Giving a shout of laughter, Ivy hugs me. "Don't be mean. You're such a typical older brother, Banner. Now, without further chitchat, tell me about this blackmail scheme. Has it got something to do with Julian Stratford? Because if you're ready to take him on, then so am I!"

At that moment, I know Ivy is not involved. The dangerous scheme targeting men like me was not able to pull Ivy into its wicked web.

She was never caught up in that prostitution ring. The scorn in her voice when she mentions it is undeniable.

Relief washes over me like a waterfall.

Wrapping my arms around her, I hold her close to my heart.

"Fuck, I was so worried that you might have been involved with that shit, Ivy. How did you escape their clutches?"

Turning to lie on her stomach, Ivy thinks hard and then confesses.

"I always wanted success on my own terms. That meant so much more to me than money."

"That's not what I asked." I'm ruthless because I need to know the truth. "Why didn't you take the money the first time you were on the yacht? You fucked me, so, in their eyes, you earned it."

Ivy looks really pissed. Her dark eyebrows pull together into a slanted line. "All you need to know is that I didn't take the money, Banner! I don't have to explain!"

Ivy's moods can be on a hair trigger sometimes. All I can do is shrug. "Fine. Keep your secrets."

Relaxing and beaming a smile, Ivy looks pleased. "Full confession? I hooked up with an old yacht girl, Banner. I didn't tell you, because I was pissed you suspected me of being involved. Her name is Maxine. Poor woman. They black-mailed her to carry on doing it."

"Great minds must think alike, sweetheart." Turning onto my side, I stare at the mass of tangled hair falling down the delicate arch of Ivy's back. I like to twirl the strands between my fingers. "Why the hell do you think I wanted to get into contact with Emerald de Vine?"

Ivy shrieks with girlish outrage as she grabs a pillow to hit me with. "Banner! And there you had me all worried you were going to cheat on me!"

Fending off the playful blows, I laugh. "I had to be sure you were out of their clutches completely, Ivy. I saw those flowers Stratford sent you. I was worried."

A tragic expression creases her brow. "I-I'm sorry, Banner. I should have told you. But everything has been happening so fast—the exposure of us at Sabine, the pregnancy, the illness—I hardly had time to breathe."

I run the tip of my finger down her spine. It makes Ivy relax. She stretches like a cat, almost purring as she touches my face.

Cupping her hand around my jaw, she says, "Why are you so good to me, Banner? I've been such a mess since we hooked up."

God, this woman is so sweet when she's not trying to pretend she has all the answers. Falling in love with her is as easy as tumbling down stairs in the dark.

"Truth to tell, angel, I've been looking to fall in love with you for ten years." I can't help giving her neck a quick nuzzle. "Blame it on that red bikini of yours. I was smitten from the start."

We're on the brink of building up steam for more sex, but Ivy puts the brakes on it.

"Hang on. Don't distract me. I don't know why Stratford is trying to stay in contact with me, Banner. Do you?"

I explain what Emerald told me about women who have appeared in movies or advertisements. "They're worth more on the yacht scene. I think Julian Stratford was hoping you would be open to having a 'million dollar a night' bang with one of his wannabe starfucker patrons."

Ivy scowls. The thought of earning a million dollars holds no appeal for her.

"What a parasite that man is! But shouldn't we just walk away from it? I'd rather not poke the bear."

That's not an option for me. I've never been the sort of man to walk away from any kind of confrontation. I've had business associates who tried to maneuver me into a corner before and it never ended well for them.

"If it were up to me, sweetheart, I'd prefer to know where that film footage of us is. We met on a yacht. They obviously filmed us. We need that back."

"You want me to find some way to leverage the blackmailers?" Ivy says it before I can suggest it.

Stroking her beautiful hair, I shake my head. "I don't know. It's not right. You're pregnant."

The full force of what we are planning dawns on Ivy.

"Shit, do you think they're dangerous?"

Her hands move down to her belly in a protective gesture.

"This is not the mafia we're dealing with here, Ivy," I explain. "It's one very manipulative bastard who has found a genius way to get wealthy men to do what he wants."

"Julian Stratford? But he's a creep. Not some financial mastermind."

"It's definitely not Stratford. We need to get hold of the puppet master."

Getting up, I go fetch my phone, then I lie next to Ivy and share my screen with her.

"Check this out. Three publicly traded companies—whose CEOs happen to be billionaires—have had their stocks shorted before a sharp drop in price. That's insider trading. And these two private companies—they both just agreed to be sold to a European consortium. Why? The companies had over five billion in liquid assets. There was no need for them to sell."

Ivy pretends to be falling asleep, making little snoring noises as she collapses.

I can't help it. I have to laugh.

"You know what? You haven't changed a bit."

Ivy pretends to wake up. "What's that you're saying?

I lean in to kiss her. "The stock market bored you when I first met you, Ivy. I remember that much. But I promise you these sales are suspicious."

"So, what do you think we should do?" Ivy looks doubtful, but I can see her mind is made up.

"We are not going to do anything." Snaking my arm around Ivy's waist, I give it a squeeze. "I'm going to ask Emerald to spring the honey trap for me. She's become a real social media star since the yacht scene cut her loose. I'll use her as bait."

Pushing herself away from me, Ivy huffs. "If you think for one goddamn moment that I'm going to allow you to hook up with bloody Emerald de Vine again, Banner, you've got rocks in your head!"

God, I should have known this would happen. Ivy can be really hard to control when she gets a bee in her bonnet.

"Listen, sweetheart. There's no way, okay? Your yacht girl days are over!"

Flinging herself off the bed, Ivy goes on the warpath!

"I never was a yacht girl! Get that through your thick head! Like every single one of the poor young girls this shit happened to, I was conned. Got that?"

Giving the "I surrender" sign with my arms, I try calming her down.

"Sure. You don't need to remind me. But that's why I want to get this guy so bad. Pimping out girls who want to be models is the lowest of the low."

From the way Ivy looks at me, I can see the wheels turning in her head. "Banner, I have an idea."

"Hit me," I tell her, trying my best to look open-minded. But whenever I think about Ivy putting herself at risk with the kind of men who bribe and blackmail young girls into sleeping with them, I want to yell with frustration.

"I'm going to throw Clifford Braxton a bone. I'm going to let him think I broke up with you, Banner. And I'm going to do it in the most public way possible."

Groaning, I shut out the view by draping my arm over my face. "Gah! Ivy, why? We just got rid of the damn guy."

She pulls my arm away and grins at me. "We're going to have a fight in public, Banner. And I'm going to call you all the blue names under the sun—including that I wish I had never agreed to our fake engagement!"

"Well, that's definitely going to get Clifford sniffing around. But I don't see the point."

Ivy announces triumphantly, "Because we want him to report it. And that means Julian Stratford will hear about it."

"So?" I'm confused as to why Ivy wants Clifford Braxton, of all people, to be proven right. "Our fake engagement is our only protection against you being called a sellout for your five-star review of Sabine!"

"I no longer care about being called a sellout, Banner. All I care about is getting justice for every girl who has been forced to have sex on a yacht. No amount of money can help a woman heal from that kind of abuse."

I wait for the hammer to fall. I know Ivy is not going to let this slide.

"And once Stratford thinks you and I are no longer together, I'm going to ask to be put back onto his books. I'm going to ask him to hook me up with a starfucker billionaire, and I'm going to take them all down!"

This is what I want too, but I never wanted to involve my pregnant girlfriend in all this!

"Ivy." It's time for me to lay down the law. "There is no way I am going to allow this. You're pregnant. You're precious. We don't know what's waiting for you on the other side."

"Either you're with me or you're not, Banner. What's it going to be?"

# Chapter 34 - Ivy

Usually, I can get Banner to agree to whatever I want, but my pregnancy doesn't make it easy this time. I get the feeling Banner knows he's the baby daddy. Why don't I just tell him?

Because Mary-Kay's new bestie, Melanie, might muddy the waters by telling a rag news reporter. And the last thing I need right now is Mary-Kay going off the deep end thinking she's been cut out of Banner's will.

Honestly, even seeing it from a neutral perspective, my best friend is starting to look like a bit of a parasite for her long-suffering older brother!

And so I keep my secret for now as my lover and I plot how to take down the person responsible for ruining so many young girls' lives....

*** 

Banner had to go overseas for more property deals, so I've had three weeks to prepare for our final showdown.

Meg has booked a tasting menu evening at the Bon Cuisine office. A select invite-only occasion. Of course, Clifford Braxton is on that list. My latest article—"Time to Get Rid of the Food Police"—has gone viral on the Bon Cuisine website.

Meg is so happy. "It's about time someone had the guts to say we should eat what we like without someone telling us we're doing it wrong, Holly! Where do you get your fabulous ideas?"

"I find it fascinating how potatoes are packed full of nutrients, but somehow it never appears on any essential fruit and vegetable list, Meg. When I dug a little deeper, I found out that no one recommends them because potatoes are cheap!"

Potatoes are all I have been craving to eat for the last few weeks. When I told Dr. Renee I was worried about it, she told me how nutritious potatoes are. Packed full of Vitamin C and Iron. After learning that, the article pretty much wrote itself.

Meg laughs. "Yep. Food and special diet snobs are the worst. What are you wearing to the tasting menu tonight?"

"LBD, of course. And you?"

"Same!" Meg chuckles. "But I'll dress it up with some accessories. The editor of Bon Mode is going to be there, but I have two school-age kids at home, so I have an excuse."

It's gotta be all about the showdown tonight!

Banner says he'll meet me at the event. I love that about him. He gets so involved in his work that he prioritizes it above everything else. He's driven, just like me.

Sami is waiting for me in the lobby while Bert keeps an anxious eye out for any cop looking to issue a ticket for a traffic violation!

When we pull up outside the huge publishing house building twenty minutes later, Banner is waiting for me on the steps.

His handsome face and amazing physique tug on my heartstrings. It's been three weeks. All I want to do is roll into bed with him and show off how big my breasts have gotten.

But I don't. There's a ball that has to be set in motion, and that's not going to happen unless Banner and I break up in the most public way possible.

Running the last few yards, I throw myself into his open arms. He presses his mouth against mine after checking I'm not wearing lipstick he might ruin with a kiss. It's small gestures like that that make me appreciate this wonderful man.

"You ready?" His voice is a deep growl. He gets so steamy when we haven't had sex for a long while. I can tell from the way he bends my body towards him to connect with the growing tumescence in his crotch that he is horny as hell after our separation.

"I was born ready," I tell him playfully, giving the front of his pants a teasing squeeze after checking that no one is watching.

We pose for the photogs together. "Who are you wearing, Holly?"

Shit. I hate it when my food world clashes with the world of fashion.

"Dior. And I bought it myself."

No one sponsors me! I wear what I want because my body is not an advertising board for sale.

This dress means a lot to me. I bought it while shopping with Banner in Paris—so I suppose he was the one who bought it for me, but I don't want to get into that here.

When they ask Banner who made his tuxedo, all the photogs get as a reply is "fuck off." That makes me giggle.

"This is for my work, darling," I say, giving his arm a little pinch, "try to play nice."

"I just want to get this over with," Banner sounds bitter. "I get mad when I think of us having to fake fight with each other. And they are so silly asking me such a personal question. As if I want a bunch of wannabes swamping my London tailor with orders."

"I doubt anyone could afford your tailor," I say in a reasonable voice. "Look, Banner. There's Clifford."

"I see him," he mutters, waving away a plate of canapes. "Sleazy weasel. If he ever wants to set foot inside one of my establishments again, he better cough up the name of that grifter who took pics of us together at Sabine."

I can sense that Banner is not liking this one bit! The man hates having to rub shoulders with the rich and famous, especially knowing what they are all going to be witnessing soon.

"Let's get this started before Meg notices me not eating any food, Banner," I say under my breath.

We've talked about how to do this every day over the phone, but it's still going to hurt me emotionally. Isn't it strange how invested I am in my relationship looking successful in public? I guess it's because my image has gone from being single to being in a couple—and my image is my brand.

"Right." Banner shakes his head and then gets down to business. "I love you, Ivy. See you later."

Grabbing a fruit juice off the tray from one of the servers, I move over to Clifford with a purposeful stride.

Lifting my glass in a toast, I butt into his conversation. "Good evening, Mr. Braxton. Maybe you should put your presence here this evening to good use, and apologize?"

Clifford gets outraged. "Excuse me? I was having a private conversation here!"

"Th-that's okay, Clifford." The head of features at Bon Mode backs away from the brewing argument she can sense is going to happen. "I'll catch up with you later."

Clifford Braxton and I are left alone, facing off against each other.

"Which black market did you buy your invite from, Cliffy?" I make sure to use a real bitchy tone of voice. "This evening is only meant to be for people who are still relevant in the world of fine dining."

"H-how dare you?!" Clifford is deeply hurt by my cutting remark. "I was critiquing restaurants before you were born!"

Banner comes to stand next to me. "Is this guy bothering you, Holly?"

Clifford knows he's outgunned. He steps back, holding his hands out. "Leave me alone—both of you."

Banner has loosened his collar. The ends of his bow tie are hanging down. Looming over Clifford, he scowls like a thunderstorm. "It's because of you that I had to say I was engaged to this bitch, Braxton!"

Everyone is not even bothering to pretend they're not listening anymore. Even the Bon Mode editor is gawking at our toxic threesome.

"I knew it!" Clifford is too happy to be scared anymore. "I knew your engagement was fake!

Billionaires don't propose to women after only one night in Vegas!"

"Shut up!" Banner snarls. "You better give me the name of that photographer if you don't want to get punched in the face."

His acting is really good! Time for me to step in when Banner raises his fist. Clifford screams and flinches as I hold back Banner's arm.

"Typical!" I say in a really scornful voice. "You think you can solve everything with violence! This is why I'm glad our engagement is only fake. You can be a real bully sometimes, Mr. Banner!"

A hiss of whispers breaks out in the crowd.

Meg hurries over. "Holly, is everything okay here?"

I pretend to be hysterical. "It's Fletcher. He's ruined everything. I never wanted to be engaged, especially with a tasteless boor like him."

"Well, you don't have to pretend anymore, sweetheart!" Banner backs off, heading for the nearest exit. "I'm calling a timeout on this little farce of ours. Goodbye forever!"

The crowd parts to let him through. I act all relieved. "Good riddance to bad rubbish, Meg. Let him go. We pretended to be engaged to get Clifford Braxton off my back. Please excuse me. Suddenly, I'm not in the mood for a tasting menu."

I hurry out, holding a handkerchief over my face to hide my laughter. God, but that was actually quite fun.

And the truth will set you free.

Taking out my phone, I send a text to Meg. Sorry, dearest. I couldn't take it anymore. Please stay with the guests and tell them I'm fine. Speak soon and thank you, Holly.

Sami is waiting for me by the town car, but I can tell that something is not right. When Sami opens the door for me, I see the back of the car is empty...

"Where's Banner?" I want to know.

Sami shakes his head. "Mr. Banner has gone, Miss Ivy."

I feel cold. Did I say something wrong? Has Banner left for good?

# Chapter 35 - Ivy

My phone buzzes as I stand dithering by the car.

"Banner?"

"Hey, honey. And the Oscar goes to... did we do good?"

"Where are you? I'm at the car."

"Yeah, I thought it was best if we didn't leave together. See you back at my apartment. The car windows are blacked out and only residents can access the underground parking. Sami has a security card for you."

It's been three weeks. I know exactly what's going to happen when Banner and I are alone in the apartment together. Mm, my mind goes into overdrive with all the crazy stuff I want to do with him in bed.

"See you in a bit."

Sami smiles as he gets behind the wheel. "Home?"

Returning his smile, I say, "Yes. Home."

***

A few candles are lit in the living area when I step inside.

"Banner?" Putting my evening purse on the table and kicking off my black Louboutin stilettos, I go around the room pinching out the candles. "You in the bedroom?"

He's there, unpacking his valise and hanging clothes in the closet. "You found me. Do you think it'll work?"

I give him a small push with my hand. "Thanks for leaving me hanging by the car! I got worried you were genuinely pissed off!"

He grins. "And now you have that out of your system, you can answer my question."

His cocky attitude always manages to make me smile. "I bet they can't wait for the event to end so that they can all go back home and blog about it."

"I don't think they'll even wait that long. Check your feed. I bet a few of them have gone and tweeted what happened from the inside of a Bon Cuisine toilet cubicle already!"

Slumping down on the massive king-size bed, I watch Banner unpack.

"Do you think I should go to Stratford tomorrow? Will it have been long enough for him to pick up what happened on the grapevine?"

When I say it, I see Banner's body language change on a dime. He goes from relaxed to uptight in an instant.

"Ivy, please can we get Emerald to do it?" After easily reaching up to the luggage storage at the top of the closet to stow the valise, Banner comes to sit next to me. "So many things could go wrong, sweetheart. Please listen to me."

Giving the middle of his rock-hard chest a small tap with my finger, I tease him. "Hey, Mr. Marine, you're the one with all the right moves when it comes to taking out the bad guys. Once I've found out where he keeps the videos, I'll get out of there ASAP. The rest is up to you."

He submits to my decision—for now. Taking my hand, he kisses the top. "You look like an extra sexy suntanned Audrey Hepburn in that dress, Ivy. But you'll look even better without it."

All that crazy stuff I wanted to do to Banner in bed? I take it back. He's in a very romantic mood as he helps me pull the zipper of my dress down.

Time for us to make real love. Sometimes we don't need all the firecrackers and crazy tricks to turn us on.

Stepping out of the dress and leaving it heaped in a puddle on the Persian carpet, I lie down on the bed, waiting with bated breath.

He gazes at me enraptured. My skin glows in the light from the two Trudon candles I left burning in the bathroom en suite, making me look like a golden statue.

"I never want us to fight like that again, Ivy." Banner seems in a thoughtful mood as he unbuttons his shirt while undressing. "Argue? Yes. Shout? Sure. But I don't want us to walk out on one another again."

Now, I'm curious.

"But we've stormed out on each other before, Banner. It's no biggie."

Sitting next to me, he strokes my belly. "My parents never raised their voices in front of Mary-Kay and me. It wasn't part of their parenting style. I always felt loved and secure at home because of that."

A warmth floods through me. "Are you saying you want the baby to feel the same way?"

Leaning forward, Banner kisses me. "Can you doubt it?"

No. All my doubts fly away as he takes me in his arms. Banner has a way of making me trust him with my life, and with my baby's life.

His kisses get more passionate. We've been apart for nearly a month and our bodies have a lot of catching up to do.

My hands flutter over the bulges of his muscles, caressing the smoothness of his skin against the tautness of the flexed tendons. I thrill when I feel his arousal pressing against me, knowing that I, only I, have the power to make him rampant.

Banner is my secret sauce and I am his relish. He almost salivates as he gets ready to go down on me, the delicious scent and special taste I keep hidden between the plump folds of my pussy can drive him wild.

The way his tongue teases my clit makes the pleasure mount higher inside me. Banner finds it so tantalizing when he sees how wet I get. When I writhe, arching my back to push his mouth deeper, he does what I want with a satisfied smile.

My hands fumble for his thick shaft, urgently wanting to repay the favor, but he holds me off. He wants it to last longer and I can sense that he's close to coming hard and fast.

Lying side by side, I stick his cock between my thighs and rub my clit against his long length.

We're face-to-face and heart-to-heart. I never knew love could be this good.

Delicious kiss follows delicious kiss as the excitement builds. Banner knows exactly what to do when I roll onto my back, spreading my thighs wide.

Heaven is when he slides into me. Paradise is feeling his thrust.

All I can do is lie back and let the orgasm wash over me like a tidal wave of lust. I feel my limbs go weak as the blood pulses and intensifies in my throbbing lovebud.

The air whooshes out of me when I realize I've been holding my breath, trying to get that ecstatic peak to last longer—which it always does. Because Banner knows exactly how to drive his cock deep inside me to keep it going, pressing himself against my clit and letting me grind myself to a higher peak.

Pushing him off me, I catch my breath. It feels like I've run the equivalent of a sexual marathon.

"I have never been fucked so good in my life before, Banner!" I'm panting, almost driven crazy by the power of my climax. "How did you learn to fuck to perfection like that?"

He's all mellow after coming just as hard. "I don't kiss and tell," he murmurs.

Wrapping my arms around him, I stroke his chest. "Come on. Confess. Did you watch a tutorial? A sexy online lesson on how to make a woman scream with pleasure?"

"Okay, you naughty minx. But I'm only telling you so you don't fret yourself over it. My first lover was my mom's best friend. She was a real high-society dame. Randy as a kitten and very experienced. I stayed with her for a long while. It ain't easy finding a constant lover while serving in the Corps."

"Tickle me pink, Banner!" I give his arm a small pinch. "I didn't have you down as a boy toy!"

He grins. "Hell, I was more of a power tool—definitely not tame enough to be a boy toy. A young man needs ease and convenience when it comes to sex, and that's what she gave me. I never knew how much of a challenge a woman could be until I met you."

"Am I a challenge?" Moving my mouth over his nipple, I give it a tiny lick.

"You, Miss Holly Forrest, are like my own personal game show!"

Settling back against the pillows, Banner relaxes and continues. "That lady gave me a taste of how lovely sex can be with a classy woman. That's my thing—I'm attracted to classy women. There's no shortage of those in the circles I move in."

My stomach gives a worried flip. "I wasn't a classy woman when we first met, Banner. I was on a yacht!"

"You're getting attraction confused with love, Ivy." Banner pulls me closer, holding me tight in his strong arms. "Right from the start, you fascinated me. You had the confidence and sophistication of someone far older. I guess that came from you leaving home at such a young age, but the way you handled yourself on the yacht showed you had a lot of class too. Money can't buy class, and it couldn't buy you either."

"That," I say, snuggling against him and closing my eyes in bliss, "is the nicest thing a man has ever said to me."

***

We go our separate ways in the morning. I ordered some sexy clothes from one of the top boutiques to be delivered to the apartment and Banner has to go to work. I want to make a good impression when I go to Stratford's, so the clothes are jaw-droppingly alluring.

He watches me put the clothes on, his expression disapproving. "I don't know if I'm doing the right thing by letting you go through with this, Ivy."

Shooing him out the door, I reassure him. "Go! I'll be fine. I'll keep your number on speed dial if I need you, 'kay?"

Exiting through the underground parking lot, I wobble down the street in my sky-high platform shoes. I chose platform wedge shoes instead of my usual stilettos because I want to show off the red varnish on my toenails.

My jeans are extra tight but not in a tailored way. I would struggle to put anything inside the pockets; I can't even insert a finger in there.

My peasant blouse is off the shoulder and made from semi-transparent cotton. Needless to say, I'm not wearing a bra.

I can remember the way to Stratford's so well. Mary-Kay and I were so young and gullible. Why were we so trusting when a strange man suggested we take blood tests and go on a yacht?

Maybe it was because no one had warned us not to. Well, I want to warn as many young girls as I can after this! Julian Stratford's pimping days are over!

Janet the receptionist doesn't recognize me when I push through the doors. I'm acting all super confident, like those starlets I've seen on reality TV. My long, black hair swings down to my waist and my makeup is immaculate.

"Hi there. Is it possible to see Julian, please? I know he's a very busy man, so please tell him Holly Forrest is here to see him."

Janet looks shocked when I say my name. She pushes a silent alarm and a burly security troll comes out of a side door. "Is this person being a problem, Miz O'Reilly?"

I store away Janet's surname into my memory and then act all shocked. "Listen, I'm not here to cause a problem! In fact, quite the opposite. Julian has been very kind to me in the past, but I'm not here to thank him for the flowers. I want to…."

Lowering my voice because two young girls are waiting in the reception room. "I want to earn some serious cash if you know what I mean."

After some back and forth on the phone while the security guard loiters around me, Julian comes to the door and beckons me in. "But you have to let Janet search you for wires first—and check your bag!"

Paranoid much? Jeez! "Sure, Julian. After all the shit that's been happening to you, who can blame you for taking precautions?"

With the search over, Julian begrudgingly allows me into his office and closes the door.

"You've caused a hell of a lot of problems for me, Holly, but I heard online that you managed to get rid of one of them last night."

Julian goes to sit behind his desk.

"You can say that again, darling!" I huff and pout, folding my arms and standing on one foot so that my cleavage and ass look sensational. "But I heard you're the best man for what I want to do next."

"And what is that, Holly?" I can tell that Julian is mellowing as he looks at me standing there.

"That fucking Fletcher Banner thought he owned me! I had to pretend we were engaged to get Clifford Braxton off my back. Braxton caught me accepting a bribe for rating Sabine five stars—it was the only way we could get the old dude off our backs."

"A fake engagement? That's a genius solution," Julian agrees. "But are you sure Banner has fucked off forever?"

"He's a meathead," I say, using my most scornful voice. "He thought he owned me. Thank fuck it's over. But I know one way to punish Fletcher for calling me a bitch.

A greedy gleam comes into Julian's eyes.

"I heard men are paying large for spending the night with someone famous, Julian. I am considered to be one of the top five restaurant critics in the world. I was rated in the Top Three Bachelorettes in New York. How much would that be worth to the lucky man who wants some of this?"

I let my fingers drag lightly over my neck, breasts, and belly, a cute smirk on my face.

Swallowing hard, Julian Stratford writes a number down on paper and pushes it across the desk towards me.

Seven figures.

Giving him a sexy smile, I write my phone number on the paper and push it back across the desk.

"You have a deal. Call me."

# Chapter 36 - Ivy

Bert calls me on the intercom. He sounds pan-icked.

"Er… Miz Woods. Your… I mean, Mr. Banner is here to see you."

From the doubt in his voice, I can tell that Bert has heard the news of Banner and me breaking up. Quite frankly, I'm shocked at how fast the news spread!

When I woke up this morning, I had a text mes-sage waiting for me from Mary-Kay.

Thank you, Ivy darling. I knew you'd put Daniel's needs above my creepy brother's. Love MK.

The message makes me roll my eyes just a little bit. I just bet you're grateful, old friend. It's easy to have that kind of mindset when the only ambition you've ever had is to siphon money off Banner.

"Let him up, Bert." I don't need to try and sound upbeat. I just am. It's the same kind of feeling someone has when the end goal is in sight.

I can't say I haven't fantasized about how Banner and I are going to punish the mastermind behind this yacht scam. I know Banner will have to kick the man's ass severely to get him to tell us where the USBs with the video footage are kept. As for me, I want to punch the man so hard for all the dreadful things he did to those young girls.

There was something about the helpless way Maxine accepted her pathway in life that got my blood boiling. And meanwhile, the man behind the curtain gets away with everything scot-free.

Banner sees me waiting for him at the door as he stomps down the corridor, a dark scowl on his face.

"I got your message" are the first words out of his mouth when he comes in and shuts the door. This man is such a force of nature. Tall enough to make me crane my neck and muscular enough to make an ordinary man do a double take.

And let's not forget the handsome. Oh, so wonderfully handsome. But when I try wrapping my arms around his waist, he moves away from me with an impatient gesture.

"What's wrong?" I'm kinda baffled at the blazing rage coming off him. "I told the truth in the text. Julian wants me to meet him at the marina. The same one as last time. What's not to like about that plan?"

Banner lets me have it. "If there's even a one percent chance the baby is mine, Ivy, I can't risk you getting on that yacht."

Running his fingers through his hair, Banner grips it into clumps, which makes the ends stand up and then fall.

I laugh. I can't help it. Is he trying to get me to tell him he's the baby daddy? Dr. Renee says I can tell the father next week if I want to. I'll be three months pregnant then, according to the scan she gave me, and well into the safe zone.

Even my severe morning sickness symptoms are starting to calm down. I'm in love with my pregnancy and can't wait to see how it progresses.

The last thing I need is Banner's bossy boots business ruining my serenity!

"Chill out. Nothing bad can happen. We've got it covered."

Banner starts to pace up and down. "I keep going over and over everything in my mind, Ivy, but we can't be sure. When that yacht leaves US waters, you're on your own."

Keeping the image of Maxine's tears in my thoughts, I stand firm. "I know what I'm doing, Banner. Do you think I would do anything to jeopardize Baby?"

Slumping down on the couch, Banner heaves a heavy sigh. "I can't condone this. It's crazy. And I bet those women you're worried about won't even think to thank you."

Sitting next to him, I take his hand. "It's simple. I get on the yacht. I'll text you how many crew there are, how many yacht girls, and how many male guests. You fly your helicopter and land, same as last time. I will show you who the host is. We force him to tell us who installed the cameras. And then we tell the girls and guests about the scam."

Banner shoots me a look. "I don't think it's going to be that easy, sweetheart. It never is. Murphy's Law. If something can go wrong, it will go wrong. If someone's gone to the trouble of making their trades through an offshore company, it makes me think they might be one step ahead."

Giving his shoulder a squeeze, I stroke his leg to comfort him. "You're overthinking it. This is some rich pervert who gets his kicks from sex and power. And who happens to make money from it at the same time. I'm taking that tracking kit you gave me—there is no way you will lose track of me so long as I have it—I promise."

Banner makes a gesture as if he's pushing me away. "You don't want to listen, Ivy." Standing up abruptly, he strides to the door. "I pray you do what's right for us and Baby, Ivy. Don't get on that yacht tomorrow."

And then he's gone! Jumping up, I run after him, catching him in the corridor on the way to the elevator.

"Wait! Banner, you'll still read the text when I send it tomorrow, won't you? You'll still land the helicopter?"

I need this to happen. For me, for Maxine, and for all the other poor young girls out there who were dragged into a life they never wanted to live.

For one moment, I think that Banner might punch the wall. His hands are bunched into two huge fists. "Yes, damn it! I would never leave you hanging. But I hope you don't go."

And then he's gone.

***

For some strange reason, my hands are shaking when I pay the driver who drops me off at the marina. I am totally bugging.

It's like there are two of me and they are both trying to get me to listen.

Think of the baby. Don't make this your fight. Let Banner sort it out.

Do this for Maxine, for all those girls who were forced to do things they hated. Do this for revenge.

"Revenge."

"What was that, Miss?" The driver looks startled as he pulls the pay portal back in the car.

Giving a nervous laugh, I pretend I never said it. "I was just thinking about the next Marvel movie. Don't worry."

I want the puppet master to know that he messed with the wrong girl ten years ago. I want to say that to his face when Banner finally tracks him down.

Giving Julian Stratford a merry wave, I go join him on the jetty.

"Hey, what are you doing here? Coming to check that I haven't changed my mind?"

Julian chuckles. "Well, you'd be surprised at how many women make up with their boyfriends at the last moment and then don't show."

Don't you mean girls, not women, you complete and utter waste of space?

That's what I want to say, but instead, I continue smiling. "I'm glad you're here actually. I want to straighten a few things out. I want the money transferred to my account the second I get on the boat. I don't want payment withheld on a technicality."

Julian nods, not saying anything because he hasn't checked my purse or body for wires. He lifts one eyebrow to let me know he would like more details.

"And by technicality, I mean kinky shit. I'm here for some lovely, refreshing vanilla sex with an experienced gentleman. That's it." If I don't lay down a few rules, I won't sound authentic, that much I know.

Julian nods again. I know why they are agreeing to my list of demands. They want to get video footage of me having sex with a man and then use it to blackmail me into deeper waters.

Satisfied, I look around. "By the way, where is the yacht? Are we going out on Kevin's boat again?"

Banner found out that his old friend, Kevin Hastings, leased the yacht he used to host the party ten years ago. And, the company Kevin leased it from is one of the offshore entities making stock trades with insider information.

It's one big cluster fuck of double-dealing.

This time, Julian shakes his head. "We're taking you out to international waters—the boss enjoys doing coke, you know. And he doesn't like having to look over his shoulder when he does it."

I open my mouth to say "That's not what I asked," but quickly close it again. I'm scared of sounding too nosy or suspicious.

Julian's phone buzzes. He reads the text. "They're here. Follow me."

I'm torn. I really, really don't want to follow this man. But I'm in too deep now to change my mind. So, I follow Julian Stratford down the jetty.

Suddenly, I remember how it went down last time. The yacht was too long to fit inside the marina, so all the yacht girls were transported there on a speedboat. Julian steps aside, pointing to the speedboat roped to the dock piling.

The driver is male, middle-aged, with an expressionless face. I guess if he's Julian's full-time boat driver, he must have seen a few things in his time. I hesitate. It would be so easy for him to take me down the Hudson and throw me overboard.

"I-I'm not too good with speedboats." I try making an excuse. "Blame it on all those fishing trips I had to make with my dad up north—"

"The yacht's anchored at the West Bank Lighthouse. You'll board there. Then you sail out past the New York, New Jersey Bight, Ma'am," the speedboat driver says. "I'll go slow so the prow doesn't bounce against the waves so bad."

He sounds normal! Not like a perv with a secret agenda at all! "Th-thank you." Taking hold of the hand he's holding out to me, I step onto the boat. "I'm a bit nervous."

Julian Stratford smirks. "No need to be nervous, Holly. You're making one man very happy by doing this. Have fun."

He waves goodbye as the boat chugs away from the dock. I don't smile. I pray the next time I see him, Julian Stratford will be in handcuffs.

My thoughts are in turmoil as the boat prow smacks against the swelling sea. We haven't gone more than one or two miles tops when the driver turns to me, shouting over the noise of the engine.

"Captain's orders are for me to put your purse into a mesh bag, Ma'am."

My nerves peep through again. "Is... is that in case we accidentally flip the boat over?"

The man smiles reassuringly. "There's no chance of that. I promise. But phones can be tracked, so the captain insists every guest's belongings are stowed inside a transmitter blocker bag. Don't worry. You'll get it back when we return to the marina."

Shit. Shit! "What are you saying? You think I'm some fucking double-oh-seven spy? Don't make me laugh. And besides, there is no way I'm leaving my makeup purse behind."

The driver is adamant. "There're lotions and makeup on the yacht, Ma'am."

Double shit! I know that's true. I remember it from last time. The yacht was packed with Bulgari and La Mer stuff.

"And my clothes? I have personal items of clothing in here. And my skin is delicate. I can't be slapping any old shit on it."

I know it sounds like I'm stalling, but I'm hoping it just sounds like I'm some uptight princess with an attitude.

The man holds a large mesh pouch and waits for me to put my stuff in it. "Either you bag your stuff, Ma'am," he insists, "or we turn around and go back."

But I've come so far! I can't give up now.

"Fine!" I make the fateful decision to leave my phone—my lifeline back to Banner—in the bag. "Fine! But don't you dare lose my personal belongings."

The man watches as I load everything into the wire mesh pouch, an item specially made to stop airwave signals from getting in or out.

The wind and dry sea air have already started to make my lips crack. Frantically, and before the man can zip the pouch shut, I pull a lip balm out of my purse. "Can I bring this at least? For the boat trip? My lips are drying out."

Holding out his hand, the man waits for me to put my pot of lip balm into it. He pulls out a magnetic wand and runs it over and around the pot. Then he opens it up and sticks his finger in the balm! It comes up clean, so he passes it back to me.

I am pissed. Seriously pissed. "Satisfied?" I ask with a scornful hiss.

"Yep." The man shrugs. "You'll find a red bikini below deck. Put it on and then bring the rest of your clothes to the top deck when you're finished."

Someone was paying attention! Someone knows I was given a red bikini last time I did this! There's a narrow mirror inside one of the built-in cupboards below deck. I look at my body in the identical bikini to the one I wore last time.

I am so far and away from that silly girl I was back then: belligerent, sassy, and oh-so scared.

Banner saved me from myself then. Can he save me now? I might have mellowed and gotten some street smarts since the last time I was a yacht girl, but my body tells me I'm three months pregnant. There's no running away from the fact.

Taking a deep breath, I slide the little pot of lip balm into the panty lining in the bottom half of my bikini. At least my lips won't get dry!

The man shouts. "Here we are. Do you need help going on board?" Tossing my head, I give my best impression of a pissed princess as I ignore the hand he's holding out to me.

I wrap my arms around myself as the sea breeze nips my skin. Ignoring the driver, I step carefully up the rope ladder unassisted as the speedboat bumps against the side of the yacht.

Two men are standing on deck to help me clamber aboard.

I gasp when I recognize one of the men.

"What the fuck are you doing here?"

# Chapter 37 - Fletcher

For the first time in my life, I look away from something bad when it happens instead of looking towards it. I'm hoping and praying that it's not true.

It has to be a glitch. When I've convinced myself that's what happened, only then do I open my eyes again.

I hardly recognize the agonized shout that comes out of my mouth when the truth hits me in the face. But I can no longer deny it.

Ivy's phone has gone dead.

My marine training kicks in and my body gets ready for action. I'm breathing slowly through my nostrils and holding the oxygen-rich air in my lungs as if I'm gearing up for a deep dive.

I was tracking the phone's global positioning, exactly as we agreed. But the signal has gone. As if the phone—and Ivy—never existed.

When the red mist disappears from my eyes, I notice the skin on my knuckles is broken and bleeding. I must have punched the wall.

For whatever reason, Ivy is pretending I am not the father of our baby. But she's not fooling anyone.

And now I have to go get my new family back.

There's a number I have on speed dial I keep for emergencies.

It gets answered on the first ring. "Yep." Short and to the point, with no preamble.

"Curtin. Meet me at the south pier."

"Helicopter or boat?" Curtin wastes no time asking how I'm doing. There's no time for that.

"Copter to get there and speedboat from the pier. Bring radar tracking and GPS. And weaponry—don't forget explosives."

The phone disconnects. That tells me Curtin has heard me and understands our mission para-meters.

There's no time to waste. I strip down to my underwear and pull on cargo pants and one of those tight cotton khaki T-shirts that get full of holes after only a few spins in the wash cycle.

I have to be able to pass as a sports fisherman or even some hot guy on his way to Fire Island. I need to get as close as I can to the yacht before someone raises the alarm bells.

Only stopping to grab a kit bag from the en-trance hall, I head for the rooftop.

I knew something would go wrong! Why didn't I pump the brakes before Ivy became obsessed with her crazy scheme?

Fifteen minutes later, I'm bumping fists with Curtin. He's already set up the location system to work from Ivy's last coordinates.

"She went dark here," he says, tapping the screen, "so I've brought up a live feed of every vessel within the perimeter."

"Mmf," I grunt. "They'll be heading out to international waters so everyone can let their freak flag fly."

Curtin adapts the perimeter's scope to take that into account. Glancing up at me, he says, "Gun the engine, Banner. Head for her last known coordinates. I'll start sifting through all the vessels that are visible via the satellite feed."

The boat lurches forward as I push the throttle to the max. My sunglasses hide the vicious hunter instinct in my eyes.

We are twenty minutes from the pier when I notice a speed boat heading in the opposite direction towards the pier, not away from it....

It catches my eye, and not just because I'm suspicious of everyone. Single guy. Middle-aged. No sign of watersports or fishing equipment on deck.

There's something off about him. He's not wearing one of those jaunty captain hats most guys his age favor.

I've seen enough of those middle-aged men swabbing the decks of their expensive cruise boats to know that this guy isn't one of them. No jacket, no hat to hold his toupee, or new hair plugs down.

From the off-brand clothes he's wearing, there is no way he could afford to own and operate an expensive speedboat like that. He reeks of middle-income lower class.

And instead of lifting his hand with a merry salute when I swerve my boat towards him and wave, he looks at me stony-faced and gives me a dead stare.

My hackles rise. My instincts are telling me this guy has just come from the yacht. Delivering my fiancée into the hands of a bunch of perverts.

I make a mental note of the boat's registration number.

How far can I follow the wake of that man's boat? It's too late for me to change course and follow him. Their operation is way too slick for one of them to travel with evidence on board.

I decided to follow the same direction as the wake.

***

Ivy

"Ha! Were you expecting Kevin Hastings? Or Amir Hava?" The man crows and chuckles as if he is the slickest dude on the block for managing to lure me out here. "No, sweetie. You escaped me once. The only one. Just about drove me mad to know you managed to get away from me."

I can't remember his name. I tried so hard to block out what he did to me all those years ago.

The smelly hot fug of his breath blasting in my face as he tried to pin me down and force himself inside me.

I have to keep it together. Long enough for Banner to locate me. He saved me once, I know he can do it again.

That thought brings me hope.

Somehow, I manage to smile. "Call me stupid, but I've forgotten your name. I can't even remember much about that yacht trip I did ten years ago."

Biting my lower lip, I push my hand out towards him. "Holly Forrest. Pleased to meet you."

He's sulking because I don't remember him. "Brent Morecambe. Considering I'm paying you seven figures to be here with me, I suggest you don't forget my name again."

Shit. He is pissed. I gotta do better. "Of course, I remember your face, Brent. But I don't think we introduced ourselves properly last time, or did we?"

He seems pleased by my explanation. "I was so hot for you, it might have slipped my mind. You were Forrest back then. I've been following your career for years."

Creepy. "How nice. What do you think of my restaurant recommendations?"

"Fuck all that." Brent waves one pudgy hand, dismissing my career just like that. "Come with me to the cabin. Sex first, then we can take a break, and give me time to catch my breath. You look so hot in that bikini. Just like you did that first time. Only this time, no one is going to be interrupting us."

I want to cry. I want to burst into tears and howl my eyes out. Why didn't I listen to Banner? But I have to see this through to the end.

Time for me to stop acting like a victim! I am no longer that silly little schoolgirl!

"You tried to cornhole me dry last time, Brent." I force my lips to sneer, even though my mouth is jumping with nerves. "Let's not make the same mistake twice. I need a cool drink and some suntan lotion. Where's the sun deck?"

As I walk away, I shoot a look over my shoulder. "You coming? I hate fucking strangers. Let's get to know one another first."

Ugh. He's loving this boss bitch persona of mine. I can tell he's excited from the bulge under his belly.

"Sure thing, sweetie." He's almost panting with lust. "I'll get the cool drinks myself. The captain needs to stay at the helm."

"Send one of the servers," I order him to follow me, pointing to the space by my feet. "I don't like being alone." And I also don't trust Brent Morecambe not to spike my drink!

Brent runs to obey me. "I've had to downsize my operation," he explains as he trots beside me. "Too many of the crew were squeezing me for money. That's why I only host one-on-one parties now. The only crew I need for that is the captain and the speedboat driver—and they're on a retainer."

My belly flips at this bad news. I'm all alone with a man who is desperate to maintain his secret blackmail ring.

Keeping the smile fixed on my face, I look intrigued. "You mean to say it's just going to be me and you? No yacht girls. No male guests?"

Brent takes my hand as he leads me to a sun lounger. "Yeah. There are only so many stupid, sex-mad billionaires on the East Coast, Holly, you know? But if you want to carry on doing this, I can set you up with some guys in Europe or the Middle East."

His eyes travel up and down my bikini-clad body. "You grew up so beautiful, girl. I'm kinda glad I waited. You could make a fortune doing this overseas."

Settling down on the lounger and patting the one next to me, I act all interested in what he has to say when Brent sits down.

"Well, Brent, I'm only doing this once, I think. Got to buy my parents a retirement home and get them off my back. Does Julian organize the girls for Europe as well? Should I tell him when I want to do this again?"

I'm passing the time, trying to think of a way to gather information, but Brent is surprisingly forthcoming.

"Julian is New York only. He's too handsy with the girls for my liking. Too many nice little virgins are getting scared off by him."

"I wasn't a virgin when you first met me, Brent." I guess he's so chatty because he knows I have no way of recording him! "So, why did you want me so bad?"

He grunts, shifting his oversized body closer. "I like to be first with all the girls. Virgins or not. I'm proud to say that I've never fucked the same female more than once. If she's up for a second time on the same night, then it's got to be anal or bondage. Something more spicy."

My mouth goes dry. Inside, I'm crying for Banner to rescue me.

"Okay, I see your point. As for me, I like vanilla, plain and simple."

A greedy smile spreads over his face. "But it's not about what you want any more, is it?"

Something Maxine told me pops into my mind. I try to think of what she told me—what she does to get paid upfront....

Walking my fingers up Brent's arm and fluttering my eyelashes, I pout and speak in a husky voice. "Darling, I'm up for anything you want, but I think there's one little thing that you're forgetting?"

Brent grunts again, sitting up from the lounger and then standing and stretching lazily. "Oh, yeah. Payment. I'll get my phone. Do you know your account details by heart?"

"Yes, I have the details." I tap the side of my head.

Brent sneers. He's scammed billions off his guests, but his mouth is all pooched and sulky because I want payment in advance.

"I'll tell the captain to lower the anchor," he says, "then he can fetch us drinks."

It worked! Maxine was right. Asking for the money upfront like that is way easier.

I nod and wave sweetly as he leaves. I keep the smile on my face because I know he's probably going to be watching this through one of his video feeds.

The yacht has Wi-Fi. That's how he can make a transfer payment into my account. That's all I needed to know. I have to act fast the minute he comes back after the anchor has been lowered.

The moment I see Brent Morecambe waddling up to the top deck, I bounce out of my sun lounger.

"Coo-ee! Brent! How about a dip?"

The yacht has crossed over the international boundary. Whatever happens on deck now, the US Coast Guard will hold no jurisdiction.

Dashing to the prow, I look down. There is no engine or propeller. Only a very long drop to the choppy water below.

I have to trust that Brent's desire to sleep with me is as strong as he claims it is.

And then I jump.

# Chapter 38 - Ivy

It stings so bad when I hit the frigid water.

I grew up by the sea, so I know what to do to make the pain less. Crossing my arms over my breasts and pointing my toes, I try to make my body a narrow shape as I enter the water feet first.

Even like that, it feels as if the skin is peeling back off my muscles. The pain is real, but I can take it. Looking for where the water gets lighter from the sunlight, I wait for my body to float upwards.

But I've lost too much weight! I no longer have all those lovely curves and fat pads that would help me float to the top.

Rule one of swimming in water. Fat floats, muscle sinks.

Shit! I'm too lean. I'm going to have to swim to the surface.

I feel that panic. My body is telling me I don't have enough oxygen. Pushing down the fear, I kick my feet and stroke my arms, swimming up to the lighter water, slowly blowing spent air out of my mouth.

It's so scary to think about all the horrible sea creatures that might be staring up at my splashing body right now. Will Brent have thrown a lifesaver over?

Sputtering and spitting, I look up.

His plump face is staring at me from the prow. He looks horrified.

"Are you batshit crazy?!" he screams down to me as he casts the lifesaver into the water on a rope. "The water density could flay you from this height!"

Maybe you, Mr. Overweight Morecambe, but not me.

"I'm sorry!" I laugh as I catch the lifesaver. "Be a doll and lift me up."

Brent winches up the lifesaver, chittering and scolding me like an irate ape.

Halfway up the side of the yacht—when Brent's line of sight is obscured by the hull's curve—I dig the pot of lip balm out of the crotch of my bikini bottoms.

Using my teeth, I screw off the bottom of the pot. I'm terrified I'll drop the smart tag back into the ocean, but I don't. Fiddling with the tiny tag, I slap it on the side of the yacht after activating the tracking device.

Now, all I can do is hope Banner is close enough to pick up the tracking beacon.

*** 

Fletcher

Curtin beckons me over and taps on the satellite image. "She's activated the tag."

There's no time for me to celebrate. I steer towards the coordinates Curtin gives me. My hunch paid off—by following that boat's wake, I headed in the right direction.

"I wonder why she took so long to do it?" My old buddy from the Corps wants to know. "Why use the tag and not the phone?"

"Just about every item Ivy took with her had a tracking device in it. I'm guessing they only left her with the one."

Curtin manages a brief smile. "I never should have doubted you, Major."

"I'm dropping anchor a good distance away. Ivy was meant to send me details about the crew, but I guess that's out of the question."

"Fuck that," Curtin growls. "Let's shoot out the hull and take the motherfuckers down! They're in international waters—ain't nothing they can do."

I'm dying to be able to tell my friend that Ivy's carrying a baby I'm absolutely certain is mine, but I can't make that call until she allows me to.

"That's a negative. Those girls on board might panic and jump overboard. There might even be female crew. Hold the firepower for now."

It's not a good feeling operating in the dark like this. Ivy was meant to relay information to me from the time she embarked. I have to do this blind.

Climbing on the hardtop of the cabin, I lie down and prop up my hands with my elbows. When I am level, Curtin hands me a rifle scope on a tripod.

"Just like old times, Major," he says. Curtin was my spotter when I was a sniper.

Blanking out everything else, I attain my target.

All the people on the yacht will see is a boat bobbing on the horizon far off. But I can see everything on deck.

I recognize the man's corpulent outline immediately. It's Brent Morecambe. He was always inviting me to his shitty poker games and parties, but I never went.

It makes my blood boil when I think of him having access to Ivy again... wait a minute.

Sweeping the scope over and along the yacht deck with meticulous detail, I am slowly starting to realize something.

"She's there alone," I tell Curtin. "I'm not picking up any crew or guests."

We observe the yacht through our high-tech scopes for a long while. Only then does Curtin reply. "That's an affirmative. Picking up no other heat signatures."

All I can do is watch as Ivy accepts a can of cool drink from Brent and then turns on her side so they can chat and laugh together.

Clever girl. You remembered to only take drinks with a closed tab from him.

"The captain is goofing off," Curtin reports. "Wait... he's actually watching something on a monitor."

"They're already secretly filming her," I take a guess. "I bet those are video feeds he's watching."

"Bastards" is all Curtin says by way of reply.

"At least we know where the control room is." I try looking on the bright side. "There's a good chance he keeps all the footage on hard drives in there too. There's too much risk bringing it ashore."

"That fat fuck thinks he's king of the world with his yacht and hot girls. Did you suspect him of being behind this?" Curtin asks. His blood is probably boiling too.

I have to give that some thought.

Brent Morecambe does not give off mastermind vibes at all. That is why he got away with it for so long. He owns the company that leases the yachts—the sailing vessels that are so conveniently set up with hidden cameras.

He's best buds with Julian Stratford who supplies him with a steady stream of underage girls.

Once he connects a billionaire guest with an underage girl and films the whole thing, he's got his hand deep in the cookie jar.

No businessman is going to say no to someone if they have footage of him screwing a school-girl.

Then it hits me. The only reason why I'm not one of Morecambe's victims is because my heart was lost the first time I ever landed on a yacht. I took one look at that sassy girl with long black hair and red bikini and that was it.

No one could ever measure up to the girl I called "Forrest" in my dreams for ten years.

"No, Curtin. He's a vampire in pink lamb's wool. Not even a wolf in sheep's clothing! He didn't even register as a threat on my radar when I pulled him off Ivy all those years ago. I just had him down as some pathetic bully loser."

"That's why he's so successful," my old Marine buddy says, making a judgment call. "The sniveling worms are the last to catch our notice."

It's torture having to watch Ivy on the lounger, so close to Brent. He keeps trying to reach out and touch her, but she always pulls away, laughing, giggling, and pouting.

He's hot for her, but it looks like she can handle him. When he gets handsy, she stands up and does a sexy shimmy dance for him, swaying her hips and touching her breasts in a suggestive way.

I know men and I know she is only going to be able to keep this up for so long before he wants more.

Jerking my head, I signal to Curtin. "Time to go in."

He takes one look through his scope and agrees. "Yep. The dude has just made his move. He's dragging her to the cabin. She's only going to be able to prolong the inevitable for another thirty minutes, max."

"Let's go."

We have a compact military inflatable tied to the back of our boat. Curtin loosens the rope while I begin hauling equipment and weapon cases into the hull. It makes the dinghy lie low in the water, but the engine capacity makes the inflatable skip over the waves easily.

I cut the engine so the captain can't hear it when we're still a hundred yards away. Using the oars, we pull closer.

Amazingly enough, Morecambe hasn't bothered to haul the lifesaver back on board. The rope is hanging a few feet over the railings where Ivy must have used the lifesaver to step back on board.

I squint a little bit as I take measurement of the distance, and then throw a grappling hook through the lifesaver's middle.

The hook makes a dull thud as it catches against the lifesaver.

"Go!" Curtin urges me to go up as fast as I can. If the captain was alerted by the thud, our only chance is to make it to the top before he can walk to the prow from the helm.

The muscles in my arms scream as I clamber up the rope. I'm a heavy man. My arms are having to carry all 225 pounds of my bulk.

Left, right, left arm, right arm. One over the other. Once you learn a skill like rope climbing, you never lose it.

I'm climbing over the yacht railings when two things happen.

I hear Ivy scream from below deck.

And the captain is racing towards me with a large wrench in his hand.

# Chapter 39 – Ivy

I tried putting this off for as long as I could, but this sleazebag has got only one thing on his mind.

All I can think about are all those poor girls who flirted with strange men on the top deck, believing that that was all they had to do to get paid.

I replied in a fake, coy way to all of Brent Morecambe's lewd comments. Leaning closer to him and batting my eyelashes. Pouting my lips and pretending to sulk. Flicking my hair.

All those things that tempt a man into thinking he's gotten lucky—and all he has to do is wait for the night to come so he can eat his cherry on top.

I do it all. Demand unattainable food. Ask for another soda. Try to lure him into talking about politics and religion. Anything that might be able to postpone going through to the cabin with him because he's distracted.

"Don't rush it!" Standing up, I do a sexy shimmy for him on the deck. "Think of this as an appetizer, Brent. Or an amuse-bouche. Why do you want to get to the main course so fast?"

I really don't like the fanatical gleam in his eye.

"I've waited ten fucking years to stick it to you, Holly Forrest. Don't tell me to slow down."

Out of the corner of my eye, I catch sight of a boat on the horizon, hidden by the swell of the waves. It's not moving. As I dart a look at it—careful not to draw Brent's attention—I catch sunlight bouncing off something shiny.

Binoculars? A telescope? Suddenly, I don't feel so alone anymore.

Brent grabs my hand. "This is what you tried to do last time, you prick tease! Either you come down to the cabin right now or I'll call Roy up here to help me tie you up!"

That boat on the horizon has made me brave.

"I didn't try anything with you last time, you fleabag! You pushed me into the cabin as I was going to the bathroom! Without so much as a 'how do you do?' Do you know how it feels to have a complete stranger trying to insert his penis into you? Well, do you?"

My voice is shrill. All the trauma from last time is flooding back into my memory.

Brent says nothing. He just reaches for something under a towel.

It's a gun. A pistol.

"I knew you would chicken out, you greedy ho!" Brent doesn't even try to sugarcoat what's going on anymore. "The minute the money went into your account, you've been trying to delay this. Well, not anymore. Move!"

He grabs my hand after picking up the towel and pistol. Two emotions fight within me. Fear and rage.

That is the wrong combination of emotions to have in a bad situation. Tamping down the rage, I keep my focus on being afraid and respectful.

I've read about that "fight, flight, or fawn" method of survival. My only chance is to fawn.

"You don't have to be rough," I explain, amazed at how calm my voice sounds. "I like to get to know someone before having sex with them, that's all."

All that makes Brent Morecambe do is cackle like a crazy person. He pushes me into the master suite so hard I trip and tumble onto the bed.

"That's not how I remember it, sweetie. You didn't know jack-shit about Jay before you let him fuck you every which way but loose after you met him on the yacht."

Ooh, I am so tempted to tell this horrible little man the truth. But I can't because he makes sure to keep the pistol close by.

The difference between you and Banner is that you have to bully, con, and blackmail women to sleep with you, you lowdown, fugly, evil, little man!

I have concrete proof that Morecambe filmed everything that went down on his yachts.

Brent Morecambe tries to bring everyone down to his level. He can't get away with this.

How long will it take that boat to get here? But I don't even know if that is Banner.

Ugh! Brent begins to wiggle out of his speedos. It's a good thing I didn't eat too much or else I might struggle to keep the food down.

Waddling towards me, he lunges and manages to get hold of one of the ties hanging down from my bikini top. He yanks on it hard and my top comes off.

I can't help it. I scream as he reaches for my breasts.

***

Fletcher

The man swinging the wrench at me is an amateur. Pivoting on my left foot, I step outside of the arc of the swing, watching it sail past me as the weight of the wrench pulls the man off balance.

When his swing has reached its lowest point, I step back inside the arc, clench my fist, and punch upwards, using all the force from my torso and arm.

The snapping sounds as his jaw breaks are very satisfying.

I wait to see if the urge to fight has flooded his body with endorphins. That sometimes happens, and it stops the attacker from feeling pain. Or he might be on some stimulant drug that keeps him in a combative spirit.

The wrench clatters to the deck as the man gives his head a confused shake. He must have one hell of a headache coming on right now.

I decide to end it. Lunging forward, I bring my elbow down on the back of his neck. I don't want to use my Glock 19 until I'm sure no one is going to be alerted by it.

They haven't really thought this through. A yacht is one of the noisiest places to be if you want to hear if someone is coming. The vessel is full of creaking side panels and waves slapping against the hull.

The man who attacked me must have been clearing up the soda and towels on the top deck.

All of these thoughts and actions happen swiftly. I'm on the move towards the cabins, leaving Curtin to search the rest of the yacht for crew or guests.

The only thing that slows me down is when I lift up the back of my shirt and take the Glock out of the belt of my cargo pants.

Ratcheting the barrel, I slide a bullet into the chamber. It is worrying me that Ivy isn't screaming anymore. That tells me old Brent has a gun as well.

Sidling along the side deck, I have a pretty good idea of where to find the master suite. All yachts have the same layout. Nothing spectacular, no surprises.

The master suite will have the best views, meaning it will have windows everywhere. Using this to my advantage, I do some recon before blasting in there, guns blazing.

Ivy is lying on the bed wearing only her bikini bottoms. Her arms are covering her breasts.

"I'll transfer the money back into your account, Brent." She's saying the words without much conviction as if she's already given up hope. "But please don't force yourself on me."

Brent Morecambe is wearing one of those expensive silk bathrobes with no briefs or boxers underneath it. He's no longer trying to hide what is uppermost on his mind. I can see the power he has over Ivy is exciting him.

There's a pistol in his hand. A 9 mm SIG P365. Ten rounds. Micro compact 3.1-inch barrel.

That three-inch barrel is the longest thing you're packing, buddy.

From the lax way Brent is holding the gun, the man has no fear of being interrupted. He truly believes that this time, he's going to get his money's worth.

I can't risk shooting through the window. I don't know what kind of glass the yacht has and I don't want to risk a ricochet.

"Get on your hands and knees and face the wall," Brent snarls. "Lift one hand off the mattress and it will be the last move you make. You don't want to know how many disobedient young girls have gone overboard with a stone around their necks!"

He's getting off on Ivy's fear and disgust.

I wait for Ivy to do as Brent says. The moment the man puts down the pistol to take off his robe, I'm through that door and have the Glock pressing into the skin behind his ear.

"Hands up, nice and slow, Morecambe," I say, choosing my words carefully so he doesn't try to make a move for the gun. "Reach for that peashooter of yours and I'll blow your brains out."

I know men like Brent Morecambe so well. They believe their money will save them from anything. They think they can buy themselves out of every trouble. They are convinced they are invincible.

Morecambe lifts his hands and laces his fingers behind his neck. He believes his life is too precious for me to waste it.

Ivy cries out but doesn't move, staying on her hands and knees in front of us.

"Banner?! Thank God!"

Her head is bent, tears falling onto the bed linen in a long stream.

Secure the prisoner first. That's my priority. "Go out to the top deck, Ivy." I know I'm using a rough tone of voice, but I can't risk her being in the same room as two guns. "The man out there—his name is Curtin. If you're injured, tell him. He will know what to do."

Shaking, she obeys me. Crawling off the bed and running out of the cabin with her arms still covering her breasts.

Kneeing Morecambe in the middle of his back, I push him down onto the bed as I kick the SIG off the mattress at the same time. Only when I have my knee on the back of his neck do I reach for the silk dressing robe he left on the floor.

Using the silk belt, I tie up Morecambe's hands and wrists. Then I find the SIG and put it out of commission. Typical of a bully, Brent had the pistol's safety on the whole time.

He hasn't got enough hair for me to grip, so I drag him to the chair and pin him there instead.

Flipping open the closet, I find a windbreaker. Pulling the cords out of the hem, I tie Morecambe fast.

Then I go out to see how Ivy is doing. She's amazed to see how calm I am, but she's living for it. I see the triumph shining in her eyes. We're both thinking the same thing—we did it!

"Thank you, Banner! I've been thanking Mr. Curtin too. I would have been so lost without you."

She hugs me. After kissing the top of her head and giving her a reassuring hug to let her know how proud I am of her bravery, I jerk my chin at Curtin. "You coming? Your interrogation skills are the best."

Giving a businesslike grin, Curtin follows Ivy and me into the master suite. Brent is making muffled moans, but he shuts up when he sees the three of us come back in.

"Are the servers in the cockpit helm where you keep the video footage? And does it hold the only copies?" Curtin doesn't waste time getting straight down to it.

All Morecambe does is nod before hanging his head and staring at the floor.

"Right. We're going to need a list of all the men you've blackmailed. If we see someone on the video footage who you forgot to mention, I'll be coming back in here with a battery and some jumper cables. You got that?"

I watch as Ivy calmly takes a notepad and golf pencil out of one of the drawers. She sits down on the bed and jots down every name that comes out of Morecambe's mouth.

When Morecambe is finished, Ivy has one question she wants answered.

"I know you probably manipulated Amir Hava to set up his meeting with Jay on Kevin's leased yacht so that you could get video of Jay screwing a yacht girl. So, why couldn't you use the footage of him and me?"

Heck. That's a good question! Not that it kept me up nights, but it would still be nice to know.

Brent scowls. "Don't act the dunce. I deal in blackmail. If a man and young woman fall in love at first sight, there's nothing illegal about that. You were eighteen and not even a virgin. The footage shows two people making goo-goo eyes at each other before acting on their impulses."

I'm amazed. I never even realized that might be the reason.

Brent continues complaining like it's our fault. "I thought I might get something on Jay if you had taken the fifty thousand dollars from Kev. I could have blackmailed the famous fucking cowboy of the conference room by saying he slept with a prostitute. Only you refused to take the money, didn't you, Miss Priss!"

Ivy blushes. "It would have been a conflict of interest for me to take money for doing something so beautiful."

Brent scoffs loudly as he sees me looking at Ivy with deep affection. The girl saved my life—my business—everything.

"Don't think I wouldn't have loved the two of you to do something kinky or sick. Especially after you pulled me off her, Jay! But that's you all over—always sticking your nose where it doesn't belong. You haven't put a foot out of line since then. Both of you."

Ivy gets a little misty-eyed. "Love at first sight."

I have to laugh. "Damn, sweetheart, but you were so sassy to me—I never would have guessed!"

Ivy has the grace to blush. "Maybe all we needed was a nice meal together for me to realize I'd met my match."

I want to hug her so tight and never let go. Booping the end of her nose, all I have to say is "Maybe."

Nodding to Curtin, I ask him if he's able to clean up here without me. He salutes. "Yessir, Major. I've got this. Just bring the inflatable back to the yacht and tie it to the anchor once you reach the speedboat. I'll use that to get ashore. Will you handle Stratford's?"

"Looking forward to it." I grin and return the salute. "And I'll stop by the marina and get Ivy's phone back from the speedboat driver too."

Laying my arm over Ivy's shoulders, kind of like I can't believe I'm finally able to stop protecting her, I start to guide her out of the cabin.

"Hey!" Brent shouts out. "You're not leaving me here with this psycho, are you?"

"That's what I've been saying to myself since I got on board the yacht with you, Mr. More-cambe," Ivy says. Giving him a cheerful wave goodbye, Ivy and I head back to the speedboat.

# Chapter 40 - Ivy

It makes front page news when the police raid Julian Stratford's agency. They make the connection to the luxury yacht that mysteriously exploded in international waters fairly easily the moment Julian begins shooting his mouth off.

I sit back and watch the flat screen as footage of Janet O'Reilly and Julian Stratford being handcuffed and marched to a stationary police vehicle unfolds. Box after box of laptops and hard drives get taken away into white panel vans.

Maxine still has my phone number. I get a text from her.

Are you watching this? I can't believe it! I'm so happy. I no longer have to live in fear.

I text back: You'll be eligible for victims comp if you reach out to the prosecutor's office.

I get a text back immediately: Screw that! I'm moving to Florida. Found a nice, cheap apartment there. I'm enrolling in college to study art. I've always wanted to create stained glass windows. Thanks for everything. M xxx

Lying back with a sigh, I continue watching the news. I have velvet cushions under my feet and my knees. And a tray of potatoes and butter toast within arms' reach.

Whatever I feel like eating, Banner provides for me.

I guess it's because I told him I'm pregnant with our baby.

He was sanguine. "Yep. I kinda knew already. Why didn't you want to tell me before?"

There is a reason, but I can't tell him. I have to make a phone call before I do.

"Hey, Mary-Kay? Can you please come and visit me?"

Typical MK, she gets suspicious. "Where are you? If you've made up with Fletch the Wretch and shacked up with him, I don't think we can be friends anymore."

I sigh. "Yes, I'm at your brother's, MK. Please come over. He's not here."

She grumbles and cusses, but says she'll be over in a bit.

I'll just bet you'll be here soon, Mary-Kay Banner. Your brother bought you a brand new apartment in the most luxurious building on the Upper East Side, right by the park. You're literally five minutes' walk away from us now.

The doorman knows to let Mary-Kay in and let her have access to our floor. I look up when she slouches into the bedroom, staring around at the decor with a critical sniff.

"You sick again?" MK sits on the edge of the bed and glances at the flat screen. "Looks like something's going down! An office is being raided! I wonder what it is?"

I ignore her. "MK, why do you hate Fletcher so much?"

That gets my friend's attention. "Is that why you called me here? Jesus! It's like you weren't even listening to me at school when I told you how mean he was to me after my parents died."

"They were Fletcher's parents too, MK!" I can't believe how self-absorbed my friend is. "He was hurting just as much, only he didn't have the luxury of being able to act out like you did!"

Her eyes narrow. "What lies has Fletch been telling you?"

"Lies?" I snort. "So, he's lying about you hooking up with a pimp and getting into drugs when you were still a kid? And is he lying about you not being able to name who Daniel's father might be because you slept with over fifteen men during that time without using precautions?"

Mary-Kay begins to cry. "I was lost, and all Fletcher could do was moan about what a horrible responsibility I was. I've been waiting for you to tell him that it was my idea for us to become yacht girls, but you never did. I was petrified of you holding that over my head."

Leaning to where Mary-Kay is sitting, I pat her hand. "Isn't it time for us to say that it all worked out for the best, MK? Daniel can't be alienated from his cousin."

Giving up her pride and anger, MK places her face in my lap and cries her heart out. It's cathartic. We hug it out and make friends.

I can tell she's lonely because Melanie doesn't come around so much anymore, being based in Brooklyn.

We chat about names for the baby and what new furniture MK wants to put into her new apartment. Before she leaves, I have one more question.

"Why didn't you and your brother go to therapy? Grief counseling or a psychiatrist?"

Mary-Kay gives a shout of laughter. "Can you see Fletcher talking about his feelings to a stranger and then having a breakthrough?"

I nearly fall out of bed, I'm laughing so hard.

***

That's the thing about love. You never realize how much you miss it when it's not around, but when it comes back, you never want it to disappear again.

Banner is in the bathroom when I tell him this.

"What's that you're saying?" He's got the faucet blasting cold water into the sink as he cleans his teeth.

"Nothing," I holler back, "I was just musing out loud."

Climbing onto the bed in just his briefs, Banner grins at me. "Are you up for a little musing in my direction? I'm always up for some musing with you, sweetheart."

"You're such a greedy boy." I pout. "We muse an insane amount of times, you realize."

Pulling the sheets down to expose my legs, he licks one of my feet like an eager puppy. "Love is the food of life. Or is it 'life is the food of love'? I forget."

He makes me laugh. He really does. "It's—'if music be the food of love, play on'—you bar-barian!"

Edging closer, he gets near enough to plant a sweet kiss on my lips. "If I'm a barbarian, then you're my damsel in distress. I'm here to save you from the ravenous hordes."

I like that image very much. "That's the problem with getting into a sticky situation, Banner. I'm addicted to you always being there to rescue me."

His kiss gets deeper. "I promise I always will. For better or worse. Sickness and health. Anything else that tries to hurt you or the baby better watch out."

I'm so in love with him when he says such sweet things. Sinking down on the bed so that we are at the same level, I return his kisses.

His hand rubs over the soft swell of my belly and I want to press myself against him. When I wrap my arms around his neck, the urge to meld my body to his gets stronger.

My breathing quickens, my heartbeat gets faster, and my imagination runs riot as I anticipate all the lovely, lovely things my protective cowboy of the conference room is going to do to me.

Hooking my finger under the band of his briefs, I indulge myself by tracing the long length of his cock with my finger. It's thick and bulging, so rampant with desire. The touch makes me wet in an instant.

Banner knows what I like, and he's an expert in being able to predict what I want before I've even thought about it. He inserts his finger—did I mention he's got large hands?—into my slit, gently moving it in and out as he relishes the wetness and tightness.

I feel his cock jerk with excitement as I flex the muscles inside my pussy, squeezing his finger like a velvet vice.

He murmurs his approval in a deep voice. "Carry on like that, darling, and this isn't going to last too long."

That's how we make love. Never the same way more than once. It's as if sex is our paint box and we can use all the colors of the rainbow.

"Short and sweet is good." I don't bother moving my lips away from his mouth as I whisper my suggestion. "We've got the whole night ahead of us."

I wait with eager excitement as his mouth lingers over my luscious nipples. I never knew how obsessed a lover could get over the changes in a woman's body as her pregnancy progresses. But that's definitely Banner. He can't get enough of my large nipples and dark areolas.

And when he inserts his throbbing erection into me, it thrills me just like it did that first time. I don't have to work hard for my orgasm to start coming because it's always there. Lingering under the surface every time Banner touches me or kisses me.

His thrust drives me to the edge of exquisite madness as he slides himself against the sensitive lovebud hidden between the plump lips of my pussy.

My fingernails scrabble at his back as the euphoria of my climax begins to mount higher. We are both lost in the primitive urge to express our love for one another in this most basic way.

When it is finished, we fall back against the pillows, too overwhelmed with ecstasy to speak for a long while.

Eventually, Banner breaks the silence. "It's like you've completed my family for me, Ivy. If I'd known it was this easy to be happy, I would have never been so flippant with you."

Snuggling up to the wonderful man I love with all my heart, I whisper in his ear, "We always had the same goals, love. We just had to get rid of everyone who was trying to get in the way."

His growl is so low it makes the bed tremble. "Line 'em up and shoot 'em down. That's how I will treat anyone who tries to hurt my family in the future."

And from the way he says it, I have no doubt that's exactly what Fletcher Banner would do!

Printed in Great Britain
by Amazon

60595339R00302